MW01038031

MY COVER MODEL

A LOVE LIKE THAT NOVEL

R.L. KENDERSON

My Cover Model
Copyright © 2019 by R.L. Kenderson
All Rights Reserved

ISBN: 978-1-950918-21-8

Editor: Jovana Shirley, Unforeseen Editing, www.unforeseenediting.com
Cover Designer: R.L. Kenderson at R.L. Cover Designs, www.
rlcoverdesigns.com

No part of this book may be reproduced or transmitted in any form or by
any means, electronic or mechanical, including photocopying, recording, or
by any information storage and retrieval system without the written
permission of the author, except for the use of brief quotations in a book
review.
This book is a work of fiction. Names, characters, places, and incidents either
are products of the author's imagination or are used fictitiously. Any
resemblance to actual persons, living or dead, events, or locales is entirely
coincidental.

MY COVER MODEL

ONE

SYDNEY

I PULLED into the driveway of one of my closest friends, Harper Stone, and honked the horn. We were on our way to a book signing where I was an author and she was my assistant. It also a chance for us to have some much-needed girl time this weekend.

I felt rude, not going in and saying hi to her husband and son, but she had given me explicit instructions to get her out of there right away.

While I waited, I looked at images on my phone of the cover model who was making an appearance this weekend. His name was Travis Zehler, and I had never heard of him until this signing.

He had a nice enough face, but I wasn't awestruck by him. He had dark blond hair and green eyes. I liked men with dark hair and dark eyes. Or at least, blue. I had green eyes, so I kind of thought of them as boring.

I'd been told more than once in my life that I was too picky. I didn't mean to be, but you couldn't force attraction.

I was kind of a hypocrite though because I was no

supermodel. I was cute, and there were times I got dressed up and thought, *Damn, I am sexy.* But I had the apple body shape, and I had no illusions about it being the female shape of choice. I had large breasts but no hips or ass. So, while I was attractive, I would never be anyone's trophy wife. And I would never be a model's girlfriend.

A few seconds later, Harper came running out of the house like her spiked pink hair was on fire. She threw her bag in the back of my SUV and climbed into the seat beside me.

"Let's go."

I put the vehicle in reverse and backed out. "What's going on? Is everything okay with you and Ian?"

Just as I put the car in drive, her front door opened, and Ian stepped into the doorway. He had a grin on his face, his oversize glasses halfway down his nose, as he eagerly waved his hand back and forth.

Harper rolled down her window and yelled, "I'll miss you, you big goof." She blew him a kiss.

"Miss you, too, honey. Have fun. Hi and bye, Sydney."

I leaned down and waved. "Bye, Ian. Give baby Wyatt kisses for me."

"Will do," he shouted back.

Harper pushed the up button on the window and pointed forward. "Let's get out of here."

We drove away with one last wave to Ian, and Harper dropped her head back against the seat and sighed.

"Is everything okay?" I asked again.

She opened an eyelid. "Yeah. I just need a break."

"Being a wife and mother is exhausting, huh?"

She sprang up in her seat. "*Yes.* A few years ago, I

thought I was going to be single forever. Happily single, I might add. But then I had to meet Ian, and that dork convinced me to marry him and have his baby."

Harper was a bit of a free spirit. She bleached her dark hair white blonde and dyed the ends pink or whatever other color she felt like that month. She was a massage therapist who set her own hours and worked out of people's homes. She refused to be employed by anyone but herself.

She'd met her husband at his job where he worked with computers and electronics—I still didn't know exactly what he did—when his company brought her in to give massages to the employees for Employee Appreciation Day.

Ian had convinced Harper to go out with him. I thought she'd agreed because she felt bad about turning him down. Instead, she'd fallen in love.

I laughed. "Does this mean you want a divorce?"

"Not on your life. He's a dork, but he's my dork. And I wouldn't give up Wyatt for the world. I just need a break."

"I think you're very lucky to have him, but I get it. You need time away, and we needed some girl time anyway."

Harper turned her head toward me. "Hey, what about you?"

"What about me?"

"You and men. I thought something was going to happen between you and that guy from your gym?"

"Alan? Yeah, he texted me about a dozen times, and then—*poof*—he was gone."

"No way. What was the last thing you two talked about?"

"Nothing big. Very benign. I think it was something

about the latest Marvel movie. And that was it." I rolled my eyes. "It's probably better anyway."

"Why?"

"Because I've seen him work out. He's kind of a fanatic. I work out the bare minimum. I only do it because it's healthy for me. He's the kind of guy who loves to work out. I do not. In the end, it wouldn't have worked."

"You don't know that," Harper said with a disappointed voice.

I shrugged. "I guess we'll never know since he ghosted me."

"I'm sorry, hon."

I laughed. "Don't be. It's fine. I wasn't in love with him. I wasn't even in lust with him."

"He didn't deserve you anyway."

"You're just saying that because you're my friend."

"And because it's true."

The book signing event was about four hours away in Iowa from our home in the Minneapolis-St. Paul area, so by the time we arrived, it was after eight at night. We checked into our hotel and put our stuff in the room.

"I'm sorry we got here so late," Harper said.

"Don't sweat it."

"I know you wanted to check in and go to the dinner tonight."

I shrugged, not wanting her to feel bad. "I did. But it will be okay. We're supposed to have breakfast tomorrow. Hopefully, we'll meet some people there."

"We could always go look and see if anyone is still wandering around."

"Might as well."

"Why don't you message the ringleader? Maybe we can still check in tonight."

"Good idea." I pulled my phone from my purse and sent Nicki, the person running the event, a message.

My phone dinged.

"Great news. They're just getting ready to put their stuff away, so if we hurry, we'll make it."

We rushed down to a small room just off the main lobby. Inside were some people milling around and a table with a woman sitting at it.

The first woman, a brunette with shoulder-length hair, smiled at us. "Hey, are you Sydney Hart?"

"That's me."

"I'm Nicki," she said as she handed me a purple-and-white name tag attached to a purple lanyard.

"I love your author name," Harper said to me.

I laughed. "All I did was shorten my last name."

When I'd first started writing, a lot of authors had talked about using a pen name. I hadn't really felt like I needed one, but I had decided that Sydney Hart sounded better than Sydney Harting.

"Yeah, but Hart and heart. It's perfect for a romance author."

"Thanks, Harper. That's why I did it." I looked at Nicki. "This is my assistant, Harper."

"Hi, Harper," Nicki said. "Give me one sec." She moved to a different pile and looked through them. She pulled out a red-and-white name tag attached to a red lanyard and handed it to Harper.

This was only my third author event, but so far, they were always color-coded. It looked like authors were purple, and assistants were red. There were also a few green-and-white name tags.

"What are the green ones?" Harper asked.

"Oh, those are the VIP ticket holders. They get to come to all the events that you two will attend."

"That's cool."

"And then we have one blue name tag." Nicki pointed to the end. "That's for our one and only model this year."

Harper looked at me and wiggled her eyebrows. "I can't wait to meet him."

I'd honestly kind of forgotten about him.

The model's name was Travis Zehler, and I had done a quick Google search on him back when I learned he'd be coming. From what I remembered, he had a nice enough face, but I hadn't been awestruck by him, like I had been expecting to be.

It wasn't that I wasn't curious or that I didn't like men. As a woman in her mid-thirties, I was completely aware that my biological clock was ticking, and unlike Harper's previous happily single status, I wanted to get married some-day, so there was a part of me that was always on the lookout for single men. But this model was so far out of my league that I hadn't really given him a second thought.

"Didn't you tell me you were happily married as we drove down here?" I jokingly asked her after we said goodbye and walked away.

"I can still look," she said. "I'm not dead."

"That you can."

She looked at me. "Aren't you excited?"

I shrugged a shoulder. "Maybe a little. It is kind of cool to meet someone who's on book covers. But I'm sure he won't give us the time of day. Besides, he's just one guy."

Harper smiled. "Whatever. I'm still going to gawk. A lot."

TWO

SYDNEY

THE COMBINED noise of two phone alarms with completely different songs woke us up at six fifteen the next morning.

I quickly shut mine off, as did Harper.

"That was a horrible noise," I commented from my bed.

"Yep, I'm up," Harper said. "Although I'm wondering now why we stayed up late, watching movies."

"I'm wondering whose idea it was to schedule a seven a.m. breakfast on a Saturday."

Harper sat up. "No kidding. It's my day to sleep in. What the hell, people?"

I pushed my covers off me and sat up as well. "We could always skip it?"

Harper's eyes widened. "And miss free food?"

"You're right. I don't think they have coffee though. We'll have to go and get one before."

Harper stood. "I'd better get ready then."

"Are you showering before you go?" I called out to her.

"No, I'm just going to get dressed and go. I'd rather shower after, so I can look pretty for the book signing."

"Thank God. I didn't want to shower either."

I spent most days sitting in front of my computer or running errands. Most of the time, I didn't even bother with makeup, doing my hair, or putting my contacts in. My outfit of choice was a T-shirt and yoga pants.

So, when it came to book signings, I always liked to look a little more professional. But I really didn't feel like doing all of that before seven in the morning if I didn't have to. Besides, I didn't have time.

I brushed my hair and my teeth and put my hair up in a ponytail. I put on clean clothes, and, yes, I decided to go with yoga pants because I wanted to be comfortable.

"We'd better go. I don't want to be one of the last ones there and have to sit with people we don't know."

"What's wrong with that?" Harper asked.

She could make friends with a wall.

"Nothing, except that I hate imposing on people." I grabbed my name tag and my key card.

"But you're an author. People want to meet you."

"I'm a non-famous author," I reminded her.

Harper grabbed her things and looped her arm with mine. "Then, let's go make them want to meet you."

We went and got large lattes first before we headed to the area where we were supposed to meet for breakfast. There weren't that many people around, but there also weren't many tables.

"See, it's a good thing we came early."

"Yeah, yeah," Harper said with a smile.

After the food was rolled out, we filled up our plates and brought them back to our table. I wasn't a health food nut, but I did try to eat well most of the time to keep myself from gaining too much weight. But I was on vacation, and I was eating as much breakfast as I wanted.

"Oh my God," Harper said with a moan. "These are the best muffins."

"Crap. And I didn't get one."

She broke off a huge piece. "Here, try some."

I opened my mouth, intending to take a bite, but she shoved the whole thing in my mouth. Both of us started laughing, and I had to turn my face toward the wall behind me. If I kept looking at Harper, I wouldn't stop giggling, and I didn't want the room to stare at my chipmunk cheeks.

A close female voice said, "Do you mind if we take your other two chairs?"

Out of the corner of my eye, I saw Harper wave her arm at our empty chairs. "Go ahead. Those seats are free."

"Thank you," a male voice said.

I finally managed to chew half of the food in my mouth and swallow it. "You bitch," I told Harper as I turned around.

She laughed again, and I probably would have, too, except I was stopped dead when I saw who was about to take the seat across from me.

It was Travis Zehler, and holy shit, but the few pictures I had seen online did nothing to prepare me for him in real life.

He was tall with broad shoulders and a trim waist, and when he turned to point to something, talking to the woman beside him, I noticed he had a gorgeous ass, too. I wouldn't have even needed to look up his picture to know this was him. He carried himself in such a way that there was no other word for it than modelesque.

Now, I remembered how I'd thought he wasn't the cutest guy I'd ever seen. His hair was shorter than the few pictures I'd seen, and he had a trim beard. When he smiled at us, I knew I wanted to have his babies.

Why did I decide not to look pretty this morning again?

Harper kicked me under the table, and I realized I'd been staring. With my mouth open. With food in it.

Travis shook his head and laughed.

I was going to kill Harper later.

The woman to my right had on a purple name tag like me and was probably about my age. She had shoulder-length auburn hair and pretty brown eyes. "Hi, I'm Angela Devlin."

I swallowed my food, composed myself, and smiled. "I'm Sydney Hart." I'd seen her name around on social media, but I hadn't read any of her books yet.

"I'm Harper, I'm Sydney's assistant."

"This is Travis," Angela said, pointing to him. "He's my assistant-slash-model."

"So, when did you two get in?" Harper asked. "We saw your name tag still on the table last night," she said to Travis.

He smiled, but Angela was the one who said, "We got here about midnight."

Harper winced. "Ouch. And you both got up so early?"

"I slept almost the whole way here from Minneapolis, so I had plenty of rest. But I did just throw on some clothes this morning," Angela said.

"Us, too," I said with a laugh. "That's where we're both from."

Although Travis looked great for someone who had driven for hours and gotten no more than six hours of sleep.

"Are you both from Minneapolis?" I asked. I thought I had read Travis was from somewhere farther away, but maybe I was wrong. I hadn't given his bio my full attention the night I looked him up.

"I'm from Michigan," Angela said. "I flew into Minneapolis and drove here with Travis."

"But you're from Minnesota?" I asked Travis.

"Yep. Born and raised." He grinned, and not one, but two dimples appeared. *Figures.* "I grew up in a small town, moved to the Cities in high school, and stayed."

I couldn't believe he was from the same place I lived. Despite just meeting him, he gave off this aura. I didn't know how to explain it, and it was kind of like finding out a famous actor lived near me.

"That's so cool that you decided to attend," Harper said.

"Yeah, Ang convinced me," he said, and I noticed the nickname he used for her. They must be close.

"How did you do that?" I asked Angela, half-joking, half-serious. "I think he's the only model to attend this weekend."

She laughed. "I did a lot of begging and pleading."

Travis shook his head, but he was smiling.

"Truthfully, he's just a really nice guy."

Travis shook his head again, and mouthed, *No, I'm not.*

Harper and I both laughed.

Angela put her hand up to her mouth, so Travis couldn't

see what she was saying, but then she proceeded to speak loud enough for him to hear. "He's also a big softy."

"Shh…don't tell anyone." Travis shoved a forkful of food in his mouth and grinned.

I mentally sighed. *God, he's beautiful.*

Harper leaned over to me and whispered, "Just a guy, huh?"

THREE

SYDNEY

A COUPLE OF HOURS LATER, Harper and I were showered, dressed, and prettied up. Now, we needed to haul all my book stuff down to the banquet hall where the book signing was taking place.

My stuff was all packed into a couple of rolling carts to make everything easier to take everywhere. We pulled the two carts into the elevator and let the doors shut.

"So...are we going to talk about you drooling over the male model?"

"I did not drool."

Harper snorted.

"I didn't. But I totally admit, he's hot."

She grinned. "I know, right?"

"His pictures don't do him justice."

Harper's brow wrinkled. "I think you've been looking at the wrong pictures."

I shrugged. "Maybe." But I made a mental note to check him out later.

The elevator doors opened, so the conversation was over.

"How long does it take you to set up?" Harper asked after we found my table in the large room.

"Always longer than I think it's going to. Hopefully, after I do this a few more times, I'll get the process down."

While it did take a while, I always enjoyed this part. It was fun to see an empty table turn into my display with all my books and swag. Harper mostly unpacked everything while I put stuff in their places. There were a couple of things I told her to wait on until the event started.

I took a step back to get a larger view, and then I stepped forward again and moved a couple of things around.

"This is why I didn't try to help."

I looked up at Harper. "Huh?"

She gave me a look. "Because I put your bookmarks there, and you just moved them."

I laughed embarrassingly. "I'm sorry. I'm kind of a perfectionist sometimes."

"*Noooo*," she said teasingly. "You don't say."

I stuck my tongue out at her, and she laughed.

"I can't help it. I want it to look great."

"You're an Aries, right?"

"Yeah. So?"

She shook her head. "Figures." She looked around.

Our table was at the end, and the table next to us was still empty with the name of an author on it I didn't recognize. The table behind us was also vacant.

"Is your banner okay where it is? That's something I did all by myself."

I patted her shoulder. "I know, and I'm so proud of you."

It was her turn to stick her tongue out at me.

"It's fine, I think." It was behind the outside chair and off to the side. "I don't think it'll bother whoever is sitting behind us, but we can ask when they show up." I looked down at my Fitbit. "But we should maybe go get something for lunch. I have to meet up for the group picture at twelve thirty, and the doors open at one." It was a few minutes after noon now.

The hotel had a restaurant, but they also had a bar area in the front where we could order food with a lounge area for people to sit. We decided on an appetizer to split since we'd had a big breakfast.

"Sydney?"

I turned around from my seat at the bar to see who'd spoken my name. It was a fellow author I had met once in the past. He was average height, probably around five-ten or five-eleven, with brown hair and hazel eyes. He was probably a little older than me, maybe about five years, and he was cute.

"Oh, hey, Derek." I smiled. "I didn't know you were going to be here."

"I got a spot at the last minute."

Harper raised her brow.

"Derek, this is my friend and assistant, Harper."

She held out her hand.

"This is Derek. He's a male romance author from the Twin Cities, too. We met at my first book signing."

Derek took her hand and shook it. "Nice to meet you. You're a little different from her last assistant."

He was referring to my sixteen-year-old niece, Lexie. My first book signing had been at the last minute too, and she had been the only one available. We'd both had fun, but it was hard when I wouldn't allow her to read my books. Too much sex. She had to wait until she was eighteen, and even then, my brother would probably kill me.

Harper laughed. "Yeah, she asked me to go, but my husband had to work, and I couldn't find a babysitter."

"Bummer."

"Yeah, but I'm here now." She smiled. "And I've always wanted to read a book by a male romance author, but I've never known where to start."

"Now, you can start with mine." Derek grinned.

I nodded. "I read one. It was good."

Derek turned to me, surprised. "You did?"

"Heck yeah. I was curious, too. I'd probably read more, but you know how hard it is to get reading time in when you're writing all the time."

Derek's cheeks might have turned a slight shade of pink, but I wasn't sure. "Thank you." He looked down. "I'm embarrassed to say, I haven't read yours yet."

"What?" I pretended to be offended. "How dare you."

"Uh…" His eyes got huge.

I touched his arm. "I'm kidding."

His shoulders sagged, and he smiled. "Put me on the spot, why don't you?"

"Hey, Derek," someone called from a few feet away.

I pointed behind Derek. "Is that Eric?"

Derek looked behind him. "Yeah."

"Eric is Derek's assistant," I told Harper.

"You're joking. Your name is Derek, and his name is Eric?"

Derek threw his hands up in the air and laughed. "I know. But we can't help what our mamas named us." He put his hand on my bicep. "I'll talk to you later, okay? I wanted to tell you about a writer group that meets once a month."

This piqued my interest. "Ooh. Yes, please do."

Derek walked away just as our food came, and Harper and I dug in since we now only had about fifteen minutes to spare.

"I think you should go for him," Harper said.

"What?" I looked in the direction Derek had gone, but he was nowhere to be seen. "I don't know about that."

She nodded. "I do. What would you think if he was interested in you? Would you be interested, too?"

I swallowed my food. "I don't know. He's cute, but he doesn't really do anything for me." I tilted my head to the side. "Of course, I haven't gotten laid in a long time, so there's also that."

Harper laughed. "How are his sex scenes? I've always wondered how a man would write them."

"Good," I said. "They're not the hottest I've ever read, but they are better than some."

She wrinkled her nose. "Bummer."

I held up a finger. "But his hero was definitely on the giving end of things and not always receiving."

Harper grinned. "Well then, you might have something to work with after all." She set her food down and moved her hands around. "Maybe you can mold him into the perfect lover."

I laughed. "You're horrible."

She shrugged. "He's probably better than Travis Zehler."

This comment surprised me. "Really? Why would you say that?" I bet Travis could make a woman come with just his smile.

"Because he's hot. He probably doesn't have to work for it. Women are so grateful that he'll sleep with them; they do all the work and give him all the pleasure." She tilted her head back and forth. "Not that I would complain too much if I got to see that man naked. I'd probably do all the work, too. But it does get old."

"Hmm."

She shoved her last bite of food in her mouth. "There is something to be said about having an average-looking guy in your bed. He wants to make you happy and will do everything he can to ensure that." She bit her lip and lifted her eyebrows. "Trust me; I know."

My jaw dropped. "You hardly ever say anything about your and Ian's sex life."

And this was someone who had told me every little detail about past lovers.

She smiled. "That's because Ian's special."

"Aww."

She elbowed me. "Knock it off. That's why I didn't tell you."

I laughed. She tried to be tough, but inside, she was a softy.

FOUR

SYDNEY

WE ALL HUDDLED in a group to get our author picture taken, and I tried to hide toward the back. I was five-six, and I tried to sneak behind some other people who were taller than me, but the photographer wasn't having it.

"You, in the black-and-white shirt," the photographer called out, looking in my direction.

I looked around, hoping someone else had a black-and-white shirt on, but no luck. I pointed to myself, and he nodded. *Rats*. I already knew what he was going to tell me.

"Come forward a little. I can't see you back there."

I reluctantly stepped forward, and out of the corner of my eye, I saw Harper laughing. She knew my revulsion to my picture being taken. She was probably enjoying this.

After about a million pictures were snapped and my face hurt from smiling, we were allowed to go.

"You should have seen your face when the guy called you out. Pure panic."

"Ugh. I hate pictures. No matter what I do, I don't look good in them."

"You are way too hard on yourself."

I disagreed. "I don't think so. I look in the mirror, and I think, *Damn, girl, you look nice today.* But then, when I see my pictures, I'm like, *Damn, who is that imposter who took my place?*" I wrinkled up my nose.

Harper laughed. "You crack me up."

We headed to my author table. On the way, we said hi to the author and her assistant who was next to us. She had baked goods at her table.

We took our seats, and Harper said, "That is a good idea."

"What is?"

"The food. I saw some other authors who had candy and chocolate."

I smiled devilishly at her. "Oh, I have something even better." I pulled up the long tablecloth and pulled out a box I'd told Harper to leave alone earlier.

"Ooh…what is it?"

I opened the box and grinned.

"Holy shit." She looked up at me. "Are those penis pops?"

"Hell yeah. They give a whole new meaning to *cocksucker.*"

Harper pulled one out. "I wanted these for my bachelor party, but Wendy said no." She curled her lip.

Wendy was her sister-in-law and the person who'd been in charge of Harper's bachelorette party after Ian begged her to let his sister do it. Harper had regretted it ever since.

I pulled out a handful and set them on the table. "It's not the same, but now, you can have a little fun with them." I wiggled my eyebrows and sat back in my chair.

"Hold that thought. I'm going to run to the restroom real quick," Harper said. "I drank too much Diet Pepsi."

"Okay."

"I'll be right back," she said before sprinting out of the room.

I felt the chair behind me tap mine.

"Penis suckers, huh?" a smooth voice said.

A shiver went down my spine, and I slowly turned my head to see Travis. He smelled amazing. Like man with a hint of cologne.

His eyes were on my table, so I took the opportunity to study him. Even up close, he was gorgeous. Barely any skin imperfections. This guy must have great genes.

His gaze met mine, and he smiled, his lips full and his dimples popping out. I wanted to touch one for some crazy reason.

He raised an eyebrow, and I realized that he had just asked me a question.

"Oh," I said as I blushed. "Yeah. You know, romance author, romance books, sex"—I held up a sucker—"cocks. It all ties together."

He looked like he was trying not to laugh.

"What's funny?"

His brow went up, as if he was trying to make himself look innocent, and he shook his head. "Nothing."

I dropped my hand. "You think it's stupid, don't you?"

Why do I care? I just met the guy.

"No. Not at all." He bit his bottom lip.

"What?" I smiled. "I know you want to say something."

Travis shook his head.

"Okay, I know you're thinking something."

"I don't know if I should say."

"Just say it."

He looked around and then met my eyes again. He lowered his voice. "I'm just picturing all these women sucking…" His gaze moved down to my mouth.

"Cocks?"

That same look crossed his face. The one where he looked like something was funny, but he didn't want to share.

I rolled my eyes. "You just wanted me to say cock again, didn't you?"

This time, he didn't hold his laugh in.

I rolled my eyes. "Don't you have anything better to do?"

"Nope." His eyes widened. "Hey, your one eye…"

"I know," I said, a little embarrassed. "It's two different colors."

For as long as I could remember, my right eye had a large spot in it that was almost half-brown. My parents didn't remember when it'd first appeared either.

"Wow. That's so cool. I didn't notice it this morning."

"Thanks. And I had my glasses on. It was harder to see then."

"Hey, Travis, I found my markers," Angela called out.

I looked to see her approaching her table.

"Talk to you later." He smiled at me and scooted his chair back up to his table. "Where were they?" he said to Angela.

I faced forward, tuning out their conversation, and saw Harper walking up to the table. She sat down and leaned toward me.

"Was Travis just talking to you?" she whispered, excitement on her face.

"Yeah. He was giving me crap about our suckers."

"What?" She straightened, and in a loud voice, she said, "Our suckers rule."

We both looked over our shoulders to see if Travis would respond. He shook his head, but I didn't know if it was at us or at Angela.

I laughed. "I don't think the kids say *rule* anymore."

"What would you know about that? You're a year older than me."

"Research." My last book was about two people in their early- to mid-twenties. Not quite New Adult, but I'd still wanted to make sure I had the lingo down.

"Whatever." Harper took out her phone and shoved it in my hand. "Look at what I found."

I looked down and sucked in my breath. "Holy crap."

It was a photo of Travis. He was wearing only a pair of dog tags. The picture only went down to the waist, but it was low, and I was pretty sure he wasn't wearing any pants. He had spectacular arms, pecs, abs, and the famous V on his hips.

I pulled the phone closer. "How did I miss this?"

"I don't know, but it's good, right?"

I quickly peeked behind me. "Oh my God, yes. How did I not know he existed?"

"No idea because I found about five books he's on the cover on."

"I need to come out of my writing hole a little more often."

Harper laughed and took her phone back. She hit the

screen a few times and showed me another. And another. In a couple, he had shorter hair. In some others, his face was free of facial hair.

"I think I like him better with the beard," she said to me.

"Me, too," I said, amazed.

"Wow. I'm surprised to hear you say that after Andrew."

Andrew was a guy I'd dated a few years back who'd let his beard grow. And grow and grow. I'd hated it. It had almost ruined any sort of beard for me on a man, no matter how short. Even Harper didn't like beards as much after knowing my ex.

"Me, too."

Travis was different from other guys I'd been interested in before, minus the hot body. I wasn't going to lie. I'd always liked muscular men.

But there was no denying that I was attracted to Travis. I'd thought I was past the age of feeling boy-crazy, but he just did something for me. And my body. I wanted the man.

I put Harper's phone down. "I'd better stop looking, or I'll be the one who's going to need a restroom."

Harper frowned for a second until she got my joke. She laughed until the first reader walked up to our table.

FIVE

TRAVIS

I SAT BACK in my seat as the readers started coming into the room. This part of a book signing always got me a little excited. I really enjoyed interacting with fans, whether it was fans of mine or fans of the author I was with.

"Okay, Trav, it's time for you to smile that beautiful smile of yours and lure some readers in," Angela said.

I laughed because I knew she was joking, but she was also serious.

Angela was one of my favorite authors to attend signings with. I'd met her a few years earlier at an event like today's, and we'd hit it off. I considered her and her husband, Dave, close friends despite living a state and a Great Lake apart.

I plastered the cheesiest smile I could on my face. "How's this?"

"Perfect. You'll have them all running to the table."

At that moment, a reader did approach Angela's table. "Hi."

"Hello." Angela always greeted readers with enthusiasm. "How are you today?"

"Good," the reader said a little shyly.

"Have you ever read anything of mine before?"

The reader shook her head.

Angela had her books in piles in front of her, and she pointed to the one on the reader's left. "My books are part of a series, and this is book one." She guided her hand down the row of all four piles. "Book two, three, and four. They are sports romance. All the characters are on the same NFL team."

The reader picked up book one and looked at the back and then the front. She looked up at me. "Is this you?" She pointed to the cover where I stood with a blonde woman in my arms.

I smiled. I was always a little embarrassed when someone asked me that. I'd been taught to be humble, so I always felt like I was bragging a little when I said yes. "That's me."

"That's so cool," the reader whispered as another approached.

"Actually, Travis is on all the covers. Each book is about a different couple, so that's why you really see his face on book one and why each book has a different female model. It also helps that he has different hairstyles in a couple of them."

"Wow. You get around, don't you?" reader number two said.

They all laughed, but her comment bugged me a bit.

I shrugged. "They're just pictures. It's all part of the job. It's not like I dated any of them." I made sure to smile as I said this.

I had only really dated one fellow model, and it had

been bad from the start. I much preferred seeing someone who didn't work in the industry.

"I just hate to see Travis starve, so I buy his photos."

I bit my cheek, so I wouldn't laugh too hard.

But reader number two was unfazed by their comments. "I'll definitely buy book one. Will you both sign it?"

"Of course," Angela said. Then, she looked out of the corner of her eye at me. "Maybe."

I laughed again and grabbed the book first, so the reader could pay while I signed. Sometimes, I put little quotes or lines in with my signature, but nothing came to me, so I just wrote my name this time.

"I'll take the first two books," reader number one said after number two was gone.

"Thank you," Angela said.

The reader paid, and we both signed the insides.

After number one was gone, Angela pushed her shoulder into mine. "Thanks for helping me sell books."

"That's why you brought me."

"That, and your charming personality. Sorry about that reader's comment."

I smiled. "It's not your fault. And, yeah, it irked me a little, but it's really not that big of a deal." I lifted my brow. "Now, if she starts stalking me, then I'm going to blame you for bringing me here."

Angela laughed.

"You joke, but if I get any naked pics, I'm forwarding them to you."

Angela just continued to laugh.

The signing went on, and readers came and went. Some of them didn't pay much attention to me, and some were fascinated by me. I never really understood that because I was just a person like them. I wasn't anything special, no more than anyone else anyway.

The table was empty for the moment, so I took the opportunity to look at my phone. A few texts had come in, but I'd ignored them while readers were at the table.

"I always feel bad, saying this to another author, but I haven't read your books. Tell me about them," a musical voice said.

I looked up to see Sydney Hart.

She glanced at me for a second and smiled but turned her attention back to Angela. This let me look at her without her knowing.

She had the girl-next-door look going for her, and that was totally my thing. Women who wore a lot of makeup and fancy clothes never really did it for me. In fact, even though Sydney looked good, I actually preferred her the way she'd looked that morning at breakfast. No makeup and her glasses on. She had beautiful porcelain skin she didn't need to cover up with anything. Although I had overlooked her cool-ass eye that morning because of her glasses.

I was also a breast and a leg man. Maybe that made me a pervert, but I wasn't dead. I'd noticed Sydney's ample chest. And, while she wasn't very tall, I could tell she had long legs for her height. For a moment, I let myself picture them naked and spread open for me while I—

"*Travis.*" Angela smacked my arm.

"What?"

Angela gave me a *seriously, dude* look.

29

I shrugged. "Sorry. I wasn't paying attention." One thing I'd learned in life was to own up to things even if it made me look less than favorable. Life was too short to lie, especially about petty shit.

"Sydney is buying books one and two and an extra book one. So, get to signing."

Wow. I really had missed a chunk of the conversation. "Why two?"

"I'm buying a set for myself and book one for my reader group. I like to do giveaways, and they love getting signed books from other authors even if they've never read them before. Plus, it helps get author names out there."

"I love that idea," Angela said. "I'll have to come over and get one of your books and do the same. I'm always looking for a way to engage my readers."

I took one copy of the first book and wrote, *Never give up on your dreams*, and then signed it. The book was about a football player who got injured and was worried that he'd never play again. *Don't give up* fit with the story and was inspiring, too.

I slid the book over to Sydney. "This one is for your reader."

She opened it up, read the inside, and smiled. "Thank you." Then, she pushed the book over to Angela to sign.

"Damn it, Travis. That's what I was going to write."

I laughed. "You can write that in the next one." I gave her the second copy of book one. "I'll even let you write in it first."

"Wow, that's so magnanimous of you," she said sarcastically.

I crossed my eyes. "I sorry. Me dumb model. Me no understand big words."

Sydney laughed. "You two must have a lot of fun together."

Angela nodded. "We do. Sometimes, too much."

A look crossed over Sydney's face for a fleeting moment, but it passed as quickly as it'd come, and she grinned. "I bet there are some good stories there."

"There are. Someday, I'll tell you."

I opened up book two. This was a story about a nerdy girl who fell in love with the bachelor-of-the-year football player. I decided on a saying that went with the story but was also directed at Sydney:

You're more beautiful than you know.

I traded books with Angela, and in book one, I wrote,

Some things are worth fighting for.

When Sydney opened them up, her eyes widened, and she might have blushed. "Wow. I think I should maybe give these to my readers instead."

"I don't think so. Those are for you."

SIX

SYDNEY

I BROUGHT the books I'd bought from Angela back to my table to put away for safekeeping. I pulled the copy I'd gotten for my readers off the top and handed it to Harper. "Look inside. They both signed it. I hope my readers love it."

She opened the cover and looked inside, read what Angela and Travis had written, and then hugged the book to her chest. "Can you just give it to me as a present?" She batted her eyelashes. "Or let me be the winner?"

I grabbed for the book, but she held on. "If I give it to you straight-out, then that would be cheating."

She stuck her bottom lip out.

"Harper, it was ten dollars. Go buy your own."

"Fine." She let go and stuck her nose in the air. "But, now, you know that'll be one less book of yours I'm going to buy."

I playfully shoved her. "You already own all my books, free of charge."

"Oh, yeah."

We both laughed as I quickly put my book away before she stole it from me.

"Why don't you go get one now before you forget?"

"You're right. I probably should." She pulled out some cash from her purse and got up from the table.

Since my table was vacant of readers, I did a little organizing in hopes that it would help with cleanup later.

"Hey."

I looked up to see Derek. "Hey. What's up? You having fun?"

He nodded. "I always do. You?"

"Yeah. There're still some tables I want to get to before the event is over, but so far, it's been fun."

"So, earlier, I mentioned a writer group that is forming in our area. Would you be interested in joining?"

"Yes, tell me more."

"Well, you know how there are so many groups online, which is great. But a few of us have been talking and thought we should do something where we got to meet in person, too. We were thinking once a month or even once every other month, depending on people's schedules."

"I like that idea. It's so great to have writer friends online, but sometimes, it would be so much easier to talk about things in person. Especially those complicated plots."

Derek smiled. "Exactly."

"How many are going to do it?"

"So far, it's only three of us, but I know I have some other contacts in the area. I need to go through my Facebook friends."

"Do you care if I invite some?"

"No. The more, the better. I figure not everyone will

always be able to make it, so if we could get around ten authors, then we'd hopefully always have a few who could attend our meetups."

"That sounds like fun." I picked up my business card and handed it to him. "I know you can contact me through Facebook, but here's my e-mail. That might be easier. When are you looking to start?"

"That's the hard part. We don't know. Next month is Halloween, then Thanksgiving, and then Christmas and New Year's."

"That's a good point."

He smiled. "We'll figure it out." He held up the card. "Thanks for the interest. I'd better get back to my table."

"Later."

A few minutes later, Harper came back and sat down with her new book. "What did Derek want?"

"He wanted to talk about the writer group he'd mentioned earlier. It's an in-person group, and he asked if I wanted to join."

"Ooh. Maybe then you can ask him out."

I rolled my eyes. "I'm not asking him out." He was attractive, but I wasn't attracted *to* him.

"Well, you should. When's the last time you got laid?"

"None of your damn business."

"Translation: *So long that I don't even remember.*"

"Shut up."

Harper laughed at me.

"I hate you."

"You love me."

I sighed. "Unfortunately."

I laughed at Harper's scowl.

We heard some voices laughing behind us, so we turned around. It looked like some readers were getting pictures with Travis.

"We should do that," Harper said. "He's been taking pictures all day. I bet your readers would love to see some pics of him."

"That's not a bad idea."

"Not a bad idea? It's a great idea."

I stood. "Okay, let's do it."

While I couldn't deny that I wouldn't hate being close to him, I felt silly for asking for a picture with him. He had all these women gawking over him, and I really didn't want to be another one. Even if I was secretly just as bad as they were. I wanted to pretend like I wasn't like other girls, but I totally was.

Harper and I walked over to Angela's table.

"Do you care if we take pictures with you both?" I asked.

Ha. If we asked for both, it would look less like we only wanted a picture with Travis. *Way to go, brain!*

I took a picture with just Angela and then Angela and Harper. Harper took one with Angela alone. We asked another author to take a picture of the four of us. And then it was Harper, Travis, and me. Harper and Travis took a picture and then just Travis and me.

Both times, I wanted to bury my nose in his chest and breathe him in.

Down, girl.

But I settled for just enjoying his arm around me. After each picture was taken, he rubbed my back, and I was disappointed when he dropped his arm.

I mentally sighed. *Why does he have to be nice, down-to-earth, and so damn good-looking?*

Harper and I sat back at my table, and I leaned over to her.

"Did he rub your back after your pictures were taken?"

"*Yes.* Don't be doing that. Don't tease me with something I can't have."

I burst out laughing. "Right?" I expressed out loud to her about how he had a trifecta going for him.

"Remember what we talked about this morning though."

I frowned. "What was that again?"

"That he is probably bad in bed and would make you do all the work."

I laughed. "Oh, yeah."

She picked up one of the two-inch penis suckers and moved closer to me. "And it's probably only a little bigger than this."

I bit my lip as I tried not to laugh too loudly. "You are so bad."

Harper wiggled her eyebrows and grinned. "I know."

SEVEN

SYDNEY

I FLIPPED open covers of the two books I'd bought from Angela Devlin to see what Travis had written. It was only the twentieth time, but I loved his words. I understood why he'd written them because I'd read the blurbs of each book, but a part of me felt like he'd written them just for me.

Silly, I know.

That was part of his charm, and I shouldn't read too much into it.

The toilet flushed in our hotel bathroom, and I slammed the books down. I was way too old to have a schoolgirl crush on someone I would probably never see again.

The door swung open. "You ready to go?" Harper asked.

"Yep." Not only was I starving, but it would also give me something to do to keep my mind off a certain model.

The book signing was over, and we had just hauled all my stuff up to the hotel room. Now, we were in search of food.

"I can't believe how hungry I am from just sitting there,"

Harper said as we left our room, making sure the door locked behind us.

"I know what you mean. I guess socializing burns a lot of calories."

"I'd just better not eat too much since we have our fancy dinner tonight."

I looked at my Fitbit. "Yeah, we have a little over three hours until then. From what I've heard, the food is going to be good."

"Oh, me, too. That author, um...Tracey Munz, she was telling me about it."

"Did you have fun today? Would you ever want to do it again?"

Harper nodded. "I did. And I have a pile of stuff from authors I want to read. I'm excited to try some of the books out. I hope that, for your next signing, you'll ask me again."

"I will." It was September now, and it was my last one of the year. "I have some I'm looking into for next year. I'll give you plenty of warning, so you can work out what to do with Wyatt."

We made it down to the lobby and headed to the bar area.

"Where should we sit?" I asked.

It wasn't crowded, but there were only so many open seats. The back had alcoves that were almost like their own little private areas, and we walked toward them.

"Hey," someone called out to us, and Harper and I both looked over to see Angela waving her hand.

"I guess we're sitting over there," Harper said with a smile.

So much for forgetting about Travis.

We walked over to their alcove. There was a long bench in the middle with Travis sitting on it. There were two short benches adjacent to it, and Angela sat at one. I moved to sit opposite her, but Harper beat me to it.

"Sorry, Syd, but I don't think Ian would like me sitting next to Travis," she joked.

"*Hey*," Travis protested.

Harper laughed while I grudgingly sat next to him. He still smelled delicious, even after hours of sitting at the book signing, although most of his cologne had worn off. It was all him now. Pure testosterone.

I made a mental note to pick up a First Response test on Monday because I was probably going to get pregnant just by sitting next to him.

The waitress came over and asked us if we'd like to order.

"Did you two order already?" I asked.

"Only about five minutes ago."

"Okay then, I'll have the cheeseburger," I told the waitress. The menu was small, and I remembered it from earlier.

"I'll have the quesadilla," Harper said after flipping the menu over a couple of times.

The waitress took the menus and left. I looked over at Travis to see him watching me.

Oh, was this supposed to be one of those things where I only ate a salad? Too bad. We weren't on a date. Plus, I had a healthy appreciation for food. Perhaps a little too healthy at times, but I was starving.

"Are you two not going to the dinner tonight?" Travis asked.

"No, we're going. I'm just really hungry."

We were almost finished eating when I got a message from my editor about a couple of mistakes I needed to fix in my latest book. Normally, I would wait to clean up the errors until I got back home, but I had a release coming up in less than a month, and my computer was upstairs. I felt like it wasn't something that should wait when I could do it now.

"I have to go and take care of something in the room," I told Harper. "It shouldn't take me too long. Do you want me to come back here and find you?"

"Oh, well…" She looked at Angela and Travis. "How long are you staying?"

Angela sighed. "Until dinner tonight. We had to check out of our rooms already."

Harper and I both winced.

"Are you driving back tonight?"

"Yeah," Angela said. "I have to get back for my kids. We'll drive back tonight, and then I'll fly home tomorrow before my husband goes to work on Monday."

"Ouch," I commented. "That's a short trip."

"I know. And, after getting here late last night, I was actually thinking of taking a nap in the car before tonight's dinner." Angela laughed.

"I don't know why. You know I'll do most of the driving," Travis said.

Harper and I exchanged looks. I felt bad that they had to hang out in the bar area. We had over two hours to go before dinner.

"Why don't you come and hang out in our room? We

have Netflix hooked up. We could watch a movie and rest. If you want to nap, Angela, you can," Harper offered.

"We will totally take you up on that," Angela said.

"Yeah, thanks," Travis said. "It beats sitting here for two hours."

"Okay, well, I'm going to go up now. I'll see you all in a few."

"Later," Harper said.

I took off for our hotel room. Once inside, I did a quick sweep. The maids had come and cleaned up our dirty towels and made the beds. And, thankfully, we didn't have unmentionables lying around.

I grabbed my computer and sat on my bed. I had picked the one closest to the window and the heater since I got cold at night. I waited for my computer to connect to the hotel's Wi-Fi, and as it did that, I turned on the TV and started up Netflix.

I pulled up my e-mail and my latest manuscript. I fixed the few things I needed to and sent it off to my editor again.

I set my computer down on the nightstand between the beds and lay down just as Harper, Travis, and Angela walked in.

"I'll be right out," Harper said and walked into the bathroom.

"Make yourselves comfortable." I waved my hand across the room in a welcome gesture. "Sit. Lie down." I pointed to myself with two hands. "As you can see, I already am."

I hoped Harper wouldn't mind if the two of them sat or lay on her bed, but technically, she was the one who had invited them up.

Travis walked over and grabbed the remote, and then he

jumped over me to land on the open spot next to me. "What are we watching?" he said as he put an arm behind his head.

Angela sat on the outside of Harper's bed. "He always has to play couch commando. I never get the remote when we hang out together."

Travis laughed. "I suppose, technically, it's bed commando," he said as he flipped through the choices and landed on the latest *Thor* movie.

I scanned his body, which was so close to mine. *Yeah, I'd like to play a whole different kind of bed commando with you, Travis.*

When I get home, I am making a date with my vibrator.

EIGHT

SYDNEY

SURPRISINGLY, I got into the movie and forgot that a handsome model was lying on the *same bed as me*. So much so that I even dozed for a bit myself.

"Psst."

I looked up from the TV to Harper. "What?" I whispered.

Travis and Angela had both fallen asleep, and I didn't want to wake them since they had a long drive ahead of them.

"You should totally take a picture," she said so low that I had to read her lips to catch everything she was saying.

I wrinkled my nose. "What?"

"Take a picture. You know…" She held her hand above her, leaned closer to Angela, and posed as she pretended to snap a photo. She looked at me again and pointed rather enthusiastically behind me. "Take. A. Picture."

I laughed. "No way."

"Yes. When are you ever going to have a hot model in your bed again? Take a pic. It's proof."

I shook my head and hoped the bed wasn't moving from my silent laughter.

Harper pursed her lips at me like she was mad, but she couldn't get rid of the smile on her face.

She swiped her phone off the nightstand, hit the Home button, and stood.

"Smile," she said right before she took a series of pictures.

Click, click, click, click, click.

"Harper," I whispered as loudly as I could, but she ignored me.

"Those aren't that good." She held up her phone and took more.

"Stop it."

She was still ignoring me as she studied her handiwork.

I stuck my foot out and tried to kick her, but she stepped back.

"I don't know. These aren't great either."

"*Harper.*" I scooted closer to the edge of the bed. "*Stop.*"

I kicked my leg out again...and landed flat on the floor.

BOOM.

"Holy shit, what was that?" Angela yelled as I caught sight of her sitting up on the bed.

Harper's mouth formed an O before she doubled over and began howling with laughter. "Oh my God, are you okay?" she barely managed to say.

I put my head on my arm. "Kill me now."

Harper laughed harder.

I rolled onto my back to see Travis peeking over the edge of my bed.

"Is anything hurt?" he asked out of concern, but I could see he was trying not to laugh, too.

"Just my pride."

Travis grinned.

"Go ahead. Laugh."

And he did.

I looked over at the other bed where Angela was laughing.

"I'm so glad we met you. This has been the best book signing ever."

About an hour later, Harper, Angela, Travis, my wounded pride, and I went down to the dinner that the event coordinators had set up for us. The dinner had different tables sponsored by various authors who had attended, and readers got to pick whose table they wanted to sit at.

I hadn't sponsored a table and hadn't picked an author to sit with, so Harper and I had to wait off to the side.

"We're sitting at Marsha Hansen's table," Angela said. "We'll see you two later." She waved, and Travis smiled as they walked past us.

"Are you okay?" Harper asked.

I rubbed my hip where I'd landed. "Yes, I'll be fine."

"In that case, why couldn't you have waited to fall until after I started taking pictures again, so I could've gotten some good action shots?"

I sarcastically laughed at her.

She put her arm around me. "I'm sorry, babe. It was just so funny. I wish you could have seen it."

"I'm so embarrassed."

She pulled away and studied my face. "Really? You didn't act like it. Way to go." She nodded. "I'm impressed."

"It's all those years I worked with difficult clients. I built up fake face, so they couldn't see how frustrated I was with them."

"Well, it worked."

"I just can't believe that I fell like that. In front of Travis of all people." I narrowed my eyes at her. "I blame you."

"I'm sorry."

"No, you're not."

Her mouth dropped open, but she was trying not to smile. "I really am. My goal wasn't to embarrass you."

"I know. But…" I looked around. We were in a room full of people, but they were all talking, and the acoustics weren't great. I could barely hear what the people next to us were saying. I leaned toward her ear. "I know this is going to sound crazy—I mean, I know that a guy like Travis probably has tons of girls falling at his feet, beautiful girls—but I felt like we had this…chemistry."

I drew back to look at Harper's face, and she nodded in understanding.

She squeezed my forearm and leaned toward my ear. "If it makes you feel any better, I know exactly what you mean. I felt like I had chemistry with him, too. It must be part of his charm or whatever. He's just one of those guys. Somehow, he's magnetic." She pulled back and smiled sympathetically.

I nodded. "Thanks. That does make me feel better." Or at least, it should, but it really didn't.

I hadn't realized how much I wanted to feel special and that he liked me until Harper said that to me.

It was a crazy dream, but feelings were feelings, and attraction was attraction. The only thing that would help was time. There was no magic wand to make those emotions go away.

My phone buzzed in my hand, so I opened it up to see about a dozen or so pictures of Travis sleeping on my hotel bed with me with various expressions on my face. I was shocked or angry, and they all looked pretty comical.

Harper bumped shoulders with me, and I looked up at her.

"Thanks. I'll cherish them always," I said with a hint of sarcasm.

Harper laughed and threw her arm around me again. "That's my girl."

NINE

SYDNEY

FIVE MONTHS LATER

"I think that's it for me. Does anyone have anything else?" Derek asked our monthly author group.

I shook my head, as did the other five authors in attendance that month.

"All right. Let's get out of here then and go enjoy the rest of the weekend."

I stood up from the table at a local coffee shop where we met once a month. We met on Saturdays because some of the authors still had full-time jobs.

I shoved my arms into my winter coat and pulled my hat over my head. It was the beginning of February in Minnesota, which meant it was still cold outside. I had ordered a coffee when I arrived that morning, but I decided to get another for my drive home.

After getting my drink, I walked back over to the table we'd been sitting at. Derek was packing up his laptop and putting his coat on.

"What are you doing the rest of the day?" I asked him.

"I have plans with a friend, and then maybe I'll get a thousand words in this evening. We'll see."

"Yeah, I understand how that goes. Good intentions."

"What do you have planned?"

"I have to go through some edits for my next release, and then my dad and my brother and his family are coming over for dinner."

Derek strung his laptop bag over his shoulder. "Are you cooking?"

"Unfortunately."

"You don't like to cook?"

"I do. I just don't really want to take the time to do it. You know how it is when you get on a roll with writing or editing. I wasn't thinking when I planned this dinner."

"I hear ya."

We stopped at the door to say goodbye because we both knew that, once we opened it, we'd want to run for the shelter of our cars.

"I hope you have a good rest of the day. Good luck on the writing," I told him.

"Yeah. You, too."

I pushed open the door and took off. "Bye," I yelled behind me.

"See you next month."

I unlocked my car and slipped behind the wheel. It was already warming up, thanks to my automatic start.

I pulled my phone out of my purse to see if I had any messages before I took off for home.

My niece, Lexie, had texted about a half hour ago to say she was heading over to my house. She had her own key, so she could let herself in.

My brother was eight years older than me, and Lexie had been born when I was eighteen. Technically, I was old enough to be her mother, but she was more like a little sister to me, and she often came to my house to hang out. Whether it was to spend time with me or to get away from her parents and younger siblings, it didn't matter because she knew she was always welcome. My house was her home away from home.

I also had a few Facebook notifications, which I scanned through to see if there was anything I wanted to address before I left the parking lot. There was nothing that couldn't wait until I got home.

And I also had an Instagram notification that the people I followed had new stories. Travis's name was always first. I didn't know why. He wasn't the first person I'd followed, and he wasn't the last person. I thought Instagram was just trying to torture me.

Since the book signing in September, I had tried to forget about Travis. I told myself he was just another guy. Sure, he was nice and good-looking, but he was far from the only man out there like that.

Yet I couldn't stop thinking about him. It wasn't every minute of every day or anything. I wasn't obsessed. But he was definitely the object of my desire, and I did think about him often.

I had even gone on a date with someone I wasn't that into a month ago in hopes of forgetting about Travis. The date went okay. We went back to the guy's place and made out, but it was obvious that the guy couldn't find any woman's hot buttons, even with a diagram and step-by-step directions, so I called a halt to going any further.

I'd left with a nice goodbye, deleted his number off my phone, and gone home and gotten myself off. I might have looked up some half-naked pictures of Travis first, but nobody could prove that, and I wasn't going to admit to anything.

I had friend-requested Travis on Facebook and followed him on Instagram after returning home from the book signing but gotten nothing in return from him. He hadn't accepted my request or followed me back. I'd commented on a few of his posts, too, just to show him I was out there, but nothing. Every time I saw that he'd liked every single one of Angela's posts, I got jealous. I was also envious of the obvious friendship that I'd witnessed when I met them. It wasn't that I didn't want them to be friends. I just wanted to be close to him like that, too.

But jealousy was a rotten emotion, and I wanted to believe that I was maturer than that. I hated feeling that way. I'd done jealousy when I was younger. I'd been on the receiving and giving end, and it was never pretty.

I thought about unfollowing Travis, but then that seemed petty, like I was doing it because he wasn't following me. So, instead, I swiped the notification, making it disappear from my screen. I put my car in drive and headed home.

TEN

SYDNEY

"HEY, LEXIE," I called out when I got home.

"In here," she answered as I took off my wet shoes and hung up my coat.

I walked into the living room. "What's up?"

She shrugged, making her long, dark hair fall off her shoulders. "Nothing. Just wanted to come over. Do you care if I spend the night?"

I dropped down beside her on the couch. "Of course not. Everything okay?"

She pulled her legs to her chest and put her chin on her knee. "Yeah. Brendan and I had a fight."

"Oh, honey." I put my hand on her back and rubbed. Brendan was Lexie's boyfriend, and they often ran hot and cold. "Are you okay?"

"Yeah. I think we both need to just cool off. Is it bad that I don't want to talk to him right now?"

I shook my head. "No. Sometimes, it's better to talk about things later." I pulled her into a hug. "You're welcome to hang out as long as you want."

Lexie pulled away and sat back up. "Thanks."

I slapped my hands on my knees. "I wish I could stay and chat, but I have to get some work done before I start dinner." I stood. "Are you helping me?"

"Sure."

"Thank God. Come find me around four if I don't emerge from my cave, okay?"

Lexie laughed. "Will do."

I went upstairs to one of the bedrooms that I used as my office and shut the door to drown out any noises from downstairs. Maleficent pushed the door open a crack, and I left it as she jumped onto my desk to lie down next to my computer. I hit the power button, and after it started, I pulled up my latest manuscript. It was a completely different book from the one I'd been working on five months ago, and I was in love with the story.

It was a story about a young girl who fell in love with her older neighbor. She was in middle school, and he was the big, popular high schooler. He graduated, and his family moved away. Fast-forward to fifteen years later where she was a physical therapist, and she was assigned to help an injured military veteran whom no one wanted to deal with because he was a jerk. The client ended up being her former neighbor and was so completely different from the boy she used to idolize.

I had titled it *Beautifully Broken*, thanks to one of my readers, and I'd had a lot of fun writing the book. Unfortunately, I was only halfway through editing the eighty-thousand-word book, and I still had to figure out what I wanted to do about the cover. I was starting to push the deadline and needed to make a decision. I had another book signing in two months, and I wanted to have the book completed by then. I also needed to get all my information to my PR representative so that she could get my blog tour started.

With a sigh, I opened my book and made myself read through at least ten chapters before I started looking at photographs for the front of my book. I hit a good roll and actually made it through fifteen chapters before I stopped. I saved my work and closed it.

Next stop: handsome men and beautiful women.

When I'd started writing books, I couldn't afford much. So, like many authors, I'd used stock photos. I had books published with those photos, and I still loved those covers, too. However, every once in a while, someone would accuse me in a roundabout way of stealing. I would then explain that stock photos were royalty-free photographs that could be used over and over again by multiple authors. It always irked me when someone would call me a thief and then ignore my explanation.

So, as soon as I could comfortably afford it, I started purchasing exclusive photos for my books. I loved that I had a picture that no one else would have. The only downside was that I had to make sure I loved it. At anywhere from three hundred to eight hundred dollars an image, I had to make sure I was ready for it to be on my book for life. With a stock photo, they were a lot cheaper, and I could change out the image later if I wanted to.

I went to one of my favorite photographer's websites. I had been avoiding it because I discovered that Travis was one of the models he photographed. A lot. Before I'd met him, Travis had been a blip on my radar. So much so that I never even realized that I had looked at some of his images before. Now, I had been going out of my way to avoid it.

It wasn't like I didn't want to see pictures of him. I just didn't want to see a particular picture of him. It was one that I wanted for the cover of my book so incredibly badly, but there was a part of me that was so afraid that it would show the world I liked him. Like there would be a huge neon sign over my head, announcing that he was my number one crush.

I knew that was absolutely ridiculous. No one actually knew how I felt, except Harper, and even she didn't know how much I thought about the guy. Plus, it was doubtful he remembered me. He wouldn't think anything of me putting him on the cover of my book.

Sometimes, I really wished I could get out of my own head. I loved the stories it came up with for my fictional characters, but it didn't need to come up with drama for my real life. I was very happy, living drama-free.

My office door opened behind me, and Lexie said, "Wow. That's hot."

I sighed. "I know."

Travis was lying on a bed with a beautiful blonde. He was shirtless with his jeans riding low. She wore a blouse that was unbuttoned to mid-chest with a hint of cleavage showing in a very sensual way. Her head was turned away from Travis, and he had his mouth on her neck. It was very sexy.

And, man, did I want to be that woman. Surprisingly, this didn't make me jealous. I thought it was because I knew that it wasn't real. It was staged, and they were posing. But it sure as hell made me want. It made me want to be her and for his mouth to be on my neck and for it to be real.

She stepped closer. "Hey, is that the guy you met at your book signing?"

"Yeah." My face suddenly felt warm.

"And you're just sitting in here, drooling over his picture, because you think he's hot or what?"

I turned my head and shot her a look. *Teenagers.*

"Yes, he's gorgeous, but I'm looking at it because I really want it for my next book cover. Their hair colors match my characters', and there is actually a scene where it would be a perfect match."

"So, why don't you buy it?"

"Because I'm afraid it'll be weird."

She wrinkled her nose. "How?"

"Because I just met him, and then I put him on my book. What if he thinks I'm a crazy stalker or something now?"

"Are you?"

I gave her an *are you kidding me* look. "No, I'm not stalking him. But I did start following him on social media."

"Okay, but did you start following anyone else you met at the signing?"

"Oh, yeah. Several authors and I became friends even."

"And have you bought their books?"

"Some of them, yes."

"And you don't think that they think you're stalking them, right?"

"Well...no."

She was right. It was because I liked him. But, if I took a step back and objectively thought about it, there would be nothing significant about me buying a picture of him after I met him. Just like I had done with the authors I'd met.

I narrowed my eyes at her. "How did you get to be so smart?"

"It's because I come from a long line of smart people, including my aunt."

I laughed. "Good answer."

She pretended to brush off her shoulder. "I know." She nudged me. "Do it. Buy the picture. You're never going to be happy with anything else if this is the one you want."

She was right again. And he was only one person. I was going to have hundreds of fans who would hopefully love my cover.

"Okay, I'll e-mail the photographer and my book cover designer."

She clapped her hands, and her brown eyes sparkled. "Yay."

"Go on. Get out of here, so I can get that done. Then, we can start dinner."

She walked toward the door. "Just remember who helped you. You might want to dedicate this book to me."

"I've already dedicated two others to you."

"You can never have too many dedicated to me."

I laughed as she walked away. Then, I opened up my e-mail and drafted my first message.

ELEVEN

SYDNEY

I LEFT MY OFFICE, feeling very excited. The photographer had thankfully been available right away. I sent my money, he sent the photo, and I sent it off to my book designer. I couldn't wait to see the finished product.

Jessica and I had been working together since I started, and we had become friends. She told me she'd already been working on some ideas but was just waiting for the final main piece. Whenever she sent my book covers, it was like Christmas, and I was a child who couldn't wait to open my gift.

I walked into my kitchen in a great mood to see Lexie had already started working on dinner. She was peeling the potatoes because she knew I hated that job.

"You're the best niece ever. Why can't you be my kid?"

She laughed as I grabbed the two pounds of beef from the fridge. Tonight, we were having meatloaf and mashed potatoes. It wasn't a fancy dinner, but it was my late mother's recipe and my father's favorite. He couldn't cook to save his life, so I enjoyed making it for him.

I got out the rest of the ingredients, but before I got my hands dirty, I poured myself a glass of wine.

"Can I have some?"

I laughed. "No."

We got into our cooking groove, and before I knew it, the meatloaf was in the oven, the potatoes were on the stove, and my family was at my door.

"Smells good in here, Sydney," my father boomed as he came through the door.

"Thanks, Dad."

My brother and sister-in-law were right behind him.

"Hey, Ryan. Hey, Grace," I said. "Where are Ben and Gretchen?"

"Slowly getting out of the car," my brother said. "When you can't turn your phone off for two minutes, it makes normal activities twice as long."

Ben was thirteen, and Gretchen was eleven, and I thought they were worse than Lexie when it came to their phones. To me, that always seemed backward.

The two of them came through the door a few seconds later, both with their eyes on their screens.

"Hey. Nice of you to make it," I said.

They both looked up and smiled.

"Hey, Aunt Sydney," Ben said, and Gretchen gave me a hug.

Everyone took off their coats and hung them in the closet.

My father had his usual Minnesota Vikings jersey on even though football season was over. It was either Vikings, Twins, or a Wild jersey or shirt. I honestly didn't think he owned anything besides sports clothes. Maybe one button-up shirt for those rare, special occasions, like a wedding.

My brother was a pharmaceutical rep and dressed up for his job, so he liked to wear T-shirts and jeans on his days off. Don't be fooled however. They were two-hundred-dollar jeans and fifty-dollar T-shirts. No Hanes or Fruit of the Loom for Ryan.

And my sister-in-law was always dressed up and looking fancy. We got along really well, but we were so different. I was wearing Old Navy jeans and a comfortable sweater from Maurice's. My brown hair had air-dried after my shower, and I'd brushed once this afternoon. I wore minimal makeup that had probably worn off from this morning. I thought I'd gotten my fashion sense from my dad.

Grace, on the other hand, looked like she was going out for dinner and drinks with her other high-class friends. Her blonde hair was curled and styled, her makeup was flawless, her clothes were stylish, and her jewelry matched perfectly. And she had on high heels. I didn't even own high heels, and she was wearing them to a casual family dinner.

There was a time when I had tried to be someone more like Grace. I had gone through a phase in college where I tried to be cute and stylish every day, but it was such a chore. Things like that came naturally to Grace. It was just the kind of person she was. And the kind of person I wasn't.

We might get along, but we never were and never would be really good friends.

She was also the kind of woman I pictured Travis being with. Someone who always looked beautiful and was dressed to the nines. My style was comfortable and casual. That meant I had to make sure to leave the house looking like I wasn't a homeless person.

The nice thing about being in my mid-thirties was that any insecurity I'd had when I was younger about not being that kind of woman was long gone. I was who I was, and if I started dating a guy, even Travis, and he wanted me to be fancier, I would say, *See ya*. Life was too short to spend two hours getting ready every morning.

If that was your thing, awesome for you. In fact, my sister-in-law probably had her routine down to a fraction of the two hours it would take me. And, if you enjoyed it, go for it. I didn't. I'd rather, write, read, watch TV, or even go to the gym. But that was just me.

"You all know to make yourselves comfortable. I'm just going to check on the potatoes."

Grace followed me into the kitchen. "Hey, honey," she said and pulled her daughter into a hug. "How was your afternoon?"

Lexie smiled. "Good. And yours?"

"Good. I'm glad to be here now though."

"Wine?" I asked Grace.

She grinned. "You know you don't have to ask me twice."

I poured her a glass and topped off my own. Then, I grabbed a beer each for my dad and brother and took it to them like the good hostess I was. They both knew that, after that, they would have to get up and get their own.

I headed back to the kitchen again when my phone beeped. I pulled it out of my back pocket and scrolled down to the attachment.

My book cover designer was already done. I held my

breath as I opened my e-mail and squealed when I saw the results. I hurried to show Lexie what my cover designer had sent back to me.

"Lexie, look. My book cover is already done." I turned my phone around and showed it to her.

"I love it," Lexie said.

"Wow. That is gorgeous," Grace said.

I turned the phone back around. "I think so."

As I e-mailed my cover designer back, praising her for her awesome skills, Lexie told Grace about who was on my cover.

"That guy is the model she met in Iowa."

"The one you had on your Facebook page?"

"Yes," Lexie answered for me.

To be fair, I had posted all the pictures I'd taken that day on my Facebook page. It wasn't just the ones of Travis.

"You should invite him to your next book signing."

My eyes flew up, and I laughed uncomfortably. "What?"

"He's on the cover of your new book, and he's hot. You will have readers flock to your table to buy your book."

Grace had majored in marketing in college, and she wasn't wrong. There had been a lot of people at Angela Devlin's table at the Iowa signing.

"I would feel like I'm using him."

"Didn't you just buy a picture because you'd met him at the signing?"

"Yes."

She raised her brow. "See? It's good exposure for him, too. And you'd be asking him. He could always say no."

"Now, I know how Lexie got to be so smart."

Grace laughed, but it was true. She was pretty and intelligent. I used to feel threatened by women like that, but now, I was proud she was my sister-in-law.

I bit my lip. "I don't know." My next signing was right here in the Cities. It would be perfect because he wouldn't have to travel. "It's a good idea, but..."

"But what?" Grace asked.

"Sydney's got a crush," Lexie singsonged.

"Shut up, brat. I'm too old to have a crush. I have a healthy interest in him," I said and stuck my nose in the air, pretending to be snooty.

She laughed.

Grace smiled at her daughter. "Does he know you have a crush on him?"

I grimaced. "God, I hope not."

Grace pointed to my phone. "Then, ask him."

"I'll think about it."

After dinner, I remembered to send my new book cover to Harper while my family went to hang out in the living room.

> Harper: OMG. That's hot. I want him to kiss me all over like that.

> Me: LOL. Me, too. But I don't want him to stop at kissing me.

Me: Grace says that I should ask him to come to my next book signing, but I feel weird about it. She says it'll help promote the book.

Harper: You totally should. Look how many readers were at Angela's table.

Me: I know. I thought about that. But what if he doesn't remember me? What if he's like, "Who the hell is this woman, and why is she contacting me?"

Harper: He's not going to think that. He might not remember you right away, but he probably will after you remind him. He did hang out in our hotel room for a while. I doubt he completely forgot about us.

Me: That's true.

Harper: The worst thing he can say is no. You really have nothing to lose.

Me: Yeah. You're right.

Harper: *wiggles eyebrows* I know I am. So, DO IT.

Me: I'll think about it.

Several glasses of wine later, with a whole lot of liquid courage, I did it.

TWELVE

TRAVIS

I WIPED my face off with my towel and looked at my watch. I'd come into the gym to work out before I went to have a late dinner with some friends. I normally tried to be done by six, so I could intermittent fast for at least twelve hours. But it was Saturday night, and I was more lenient with myself on the weekends.

I had just enough time to hit the showers and head over to the restaurant to meet my friends.

I threw my towel over my shoulder and headed to the locker room. I rounded the corner and ran into my ex. She had on street clothes, her gym bag on her shoulder, her auburn hair was done, and her makeup looked fresh.

"Hey, Trav," Christy said.

"Hey."

We both stood there for a few seconds, staring at each other. We'd broken up over a month before I went to Iowa with Angela, and we'd managed to avoid each other since.

Christy was a fellow personal trainer. Since we basically got to pick the hours we were at the gym, so we could work around our clients' schedules, we'd done a good job of never having to stop and say more than a polite hello.

"How have you been?" I asked her.

"Good. Great. And you?"

"Pretty good." I'd gone on a couple of dates but nothing serious. And standing in front of her now, with just the two of us in the hall, made me realize I kind of missed her.

"How's work going?"

"Good. Although all those New Year's resolutioners have mostly fallen off the wagon already."

She chuckled. "Yeah. Same for me."

"Are you heading home for the night?"

"Yeah. I just finished with a client."

I was probably making a big mistake, but I opened my mouth and asked her anyway, "I was going to dinner with some friends. You want to tag along?"

Her blue eyes widened. "Uh, sure." She smiled. "That sounds like fun."

"Give me five, and I'll be out."

"Sounds good."

When we got to the restaurant, my friends—Broderick, Dan, and Lilah—didn't look happy to see my ex with me.

"Hi," they all said in strained voices.

I wasn't surprised. Things hadn't ended well with Christy and me.

"Dude," Broderick said, "I need to talk to you a minute."

"I'll be right back," I told Christy. *Be nice*, I mouthed to Dan and Lilah.

Broderick pulled me away. "What the hell? Why did you bring her here?"

I shrugged. "We ran into each other at work, and it just came out."

Broderick pinched the bridge of his nose and shook his head. "Did you forget what she put you through? All her accusations? All the times you had to walk on pins and needles around her? Did you forget how she *hacked into your phone to spy on you?*"

I winced. "No, I didn't forget." But my anger and hurt had faded some. "This is not a date. We're not getting back together. I invited her out, thinking maybe we could be friends at least. We were together a year and a half."

Broderick put his hand on my shoulder. "I hope you're right, but broken up or not, I don't think her jealous nature is going to fade. She's insecure, and she's never going to be able to handle you being with someone else." He dropped his arm. "She couldn't stand you being friends with other girls or taking pictures. I can't imagine what she's going to do when you are actually dating someone."

I sighed. "It's fine. We're just having dinner"—I spread my arms—"with friends. We're not alone."

"I hope you're right," Broderick said and headed back to our table.

I followed Broderick and sat down next to Christy. She gave me a questioning look, but I smiled and shook my head.

Dinner was going well, and I was reminded of when Christy and I had first begun to date. She had been laughing and joking all night with my friends. Maybe me breaking up with her had helped her realize that she needed to work on some things.

I did come to the conclusion that I missed being in a relationship more than being with Christy herself. She'd put her hand on me a couple of times, but the spark was gone.

My phone vibrated on the table. It was the first time it had gone off all night, and I froze.

Toward the end of our relationship, it had seemed like every time I got a phone call, an e-mail, a notification, anything, Christy would get mad. It had gotten to the point that I'd kept my phone on silent and would check it when she left the room. It was one of the reasons we weren't together anymore.

And, even though we were no longer an item, I instinctively braced myself for her reaction. But she picked up her glass like nothing had happened.

I relaxed and felt a bit of hope that she'd changed.

I picked up my phone and swiped through my notifications. I had a direct message from Sydney Hart.

I looked over at Christy, who smiled at me.

I opened the message.

Hi, Travis. I don't know if you remember me from the Iowa book signing. I was the author at the table behind you, and we hung out a little after the signing.

I frowned. Of course I remembered her.

There is a book signing coming up in two months in Minneapolis. I would love to have you attend the signing with me. Just as a model. Harper will be my assistant again. Here is the info on the event.

She posted the link below.

Just get back to me when you can. Thank you.

Another message popped up.

I almost forgot to add. I have a book coming out right before the signing, and you'll be on it. Please don't share this with anyone since I haven't done a cover reveal yet. Thanks again!

Next, an image of her book came through. It was a photo of me and Joni, a friend and fellow model. I'd like to think I was modest, but I had to admit, I looked good, and the cover looked great.

"You're still doing that?"

I frowned and looked at Christy. We might have broken up months ago, but I still knew her. She was trying to act casual, but I could tell when she was mad.

I put my phone down and sat back. "Doing what?"

"Uh-oh," Lilah said.

"The modeling thing."

I furrowed my brow. "Of course I am. Why did you think I'd stopped?"

She picked up the napkin on her lap and threw it on the table. "I thought that *maybe* all these months without me would make you see what you'd been missing."

"You mean, someone who tries to control him?" Broderick said.

I narrowed my eyes at Broderick.

Broderick held up his hands. "Sorry. None of my business."

"I didn't try to control him," Christy protested.

I sighed. She clearly hadn't changed. "Christy, you didn't even like it when female clients contacted me, and that was for work." It had gotten so bad that she started to not like it when *male* clients messaged me.

She grabbed her purse. "I can see that you and I will never agree on this."

The woman was delusional.

"No, we won't." *Good luck finding a guy who will.*

"I think it's time for me to go."

"I think that's a good idea."

Her expression darkened. She was out of her mind if she thought I was going to stop her. She was beautiful and had a great body, but she was ugly on the inside. Broderick was right. She was incredibly insecure despite the number of times I'd tried to tell her and show her that I cared about her and was attracted to her.

Christy stood and stomped out of the restaurant. All I could think about was how grateful I was that we'd driven separately.

"Wow," Lilah said after everyone watched Christy go.

"Sorry you all had to see that."

"I'm just glad you're not getting back together with that bitch."

"*Broderick*," Lilah said.

"She hacked into the guy's phone. For no reason. He wasn't cheating on her or anything even close."

It was true. I had never given Christy a reason not to trust me. I'd been cheated on, so I knew what it felt like. I'd promised myself I'd never do that to someone else. Christy just hadn't liked my modeling. Even though it was something she'd loved about me when we'd first met.

"Broderick's right. She's kind of a bitch," I agreed.

"What got her so pissed off?" Dan asked.

I opened my phone and showed him the message and book cover.

"Damn, Trav," Lilah said, fanning her face. "That's hot."

My face warmed. "Thanks."

"Are you going to do it?" Dan asked. "Do *you* remember who this author is?"

I smiled. "Yeah, I remember her."

She was so different from Christy. My ex would never have gone to breakfast with no makeup, and Christy would never have taken falling on the floor the way Sydney had either. Christy would have been pissed at everyone laughing at her. Sydney had been embarrassed, but she'd taken it in stride. I'd thought of her a few times since I'd seen her.

"So, what are you going to do?" Lilah asked. "Tell her yes or tell her no?"

THIRTEEN

SYDNEY

THANKS FOR ASKING. *I'd love to accompany you to the book signing.*

I stared at the message one more time just to make sure that was what it said even though I already knew it did.

"I'm sure he'll be here," Lexie said, trying to reassure me.

"Yeah." But I wasn't sure.

It was April, and the book signing was supposed to start in half an hour. I'd given Travis the information, and he'd agreed to come, but so far, he'd been a no-show.

I understood that things happened. Harper was supposed to come with me today but had gotten the flu. But it would have been nice for Travis to tell me he wasn't coming. I wouldn't have been mad, and I also wouldn't feel like such a fool.

I had paid for his modeling fee. I had told the coordinators he was coming. And, now, I was being stood up.

I had been so excited that he'd said yes. It was practically all I'd been thinking about for the last week. If I were honest with myself, really, the last month. And he'd forgotten.

I knew I should have reminded him since we hadn't messaged each other for a month. Not since I'd given him the final details for today. I just hadn't known what to say. I hadn't wanted to be pushy.

I'd known there was no chance he'd be interested in me, but apparently, hope was a stupid bitch who had played a trick on my subconscious.

I picked up a copy of *Beautifully Broken* from my large stack. His picture taunted me. Now, I was stuck, looking at him all day.

"I bet you'll still make some good sales," Lexie said.

I smiled at her. "I'm not worried about that. I never make more than I spend on a signing. However, I wouldn't have brought so many books with me." I looked at the box behind me, filled with my new novel. At least it would last me several signings. And I could always do some signed giveaways to my readers.

"I'm going to go use the restroom real quick. You'll be okay?" I asked my niece.

"I'll be fine."

I found the nearest restroom, used the toilet, and went to wash my hands. While I rinsed the water off, I looked up in the mirror and blushed. I had gone out of my way, doing my hair, carefully putting on my makeup, and picking out my outfit.

I felt ridiculous.

I grabbed a paper towel and got it wet, and then I

removed the red lipstick I'd put on my lips. I was a Chap-Stick girl anyway. I rarely ever wore lipstick, even when I wore makeup.

I dug until I found my brush in my purse and brushed out my hair, curls and all, and found a hair tie. I pulled it up into a messy, semi-stylish bun. It would be easier to sign books without my hair in my face.

Maybe it was a good thing Travis hadn't come. I was more comfortable now, even with just the two changes. I would, however, like my fifty-dollar modeling fee back.

I shrugged at my reflection. *Oh well. Live and learn, I guess.*

I headed back to the room where the event was taking place, thankful that I had still worn comfortable shoes. At least I hadn't let the thought of a hot guy change my footwear. I did way too much standing to put on pretty feet-killing shoes.

My table was back in the corner, so I stopped at a few tables on the way back to grab some business cards and other swag to keep track of books I hoped to read someday. The only thing I didn't like about being a writer was reading. I was always fearful of accidentally copying someone's style, and many times, after writing all day, I had no desire to look at other words.

By the time I retired, my to-be-read list was literally going to be a mile long. That was single-spaced, eight-point font size. Hopefully, I retired young and lived long.

I had my head down, scanning each table as I walked past in case something caught my eye or I saw someone I knew, so when I got to my table, I was a little shocked to see someone sitting and talking to Lexie.

Travis's hair was longer than when I'd last seen him, and

I almost didn't recognize him. Maybe I shouldn't have been avoiding him on social media because, damn, it looked good on him. It was thick, and I wanted to run my fingers through it.

He smiled when he saw me and stood. "Hey." He leaned close and kissed me on the cheek. "Sorry I'm late."

I blushed at his affection, but then I realized it was very Hollywood. I always noticed that when famous people greeted each other. He was being polite.

"Oh, um…that's okay." I scooted in between him and the table to take my seat in the middle. As I moved past him, my butt brushed against the front of his fly. My previously warm face was now on fire. "Sorry about that."

He laughed. "It's fine."

"Travis was just telling me that he had to go to his younger cousin's soccer game this morning, and that's why he just got here," Lexie said as I took my seat.

"I'm glad you could make it," I told him.

"Yeah, Sydney thought you'd changed your mind or just forgot."

I spun my head around. "*Lexie.*"

She shrugged. "What? It's the truth."

"He doesn't need to know that," I pointed out.

I could hear Travis laughing behind me, so I looked back at him. "I'm sorry about that. Sometimes, I think that teenagers don't have a filter from their brains to their mouths."

"I do, too," Lexie objected from behind me.

Travis held up a copy of *Beautifully Broken*. I hadn't even noticed he'd been holding it.

"This looks great."

"Well...you are on the cover." *Way to open your big mouth, dummy. Quick. Say something else.* "I mean, you both look good." I tilted my head to the side. "Is it ever awkward, posing with someone like that? Is it hard to pretend?" I mentally patted myself on the back. *Good job. He thinks you're just interested in his profession.*

"Occasionally, it's awkward if I don't know the other person. You have to pretend you have some sort of intimacy with a complete stranger. On the other hand, if it's someone I do know, we start to laugh and can find it hard to be serious."

I tried to picture myself modeling. "I think you all deserve more credit than you get. I know it's not easy."

He smiled. "Oh, have you ever done it?"

I gave him a deadpan look. "You're joking, right? I might be cute, but this"—I waved my hands down in front of my body—"isn't model material." Before he could think I was fishing for compliments or waiting for him to protest, I added, "I used to watch *America's Next Top Model*." I put my finger to my lips. "The older I got, the more ridiculous the contestants got, but I couldn't stop watching."

He laughed. "Will you sign a copy for me?" he said and handed the book over to me.

I lifted my brow. "Did you pay for this?"

"Uh..."

"I'm kidding. You can have it for free." I grabbed another book from my pile and gave it to him. "But I'll only sign yours if you sign mine."

"And I would like you to both sign my copy," Lexie said.

"But you can't even read it." I quickly turned to Travis. "She's only sixteen."

"Too late. I already did."

I gasped. "Alexis Harting."

"Syd, I've read all your books."

"Your parents are going to kill me."

Lexie grabbed a book and handed it to me. "What they don't know won't hurt them."

FOURTEEN

SYDNEY

"WHAT HAPPENED TO HARPER? I thought she was coming today," Travis asked about two hours into the book signing.

"Sick."

"That's too bad."

"Yeah, she was bummed. I practically had to make her stay home today."

I watched Travis's face and wondered if he was disappointed about not seeing Harper today. Maybe she was the reason he'd agreed to come.

Stop it.

I was being irrational. He came because he was a nice guy, and this was a good business opportunity for him. He wasn't interested in Harper. And, even if he were, she was married.

Travis leaned back in his seat and stretched. I found it really hard to not stare at him. I wondered if the women he dated could ever stop looking at him. I didn't know if I could. And I'd only seen him in person with his clothes on.

He rubbed his stomach. "I should have brought snacks. I'm getting hungry."

"You can go and get food if you want."

Today's event was in a hotel again, so there was the restaurant, but it was also attached to the Mall of America. And, unlike the event last September in Iowa, this one was a book signing only. Not a get-together the night before or a special dinner tonight.

"Nah. Why don't we go get something to eat after this?"

I was momentarily shocked that he was asking if we wanted to go to dinner. I'd figured he'd have plans since it was Saturday and all.

"That sounds great. But Lexie rode with me today. She has plans with her boyfriend after this. She was nice enough to postpone them to come with me today."

"I can drive your car home," Lexie exclaimed. "And Brendan can just pick me up from your place."

"That's nice of you even though I know you just want to drive, but I'm not spending money to Uber home from here. Too expensive. I'm a starving artist, remember?"

"No, you're not."

"Close enough."

"I'll take you home," Travis said.

I whipped my head around. He couldn't possibly want to eat with me that badly.

"I couldn't impose on you," I said, offering him an out. "Where do you live? Because I live all the way down in Shakopee."

I lived about forty-five minutes from the mall, and depending on which direction he lived, he could live over an hour away from me.

"I live in Minnetonka. Not that bad of a drive."

It was at least twenty to twenty-five minutes, but it definitely could have been worse.

"Are you sure?"

"Please say yes," Lexie butted in.

"I'm sure."

"Okay," I said. "Let's do it."

TRAVIS

I put my hand on the small of Sydney's back as the hostess led us to our table. We had decided to eat at one of the many restaurants in the Mall of America to make things easier, and Sydney had chosen Italian.

I loved Italian but didn't eat it too often. I had to work hard to keep my body lean and fit for my job, so when I was prepping for a shoot, I avoided it entirely. I was lucky that I worked in a gym because I had to exercise about two hours every day. At this point, I considered working out as part of my personal training and modeling jobs.

We were shown to our booth where we sat opposite each other.

"Can I get you something to drink?" the hostess asked.

"I'll have a glass of wine." Sydney frowned. "Unless it's too early."

It was a little past four.

"It's five o'clock somewhere," I told her. "I'll have a beer," I told the hostess.

We were left alone, and Sydney looked a little nervous. I hadn't realized how much I had been looking forward to seeing her until she walked up to her table at the signing.

I'd almost forgotten how pretty, in a refreshing and natural way, she was.

I'd dated other girls like her, but it had been a while. Christy made me lose sight of what I really liked and appreciated in a woman.

Our server came over with our drinks and bread basket and introduced himself. He said he'd give us a few minutes to look and be back.

"Thanks for asking me to come today," I told her when we were alone.

Her eyes widened. "No, I should be thanking you." She grabbed a piece of bread and tore a hunk off. "I almost didn't ask you."

I frowned. "Why not?"

She smiled, the corner of her mouth curving up. "I figured you'd have something better to do."

I shook my head. "No way. I was happy to do it."

She looked away, and I wasn't quite sure, but her face might have turned red.

"Lexie said you have another book signing next month."

"I do. It's in three weeks actually."

"Where's that one?"

"Chicago."

"Do you have a model lined up for it?"

She laughed and took a sip of her wine. "No. I won't have a new book out before then. And you're the only one I've ever asked to go with me."

I liked that answer. "Do you want one?"

Her brow furrowed. "Do I what?"

"Do you want a model to accompany you?"

Her mouth dropped open. "Are you saying what I think you're saying?"

I laughed. "Yeah. Do you want me to go to Chicago with you?"

"Wow. Why would you—" She waved a hand in front of her. "Never mind with that. I'm not flying. I was planning to drive."

I shrugged. "That's okay. It's only, like, six hours, right?"

"Six and a half. Maybe seven, depending on the traffic." She tilted her head. "Are you saying you want to ride with me?"

"Yeah. Why not? Seems silly to take two vehicles."

"That's true."

"Would anyone else be driving with us?" I hoped it would just be the two of us.

Her smile faltered. "Uh...maybe. I haven't found anyone to be my assistant yet."

I beamed. "Great. I'll be your assistant."

She shook her head. "I can't ask you to do that."

"You don't have to. I don't mind."

She gave me the side-eye. "Are you sure this is what you want?"

I laughed. "Yes. I think it'll be fun." I raised my brow. "Don't you?"

"Of course, but…"

"But what?"

She smiled and shook her head. "Nothing."

"So, are we going to do it?"

Her eyes widened for a second, and I had to stop myself from grinning. I hadn't meant for it to be an innuendo, but now that I'd said it…

"Let's," she said.

FIFTEEN

SYDNEY

"THANKS FOR DINNER," I told Travis as he drove me home. "You really didn't have to pay. I could have paid, or we could have split the check."

"And let a starving artist starve?"

I laughed. "Well, I might have exaggerated. I'm not exactly starving."

He shrugged a shoulder. "I figured, but I was happy to pay. I haven't had Italian for a long time."

"Really?" A thought occurred to me. "Oh no. Do you not like it? You should have said something when I suggested it."

He laughed. "No. I love it actually."

"Whew. If you didn't like Italian, I'd worry that you were a potential psychopath," I teased. "Wait. Then, why haven't you eaten it?" That was such a foreign concept to me. I loved food, and if I wanted something, I usually ate it.

"My ex didn't eat Italian."

I felt bad for him. "Oh, she didn't like Italian?"

That would explain not eating it. I had an ex who didn't like Mexican, so I'd only gone out for it with friends.

"No." He laughed like what he was about to say was silly. "She didn't eat it. Too many carbs."

I wrinkled my nose. "She's one of those, huh?" My eyes widened. "I'm sorry. That was rude. A lot of people don't eat carbs."

He laughed. "It's okay. I get it. But I don't eat a lot of carbs either. I try to stick with protein."

That would explain his chicken Parmesan that he'd ordered with a substitute of grilled chicken.

I looked away from him and winced. He didn't eat much, and his ex didn't eat any while I had eaten almost my entire bowl of pasta. He probably thought I was a pig.

"You probably work out a lot, too," I said to him.

He nodded. "I do. I kind of have to if I want to keep modeling. Do you?"

"Only the bare minimum. I do it to stay healthy, not because I like it. I have yet to experience that high that people talk about."

"Really? I love working out."

"Did your ex work out, too?"

"Every day. She's a personal trainer, like me."

"I see."

This was like the guy at my gym who had been texting me and then suddenly stopped. Travis and I were too different but in a way that made me feel like I was lacking because I wasn't as disciplined as him or his ex.

I pointed to my house. "It's the one on the right."

He pulled into my driveway, and I turned in my seat. I honestly didn't know what to do. We'd gone out to eat, but it hadn't been a date. But he had driven me all the way there, and it felt rude not to invite him in.

I wanted to throw my hands up in the air. This was too complicated.

Then, I realized that it was only about six thirty, and the sun was still out for a couple of more hours, so it was too early for him to think I was inviting him in for sex.

Not that I would turn sex down. *Hell no*. But I didn't want him to say no to coming inside because he felt like that was what I wanted.

"Did you want to come in for a minute?"

"Sure." He shut off his SUV, and we both got out.

I unlocked the front door for us and called out Lexie's name. No answer.

"I'll be right back. I'm going to make sure my car is in the garage."

"No problem."

On my way to check, I set down my purse. My car was safely where it was supposed to be. I let out a deep breath filled with relief. I trusted Lexie, but she was still a sixteen-year-old girl.

I walked back into the living room. "My car is safe and sound."

"That's good," Travis said with a nod, but he seemed different. More reserved.

Maybe he'd changed his mind about Chicago.

"I thought maybe we should exchange phone numbers. But, if you've changed your mind about going with me next month, that's okay. We don't know each other that well." I narrowed my eyes at him. "You're not a serial killer, are you?" I joked.

"No."

Yikes. He hadn't even cracked a smile. I always did tend to laugh at my own jokes harder than anyone else.

Something clearly had changed.

"I'm serious. You really don't—"

"Can I ask you a question?"

"Shoot."

"Do you have something against how I take care of my body?"

My eyes widened. "No. Not at all. Why would you think that?"

He softened a little. "In the car. I could tell you didn't agree with the way I or my ex eat or work out."

This seemed like a heavy conversation for two people who were just getting to know each other, but I could tell it bothered him.

I rubbed the back of my neck. "It's not that I don't agree with what you do." I held up a hand. "That's not entirely true. I don't understand giving up an entire food group unless it's medically necessary. But I'm not going to judge you for it. I understand that you have to look a certain way for your pictures. I actually kind of admire your discipline."

I shrugged. "But it's not something I can do, and I've been on the receiving end of being judged for liking food and for not being skinny. I dated a guy who wanted to go out and do physical stuff all the time. I like staying home. I like vegging out. Not all the time, but way more than he did. And then there were the subtle hints about my food choices. Obviously, we didn't date long."

That wasn't that bad to tell, but the next story was worse in my eyes.

"One of my good friends from college had always been like me. But, about four or five years after we graduated, she met a guy who was an exercise fiend. She started working out and dieting like crazy. I was happy for her until she lost too much weight. She wouldn't go out to eat with us anymore, and when I did see her eat, she was like a bird. There was no way she was healthy. But what was worse was that she started to make comments to me and our other friends about our weight and eating habits. I finally cut her out of my life when her boyfriend told me that no one would ever date me if I didn't lose at least twenty pounds. She didn't defend me."

Travis sucked in a breath, a horrified look on his face.

"I know, right? Real winner there. I'm sure he made comments to my friend all the time, and that's why she got so thin. We encouraged her to leave, but she was in love."

I shook my head as I remembered how hopeless my friends and I had felt at that time.

"Anyway, society has been telling girls since they were little that they aren't good enough. It took me a long time to like myself the way I am. I know I'm not perfect, but I'm happy. And I don't need someone making me feel like something's wrong with me. I wasn't judging you, Travis. It's more like I don't want you to judge me, even silently."

He stared at me for what felt like forever. Then, without warning, he stepped forward. He put his forefinger under my chin and used his thumb to pull my bottom lip down, and he kissed me. Our lips were like the fingers of folding hands, interlacing with one another. I brushed my tongue against his bottom lip, which was pressed between mine.

Travis stepped back. "Where's your phone?"

"Uh…um…uh…in the kitchen." I stood there for another second. "I'll go get it." I shuffled my feet to my purse, almost in a trance, and walked back. "Here you go."

He took my phone and turned it back to me. "Can you unlock it?" He smiled, trying not to laugh.

"Oh." I laughed at myself. I unlocked the phone and handed it back to him.

He did a few things before giving it back to me. "I put my number in there and sent a text to myself, so I know it's you. Text me the Chicago info, okay?"

I nodded. "Okay."

He grinned, and all I could see were his dimples. "I'll talk to you soon."

I nodded again. "Okay."

He pulled me forward and kissed my forehead. "Later, Sydney."

SIXTEEN

SYDNEY

"SO, NOTHING FROM TRAVIS?" Harper asked.

"*No.* And who does that? Who kisses someone and then just walks away? It's been two weeks already."

Harper carried a glass of wine for me and handed it over. "So, he hasn't talked to you at all?" she asked as she sat down on her couch next to me.

I took a sip. "Talked to me? No. We've texted back and forth about the Chicago trip, but that's it. Nothing about the kiss. No asking me if I want to hang out. The guy hasn't even returned any of my social media follows." I pouted.

Harper chuckled. "Maybe he's waiting for you to bring up the kiss."

"Then, he's going to keep waiting because he's the one who kissed me. I'm not going to go after him, begging for scraps of his attention. Been there, done that." I took a long drink this time.

"Sorry, Syd. I wish I knew what he was thinking."

I picked at the back of her couch. "Me, too. But I think, more than that, I wish I'd stop thinking about it. I've actually been thinking about canceling the trip. Or at least telling him it's canceled and going by myself."

Harper tilted her head, her eyes sad. "Don't do that."

"Why? I feel like it would relieve a lot of stress."

"How about this? Why don't you just tell yourself that the kiss didn't happen? If there's no kiss, there's nothing to obsess over, and there's nothing to worry about." She nodded.

I looked down my nose at her. "You have met me, right?"

She laughed. "Yes. And I know that you can do this." She took a drink of her own wine. "Remember the movie *He's Just Not That Into You?*"

I groaned. "Say no more. You're right. I have no idea why he kissed me, but it was obviously a fluke."

It was amazing what one sentence could do. I was still going to think about it. That couldn't be helped, but I really didn't want to be like the girl in the movie. The kiss obviously meant nothing to Travis, and it was best to let it go.

"Wow. That was kind of easy."

I chuckled. "Hey, I remember watching it and feeling so bad for the character who didn't get it that the guy didn't like her. I do not want to be like that."

"Good for you."

"Travis and I are just friends, and there's nothing wrong with that."

"That's what I'm saying."

I twirled the wine in my glass, watching it swirl around. "But, if he could just fuck me once, then I'd really let it go."

Harper threw her head back and laughed. Suddenly, she gasped, and her eyes lit up.

"What?"

"What if something happened with your hotel reservations and you two ended up in the same room?" Her eyes widened. "Even better, there's only one bed. And it's a full. You should totally bring condoms."

I smiled and shook my head. "What is this? A romance novel?"

"Why not?"

"One, I already made the reservation. It is definitely for two rooms. Two, the hotel probably doesn't have anything smaller than a queen, and if there's only one bed, it'll be a king. Three, the hotel would have to be booked full. Four, most hotels have rollaway beds. Five, I wouldn't want him to think I did it on purpose." I pointed a finger at her. "Which is why I will not be taking condoms."

Harper wrinkled her nose. "Yeah, you're right. It would be fun though."

I looked at her like she was crazy. "What? No way. I wouldn't sleep a wink with him next to me."

"You did in our hotel room."

"But that was a short snooze. And we weren't alone, and we were on top of the covers in our clothes."

"I suppose you're right. But you should still bring protection."

I snorted at that ridiculous suggestion.

"Even if the one-hotel-room, one-bed thing won't happen with you two, you should totally put something like that in your next book," she said, pointing her glass at me.

"It would have to be a really good reason because it's been done before. A lot."

"*Yeah*. Because it works, and women like to read that shit."

"Hmm. That's true," I said and immediately began brainstorming how to get the idea into my next book.

The back door opened, and we heard the pounding of little feet running toward us.

"Mommy."

A blur flew past me and landed on Harper.

"Hey, buddy. How was the park?" The hand that was holding her wine was stuck up in the air, so Wyatt didn't knock it over.

I reached for the glass, so she didn't have to worry about spilling it.

"Thanks," she said and lifted her almost two-year-old into her lap. "How was the park?" she asked again.

"Fun."

There was a large sigh behind us, and Ian dropped a bag on the counter.

"How'd it go?" Harper asked her husband.

"Good. I'm exhausted, but it was fun." Ian walked over and sat down in the recliner adjacent to us. "How's it going, Sydney?" he asked me.

"Good."

"She's having man troubles," Harper said.

I looked at her. "I thought we'd just established that I was not and that I was going to let it go."

"I thought maybe we could get a man's perspective," she said as Wyatt slipped from her lap and went for his toys in the corner.

"What's the problem?" Ian asked.

I hesitated. I didn't care if Ian knew. I liked him and

considered him a friend. But he was very logical about everything.

"Nothing really. A guy kissed me, and then that was it." I shrugged. "No follow-up."

"It's the male model who's going with her to Chicago."

Ian's dark eyes widened. "Oh."

"Oh? What does *oh* mean?"

He shook his head. "Nothing." He put his finger to his lips. "So, you're going on a trip together, but he hasn't mentioned the kiss?"

"We're going on a *business* trip together, and no, he hasn't. Harper and I decided that it hadn't meant anything, or he would have brought it up or asked me out."

"Hmm." He tapped his mouth.

"What does that mean?"

He dropped his hand, lost his thinking face, and shrugged. "I have no idea. You're asking the wrong guy."

I looked at Harper. "Your husband is worthless."

She smiled. "But he's mine."

SEVENTEEN

SYDNEY

THE FOLLOWING THURSDAY, there was a knock at my front door before it opened, and Harper barreled through. We lived close enough that we just walked into each other's houses.

"Hey, what are you doing here?"

"I just came to see how you're doing since you're leaving for Chicago with Travis today."

Our conversation had been last Saturday, and I was feeling better. "Good. Less emotional."

"Are you nervous?"

"A little. He's still a cute guy even if he's not interested in me."

"What time do you leave?"

"About one. He's working this morning. He already took off Friday, so I said it would be okay if we didn't leave until this afternoon." I looked down at Harper's hands. "What's in the bag?"

She grinned, her eyes looking sneaky.

"What are you up to?"

She threw the plastic bag at me.

I caught it and looked inside. I pulled out the box. "Condoms? Really?"

"Hey, you never know. And, if it's not Travis, maybe you'll find someone else. Maybe, if you have sex with someone else, you'll stop crushing on Travis."

"I see your point, but I don't think that's going to happen." I walked toward my kitchen, setting the box down on the dining room table as I went. "Do you want any coffee?"

"Sure. And why don't you think it'll happen?"

I pulled a cup from the cupboard. "Because I'll be working a lot." And, for some crazy reason, I didn't want Travis to see me with someone. Basically, just in case I actually had a one in a million chance with him. I didn't say it was a rational thought.

Harper pursed her lips. "You're a spoilsport."

I laughed and took a drink of my coffee. "Trust me; I know. I agree on the sex part. Maybe after I get back."

She lifted her cup and clinked it against mine. "That's the spirit."

I looked at the clock on the microwave. "Damn, I still need to finish packing and shower. I also have to run to Target before I leave town and pick up a few things."

"I can help."

"You want to help me pack?" I asked doubtfully.

"I wouldn't say I want to, but I will to help you save time."

"Okay. I have all my stuff and my clothes on my bed. I just need to put them in the suitcase."

"Sounds easy enough."

We went upstairs where I pulled a bag from my closet for Harper.

"I'll be out in ten," I told her.

Ten minutes later, I pulled open my bathroom door in my room. Steam rolled out toward Harper, who was sitting on my bed, looking through her phone.

"Hey, can you put two more things in there?" I asked her.

She looked up. "You have enough clothes for a week, but I think I can manage."

"Yeah, I know," I said as I went back into my bathroom to grab my stuff. "I never know what I'm going to want to wear." I emerged with my toiletry and cosmetic bags.

Harper took them from me, and I watched her stuff them in the middle of my two piles of clothes.

"I get it."

I picked through my hair. "Thanks for your help."

"No problem," she said, zipping up my suitcase.

"Want to go to Target with me?"

"Nah. I'll probably spend too much. Walk me out?"

"Sure."

We went downstairs and headed for the front door. Along the way, Harper picked up her present for me. "Are you sure you don't want the condoms?" she asked, holding the box up.

I laughed. "No, thanks. I'm good."

She shrugged. "Suit yourself." She gave me a hug. "Good luck with Chicago. Call me if you need anything."

I squeezed her tight. "I will."

After a long drive to Chicago, Travis and I finally pulled up to the hotel. He had insisted we take his SUV, claiming he wouldn't fit comfortably in my car with his long legs. I'd felt bad, but he'd sworn it was no big deal.

With Travis driving, I had alternated between sleeping and working on my latest novel. One of the best presents I'd ever bought for myself was a little laptop that I could take everywhere.

It was about eight at night, and I was ready to crash. I'd used up all my brain cells on the last few chapters that I pounded out on the drive.

"I think I'm just going to grab my luggage and leave my book stuff until tomorrow," I told him when he opened the back.

Travis frowned. "You're not worried about someone stealing it?"

I shrugged. "Let them. Unless they're a writer, it's going to be pretty worthless loot."

"Okay." He grabbed my suitcase and set it down for me, and then he reached for his own.

He locked his SUV, and we headed for the lobby. There were two people working, and one of them was free.

"Hello. Welcome. Can I have the name of the reservation, please?" the young woman said.

"Harting with a T. First name, Sydney."

Her keyboard clicked, and she typed in my info. "Okay. Here it is. Sydney Harting."

"Thank you."

A few more clicks, and she came back with two sets of

key cards. "Okay"—she set them on the counter—"your room is two nineteen."

No. This could not be happening.

"Excuse me, but I made the reservation for two rooms."

Her mouth formed a circle. "You two are not staying together?"

I shook my head. "No. I asked for rooms side by side, but I still asked for two rooms."

"Let me look. One moment, please."

I looked over at Travis. "I'm sorry. I swear, I booked two rooms."

He shrugged. "I've slept in some pretty crappy places while in the Army. If we have to share a room, it's not a big deal."

At least he didn't seem to think I had planned this.

"Oh, here it is." The young woman smiled. "I'm sorry about that. I didn't see it at first."

The tension drained from my body. "Thank you."

Another set of key cards were brought over. "Here you go. So, your rooms are two nineteen and two twenty-one. Do you need help with any luggage?"

"No, thanks. We've got it," Travis said.

The two of us walked away and headed for the elevator. We got on right away and went up to our floor.

"So, what are we doing tonight?" Travis asked as we walked down the hall to our rooms.

I winced. I hadn't even thought about the fact that he might want to go out and do something. "I was thinking of just staying in tonight. But, if you want to go out, we can." We reached our rooms, and another thought occurred to me. "Or you can go out on your own."

We were in Chicago. Maybe he wanted to go out and party without me tagging along.

Travis stuck his key card in the slot. "I'm good." He pushed open his door and disappeared.

He's good? What the hell does that mean?

I unlocked my own door and rolled my suitcase in. It was a good thing we'd gotten two rooms because mine had one king-size bed. I picked up my luggage and set it on a shelf made for just that.

I had only unzipped my bag when there was a knock. Except it wasn't coming from the front door. I stepped back and saw that on the other side of the television was another door. Travis and I had adjoining rooms.

I went and opened it.

"Hey. Long time no see," I joked. Lamely.

Travis smiled. "Can I borrow some toothpaste? I seem to have forgotten mine."

"Sure."

I walked over to my suitcase and flipped the top open. I pushed aside the clothes to get to the middle where I'd stuffed my cosmetics and toiletries. I reached my hand between them, looking for the bag. I had stuffed too much in my luggage.

The first thing my fingers encountered was a small packet of some sort.

I didn't remember putting anything like that in there.

I yanked on it and out flew several yellow packages all attached to each other. The end slipped out of my hand and landed at Travis's feet.

He lifted his brow. "It looks like you're going to be doing a lot more than signing books this weekend."

On the floor was a row of condoms. Not one or two, but a whole line of them.

I should have never let Harper offer to help me pack. She'd taken home an empty box.

I was going to kill her.

EIGHTEEN

SYDNEY

I SCRAMBLED over to Travis and picked up the condoms. "Harper did it as a joke," I tried to explain.

He didn't say anything as I bunched them up and set them on the desk. He just smiled.

Quick. Change the subject.

"So, you need toothpaste, right?" I went back to my suitcase, this time pulling out the right item. I opened the bag and took out one of several travel toothpastes. "Here you go."

"Thanks. I'll bring it back when I'm done," he said, halfway to the door.

"It's okay. I have more than one."

He was already in his room.

"Never mind, I guess."

Since Travis had never said anything about going out, I dug in my suitcase and found my pajamas. I carried them and my toiletries into the bathroom. I didn't know when he was going to bring my toothpaste back, and I didn't think he'd want to walk in on me mid-clothes change.

After I put on my comfortable, not-at-all-stylish shorts and T-shirt PJs, I washed my face, brushed my teeth, and took out my contacts. I pulled my hair up in a ponytail and looked at myself in the mirror.

"It's fine if he sees you like this, Sydney. He isn't interested in you and won't look twice at what you look like."

I opened the door to see my room empty, but since our two doors were still open, I went to look for Travis.

"Hey, Travis. You can just keep—" is what I started to say, but the rest of the words completely left my brain when Travis stepped out of his bathroom without a shirt on.

Sweet Mary mother of God.

His photos didn't do him justice.

He was chiseled and tan, and right below his belly button was a blond treasure trail that slipped under his jeans, which hung so low that the V of his hips looked like they had been carved out of marble.

It should be illegal to be that sexy.

"Sorry. What did you say?"

"Huh?" I swallowed and wiped my mouth to make sure I wasn't drooling.

"I couldn't hear you. What did you say?" he asked again.

"Oh." *I want to lick you all over. No, that's not it. Impregnate me. No, that's not it either.* "Uh…I was going to say, you can keep the toothpaste. It was an extra."

He smiled. "Hey. Thanks."

"Sure." I looked around his room—he had one king-size bed, too—and back at him. "Are you going out tonight?"

He frowned. "Out?"

103

"Yeah. I thought maybe you'd hit some clubs or something."

He looked me up and down. "You don't look like you're ready to go out."

I pulled on the bottom of my shirt. "Yeah. No, I'm staying in, remember? I'm tired. Besides, I wouldn't want to ruin your fun."

He cocked his head to the side. "How would you ruin my fun?"

"I'm old."

He laughed. "You can't be that much older than me."

"I'm thirty-four."

"And I'm twenty-seven. Like I said, not that much older."

"Yeah, but we're a guy and a girl. What if they thought…you know…that we were together or something?"

He frowned. "So?"

"So…you're young, hot, and single."

He smiled, taking a step forward. "You think I'm hot?"

I put my hand on my hip. "You know you are, or you wouldn't be modeling."

"Not everyone agrees with you."

"Then, they're dumb because you have, like, this magnetic pull to you. It's like any straight woman can't resist."

He laughed.

"Anyway, go out and get your groove on."

"Maybe you should go out and get your groove on."

I shook my head. "I didn't come here for that."

He lifted his brow. "Your stack of condoms says otherwise."

"I told you, that was Harper."

"But was it?" he teased.

"Yes." My face was heating up. I didn't want to talk about the condoms anymore. I turned to go back to my room. "Just let me know if you go out or not, so I don't worry about you."

Way to sound like his mother, Sydney.

I marched into my hotel room and pushed my door closed behind me. I pulled out the desk drawer and pushed the condoms inside. *There. Out of sight, out of mind.*

I turned off all the lights but the one next to my bed and turned on the television. Hopefully, I would find something to occupy my mind. That way, if Travis went out, I wouldn't have to picture the pretty, young women he might find there.

I looked up at my adjoining door to see that I hadn't pushed hard enough because the door was slightly ajar. I considered getting up and closing it, but I was comfortable in my bed.

"Hey, Travis?"

Two seconds later, he poked his head in my room. "Yeah?"

"If you bring anyone home, will you just make sure that one of the doors is closed?"

He laughed and walked away.

Hopefully, that was a yes.

I turned my attention to the TV and what I wanted to watch. Like the hotel in Iowa, I was able to sign into my Netflix account, and soon, I was scrolling through the movies. I knew I'd fall asleep, so I searched for something I'd seen before. I settled on *Empire Records*, a cult classic.

A few minutes later, the door pushed open, and Travis walked in, wearing just a pair of shorts and glasses.

Holy crap. He looked adorable with glasses on. I had always been a sucker for a man in spectacles. *Can he just stop being so damn good-looking already?*

Travis jumped on the other side of my bed. "What are we watching?"

"What are you doing?"

"You said you were staying in, so it looks like I'm watching TV with you."

I couldn't believe he wanted to stay in and hang out with me.

He waved his hand in front of my face. "Are you okay?" He tried to reach for the remote.

Quickly, I yanked my hand away. "I'm fine." *Just a little surprised.* "But you're going to watch what I want to watch," I said with a grin.

"Okay." He sank down onto the pillows. "So, what is this?"

"*Empire Records.*"

"Never heard of it."

I groaned. *Yeah, I'm not old, my butt.*

NINETEEN

SYDNEY

I SHOULD HAVE KNOWN I would dream about Travis. In my dream, instead of going back to his room to sleep, he stayed in my bed.

I roll on my side toward Travis, and my mouth grazes the top of his back. I push my nose into the back of his neck and inhale.

I could wake up to this scent every morning.

Slipping my arm around his waist, I brush my fingers over his chest. I love the feel of his muscles. I slide my palm down his wash-board stomach, admiring his dedication to physical fitness, until I hit the top of his shorts.

Reminding myself I am dreaming and I should just go for it, I slide my hand underneath until I find what I am looking for. Since he is sleeping, Travis isn't hard, but that soon changes as I wrap my hand around him.

His cock is hard and smooth, and it puts my penis suckers to shame.

I can't wait to tell Harper she was wrong.

He rolls onto his back, giving me better access. "Sydney, do you know what you're doing?"

107

I frown. It isn't exactly what I want to hear out of dream Travis's mouth. I was hoping for something like, That feels good.

He puts his hand on top of mine. "Sydney. Wake up, honey."

I opened my eyes and worked to clear the sleep from my brain.

It was still dark outside, but there was some light coming from the TV. It was the black Netflix profile screen, but it still gave off a bit of light. I turned my face away and hit male skin. *Hmm.* I leaned back and looked up into Travis's eyes.

His brow went up, and a small smile fell across his face. He squeezed my hand, and I realized that my fingers were wrapped around his very hard penis.

I gasped as I yanked my hand away. I rolled to my other side, so he couldn't see the shame on my face. "Oh my God. I am so sorry!"

I had *violated* him in his sleep.

I realized now that I had passed out sometime during the movie. I didn't remember Travis leaving. He must have fallen asleep, too.

"It's okay, Sydney."

He put his hand on my shoulder, and I jumped.

"No, it's not."

I felt the bed shift as he sat up and then stood. Fearing that he was coming around to talk to me, I covered my face with my hands and rolled onto my stomach. I couldn't face him right now.

"Sydney, I'm not mad."

"'Thank you. I appreciate that. But I still molested you in your sleep."

"*Molested* is a strong word."

"But an appropriate one."

"Will you please look at me?"

"No."

He sighed.

"Please, just go. We can talk about it in the morning."

"Okay. I will. On one condition."

"What's that?" I said from between my hands.

"You stop beating yourself up. I'm not mad. I'm not offended. If you want to know the truth, it felt good. So, give yourself a break."

He didn't wait for me to answer. His footsteps faded as he walked away.

When I was sure I was alone, I turned onto my back and stared at the ceiling.

I couldn't believe I had done that. I knew that I had thought I was dreaming, but I couldn't help but feel like I'd violated him.

What if the situation were reversed?

You'd open your legs and tell him not to stop.

Okay, I would do that but only because it was Travis, and I wanted it. It didn't make it right. Because, if it was someone I didn't want, I would feel completely different. And, despite the kiss Travis had given me, he had never even hinted he wanted me to touch his dick.

I looked at the clock and groaned. It was only a little after two in the morning. I was never going to go back to sleep.

I found the TV remote where I had dropped it in the

middle of the bed and shut off the TV. And then I began to think of ways to make my mistake right.

Surprisingly, I had fallen back asleep. When Travis woke me up, I was disorientated.

I looked up to see him carrying two to-go cups from Starbucks. "I know I shouldn't have the nerve to ask this, but please say one of those is mine."

He grinned and held out one to me.

I slowly sat up and took it from him. I savored my first sip as Travis sat at the end of my feet.

"Feel better this morning?" he asked.

I looked at him. "Well, I'm able to look you in the eyes, so yes, I suppose." I noticed that he was wearing track pants and a tank top. "Did you go work out?" I had noted the hotel had a gym when I made the reservation.

"Not yet. I went and got us coffee first. And I figured we needed to talk also."

In the light of day, what had happened didn't seem as big of a deal. But it should. "I'm really sorry. I was dreaming. Or half-dreaming." I shook my head. "I don't know really. All I know is that I didn't think I was touching you in real life. It's a flimsy excuse—kind of like, *I was drunk*—but I feel terrible about it."

"Well, I accepted your apology from last night. But you're being too hard on yourself."

"I don't think so."

"What if I told you that I woke up but didn't stop you right away? Wouldn't that change things a little? If I was awake and you were asleep, wouldn't I become the responsible party?"

He had a good point.

"I suppose you're right, and it does make me feel a little better." I took a drink of my coffee. "But that's only if it were true." I pushed the covers off my legs, stood, and stretched. "But I'm pretty sure you were sleeping before I woke you up. I bet you were pretty disappointed when you realized whose bed you were in." I walked toward my suitcase to pick out my clothes for the day. "I'm just glad you're not offended. Thanks for accepting my apology."

I picked the first few articles of clothing when I realized that Travis hadn't responded to me. I turned around to see him watching me from the bed.

"Can I ask you a question?" he asked.

"Of course."

"Why do women do that?"

"Do what?"

"Demean their worth, their attractiveness, their…anything?"

"Hmm." I took a sip of my coffee to gather my thoughts. It was a heavy question for early in the morning. "I think it's because society is always telling us that we're not good enough. We're not thin enough; we're too thin. We're not tall enough; we're too tall. Our boobs are too small; our boobs are too saggy. We have the wrong body type, we're not smart enough, we're not as good as men, et cetera, et cetera, et cetera. So, if we admit it first and say it out loud, then we don't have to hear anyone else say it, and we save ourselves from disappointment." I took another drink. "But I'm guessing you're not referring to women in general."

"No, I'm referring to your comment about me being disappointed when I woke up. Why are you so hard on yourself?"

I wrinkled my nose. "I'm not. I used to beat myself up about some of the things I already mentioned, but I'm not as young as I used to be. Life is too short to be unhappy all the time. I'm happy with my body and my looks. Would I like to be thinner and prettier? Of course I would, but I'm not going to think I don't deserve everything in life because I do. Because I also know, now that I'm older, that everyone is attracted to different types of people. I know I'm cute, I'd like to think I'm smart, and I also think I'm fun and nice. Any guy would be lucky to have me."

"Okay…"

"But—and it's a pretty big *but*—he has to be attracted to me. Even the prettiest girls in the world have guys who aren't attracted to them. So, I wasn't being hard on myself. I was just stating a fact." I leaned forward as if I were telling Travis a secret. "Tons of women love Tom Hardy. Sure, he's good-looking, but he just doesn't do it for me. So, would I be disappointed to find Tom Hardy in my bed instead of Chris Hemsworth or you? Well…yeah." I straightened. Realizing what I'd just said, I could only hope that he'd missed the part about how I would rather wake up next to him. "But it doesn't change who Tom Hardy is and that he's attractive." I gestured to Travis and back to myself. "Just like us. I'm not saying I'm not good enough for you. I'm just saying I'm not your type"—going by his lack of contact after our kiss—"and you'd probably rather wake up next to someone like Blake Lively."

I turned back to my clothes.

"I hope that helps," I said over my shoulder.

I heard Travis get up from the bed and walk over to me.

"Do you have any clothes in there for working out?"

"I can put something together." I had yoga pants, a couple of T-shirts, and an extra bra I could sweat in. "Does this mean you're going to make me go to the gym with you?" I whined.

"Yep. Get your ass ready." He slapped my butt like a coach would to his football players and walked to the door. "Oh, and, Sydney?"

I looked at him standing in the doorway. "Yeah?"

He grinned. "Blake Lively doesn't do anything for me." He walked into his room and shouted, "Be ready in five minutes."

TWENTY

SYDNEY

AS I USED the elliptical machine in the small hotel gym, I watched Travis work on his arms and thought about his Blake Lively comment. *How could he not be into her?*

I knew it was like me not being into Tom Hardy, but still. I was practically into Blake Lively, and I was a straight female.

But, more than that, I wasn't sure why he'd told me that. There was a possibility he'd caught my slipup about wanting him in my bed, but maybe I was reading too much into it. Especially since he'd never disagreed about being disappointed about waking up next to me.

And I was right back to where I'd started last week at Harper's. This had to stop, or I was going to drive myself crazy.

I brought the elliptical to a stop and watched Travis walk to the bench press. There was another guy who was alone, and it looked like Travis was offering to spot for the stranger.

The stranger nodded, and Travis held up a finger. He pulled his tank top over his head and used it to wipe his face.

With his attention on his new workout companion, I took the time to admire him. When I'd told him last night that he was magnetic, I hadn't been joking. It was like something just pulled me to him. My attention, my desire, everything. He was just so…beautiful.

I watched sweat run down his chest and remembered that I had touched him there.

Now that I was no longer beating myself up, I was letting myself recall everything I could about my "dream." He'd felt so good under my fingers, and I couldn't believe that I'd actually had my hand on his junk. Despite what Harper had said about him probably making a woman do all the work, I wouldn't care as long as he stuck that big cock in me. I would ride that thing—

Stop, stop, stop.

I was only making my situation worse. Now, not only was I sad he didn't want me, but I was horny, too.

Although…horny I could take care of. And it was a much more fun emotion than being sad about unrequited love or unrequited lust. Whatever it was that I felt for Travis.

I pulled my earbuds from my ears and stepped off my machine even though I'd only done twenty minutes. I needed to get upstairs before Travis finished working out. I didn't want to come up with a good excuse about why I had to keep the door to our rooms closed.

I'm sorry, Trav, but I need to masturbate while I think of you fucking me. I'll be done in five minutes. Later.

Even though I would be way too embarrassed to ever say that to him, I laughed at the expression I imagined on his face.

"Hey, I'm going to head upstairs," I told Travis as I walked by.

"Hold up, man," he said to his new friend and turned to me. "Are you sure? Did you need me to spot you or something?"

I could tell he was worried that I thought he'd ditched me or something.

"No, no, you're fine. I wasn't even going to work out today. So, I'm already ahead of myself even though I didn't do it long." I smiled, so he would know that I wasn't upset.

"You're sure?"

"Yes." I waved him off. "Stay. Don't worry about me."

"Okay. I'll see you in about a half hour. Maybe forty-five minutes."

"Don't worry about me," I repeated over my shoulder, already halfway to the door.

I rushed upstairs to my room. The first thing I did was close my adjoining door, but it wouldn't close all the way.

Damn it. That would explain why it hadn't closed when I shut it last night.

I wasn't going to take a chance on leaving my door open, so I shut Travis's door. I couldn't lock it, but with his shut and mine almost shut, I should be good. Plus, I still had twenty-five minutes. As the person who knew my body the best, it wouldn't take me that long.

I dug around in my suitcase for my travel vibrator, Tripp. Yes, I had a vibrator that I used strictly for traveling. After forgetting it a couple of times, I'd decided to buy a copy of my favorite battery-operated boyfriend, so I would never forget it, and I would never have to worry about grabbing the charger from my nightstand.

I pulled the shades closed and turned off all the lights, giving the room a nice, soothing atmosphere. I could only see a small amount of sunlight seeping through the slight crack between the shades and the walls.

Since I needed to take a shower after sweating from the gym, I stripped off my sweaty clothes, so I could head to the bathroom once I finished pleasuring myself.

Normally, I just lay down on my bed and went to town, but since someone could walk in, like a maid who didn't know how to knock, I got under my covers.

I turned Tripp on but soon realized that my room was too silent. I needed music.

I got up and grabbed my phone. In retrospect, I should have pulled out my headphones and just set it on the nightstand, but instead, I stuck only one earbud in, thinking I could hear if someone knocked or something with my other ear.

Then, I pulled up some eye candy and went to town.

TRAVIS

I ended my workout session a little early to check on Sydney. She'd acted a little weird down in the gym. I'd thought we'd settled everything with the middle-of-the-night incident, and I hoped she wasn't worrying about it again.

Truth be told, I hadn't wanted her to stop. But, when I'd realized that she was half-asleep, I'd known the right thing to do was to wake her up. I hadn't known she would beat herself up so much. Part of me wished I'd just taken her hand off me and rolled her away, so she wouldn't have felt so guilty.

I walked into my hotel room and threw my phone on the bed. The first thing I noticed was that my door to our adjoining rooms was closed. I frowned. I didn't remember closing it. It seemed odd because why would Sydney shut my door when she could just close her own?

Then, I heard a noise coming from her room. I paused to listen a moment. It sounded like she was crying out or yelling.

I yanked my door open, worried that someone was hurting her. The hotel we were in was nice, but I had no idea what the area was like, such as the crime rate. Maybe someone had broken in, and that person had closed my door.

Sydney's door was open just a crack, so I peeked inside. If someone were in there, the element of surprise would be best.

I didn't see anyone right away, because it was dark in her room. That didn't seem right to me either. I slowly eased her door open further. There was no masked man or intruder, but I did hear Sydney cry out again.

"Travis," she cried out.

I could see a lump moving around under the covers. I couldn't see her head, and now, I was worried that some-body was under there. That she was trying to fight someone off, and she was calling out for me to help her.

I marched over to the bed and jerked the covers off, ready to defend her.

SYDNEY

My eyes opened the second the cool air hit my body. I could only see that someone was standing over me. I screamed and used the only thing I could to protect myself.

I launched my vibrator right at the pervert and smacked him in the forehead.

His hand flew up to cover half of his face as he turned and fell back onto the end of my bed. "What the fuck, Sydney?"

I gasped and jumped out of my bed. "Oh my God. Travis?"

"That's me."

I turned on the lamp next to my bed. "I thought you were someone who'd broken in to hurt me."

He chuckled and then stopped right away. "Ow. That's funny because I thought someone was in here, hurting you."

I went to the end of the bed and leaned down next to him. "Why?"

"I heard you cry out."

It was then that I remembered I was naked, and Travis had just caught me masturbating. "Yeah…"

He sat up and looked at the floor where Tripp was still vibrating.

He raised his brow and dropped his hand. He had a big red mark on his forehead above his eye. I winced.

"I see now that I interrupted you."

I crawled over to my vibrator and shut it off, and I shoved it to the back of the cubbyhole at the bottom of the nightstand.

"Um…yeah," I admitted awkwardly. "I'd better go

shower." I stood and walked toward the bathroom with as much feigned calm as I could muster, grabbing my robe on the way. "I'll talk to you later." I went in and shut the door, and I leaned against it, letting my head fall back with a thump.

I thought I was cursed when it came to Travis. I kept embarrassing myself. And my little crush wasn't going anywhere. Thank God we hadn't discussed doing any more book signings together because I didn't think my blood pressure could handle it.

I stepped away from the door and turned on the water, wondering briefly if I could just drown myself instead of facing him again.

TWENTY-ONE

SYDNEY

I QUICKLY SHOWERED and securely wrapped my robe around me. Then, I went in search of Travis.

I wanted to make sure I hadn't ruined his handsome face. The book signing wasn't until tomorrow, but there was an author meet-and-greet tonight, and I would feel awful if he had to walk around with a lump on his forehead.

Both our adjoining doors were ajar, but I knocked before I went into his room. "Travis?"

"In here," he said from the open bathroom.

I walked over and paused when I got to the doorway. He was only in a pair of boxers, and while he looked damn good, what really caught my eye was the bruise already forming on his forehead.

I rushed inside and turned his head toward me. "Oh my God, I've ruined you."

He laughed. "It'll heal."

I brushed my thumb over it. "I'm sorry. I had no idea my...toy could be so deadly." I looked up into his eyes and blushed.

He was even more beautiful up close, and his gaze was a powerful force, watching me.

Travis put his hands on my hips and swung us around until my butt was against the bathroom counter. I didn't know where to put my own hands, so I rested them on his biceps.

"I'll accept your apology on one condition."

My eyebrows went up. I had taken for granted his acceptance, just assuming he'd tell me I was forgiven. "Okay. What is it?"

"I want an honest answer." His face was serious. Not a hint of a smile.

I took a deep breath because no one prefaced a question with that unless it was going to be hard-hitting. "Hokay."

"Why did you say my name?"

I wrinkled my nose.

He stepped closer. "Earlier. When you were in bed with…"

"Tripp."

"Tripp?"

"Yeah, it's the name of my…toy."

"Why Tripp?"

"Because it's the name of Matthew McConaughey's character in *Failure to Launch*, and I take him with me on trips."

He smiled.

Finally.

"All right then, when you were in bed with Tripp, why did you say my name?"

I pulled my hands from his arms and began toying with

the hem of my shirt. I didn't want to lie, but I sure as hell didn't want to tell him the truth either.

The serious face was back, and I knew he wasn't going to let it go.

My cheeks began to burn. But it was time to own up to it. What was the worst thing that would happen? He'd think I was depraved. It wasn't like I would die if he knew.

Fuck it.

"I was…thinking of you."

His eyes widened, and he looked at my crotch and back to my eyes. "You were thinking of me while you touched yourself?"

He hadn't had to say it so bluntly.

I raised my chin. "As a matter of fact, yes. I'm sorry if that offends you—"

Travis cut me off with a kiss.

His mouth opened over mine, and his tongue swept into my mouth.

I wrapped my arms around his neck and pulled him close. Now that his lips were on mine, I wasn't letting him go.

I kissed him back, slanting my head to the side. He was a great kisser. He knew just the right amount of tongue to give, and he tasted good. I wanted to devour him.

Travis's hands moved from my hips up my back and back down. He cupped my ass and pulled me against his erection. He managed to hit my sweet spot, and I groaned into his mouth as I grew wet.

I pulled my arms from his neck and trailed my fingers down his chest until I reached his boxers. I wanted to touch him everywhere, and I wanted him to fuck me. I didn't care if this was the only time. I didn't care if we never saw each other again. Okay, I cared, but it didn't change the fact that I *needed* him to fuck me, so I could get him out of my system.

Then, maybe I could stop thinking about him.

But later. Right now, all my thoughts were going to be laser-focused on the two of us.

I thrust my hips at him to get him to move back because I didn't want to stop kissing him long enough to tell him to back up.

He received my message, and I swiftly shoved my hand in his underwear. I grasped his cock in my palm, and we both moaned. He was hot, smooth, and oh-so hard.

I was so into touching him that I almost didn't notice when his hands moved up my sides and parted the top half of my robe. He picked up one of my breasts, which was more than a handful, and thumbed the nipple. I had never been crazy about my boobs being touched, but right now, I felt it go all the way to my pussy.

I wanted him inside me.

I pulled the bottom half of my robe apart and dragged my hand away from his shaft. I yanked him toward me so that his dick hit my clit again, and I rotated my hips against his.

He pulled his mouth away, and we both dragged some much-needed air into our lungs.

His lips were a dark red now, and I couldn't resist. I kissed him again.

He cupped my face and pulled me away. "We need to go to your room."

"Why?" I was ready to do it right there.

He grinned at me. "We need to get to that surplus of condoms you have."

I smiled. "Harper for the win."

He laughed and stepped back. I slipped off the counter and headed to my room with my robe hanging on my elbows.

Once we reached my room, I flung the robe onto my suitcase and grabbed the condoms out of the desk drawer. I turned around and waved them at Travis as I bit my lip. I probably didn't look as seductive as I wanted, but I didn't care.

Travis still had his boxers on, but his dick was trying desperately to escape the opening in the front.

"You are so fucking sexy."

I walked up to him and slapped the condoms against his chest. He clutched them as I let go. I grabbed on to each side of his underwear and pulled it down with one quick jerk.

"You don't need to flatter me. I'm already going to fuck you."

He laughed. "But it's true."

I pushed him back, so he fell on my bed. "Then, by all means, keep telling me I'm sexy."

Travis ripped a packet off the end of the row and opened it. I watched him roll the condom down, down, down.

I licked my lips.

He looked up at me. "Get your cute ass over here, sexy."

I approached the bed and put a leg on either side of him. I grabbed his cock and positioned him at my entrance.

I rubbed it back and forth a few times over my clit, and then I sank down on top of him.

"Holy shit," I said as Travis said, "Fuck me."

He sat up and wrapped his arms around me.

"I already am," I told him. I couldn't stop joking, even when I was having sex.

Travis smiled and kissed me as he nudged my lower back.

I started rotating my hips, experimenting with his length and girth, making sure I could handle him. It had been a while, but I was confident he had been made to fit inside me.

I picked up my speed and soon had to tear my mouth from his. I needed air and couldn't concentrate on both. I clasped him close to me as my orgasm neared. "Oh my God, I'm going to come," I said next to his ear.

"I can't wait."

He kissed my cheek and then down to my neck, and that was all it took.

I lost all rhythm as my climax hit me like a semitruck. It slammed into me, and I cried out. Travis continued to thrust under me until my body sagged on his.

I knew I had been the only one to come, but I needed a minute to regain some strength to keep going.

But I had nothing to worry about because Travis rolled us over until I was on my back. He pulled out of me and stood.

"Roll over, sexy. On your knees."

Despite my lack of energy, I was excited for this next step and pushed myself over.

I'd barely gotten myself situated when he grasped my

hips and shoved back into me. I moaned at the new places he was putting pressure on inside me.

"Damn, you are so wet."

"Is that bad or good?"

"Best fucking thing ever."

I couldn't see him, but I could hear the smile in his voice.

He gripped my hips as he pounded into me.

I clutched the comforter in my hands and shoved my ass in the air. I loved it when I was screwed hard, and I let him know it because I couldn't stop crying out every time he thrust inside me.

I wasn't going to come again, but I was sure as hell enjoying the ride.

I heard Travis's breathing quicken, and I knew he was going to come, too. I clenched my inner muscles down around him as he groaned and let himself go inside me. My only regret was that I couldn't see his face.

Travis collapsed on my back and pulled us to our sides.

"Holy shit. That was amazing. Even better than I imagined," he said through shallow breaths.

"You imagined what it would be like to have sex with me?"

"Hell yeah."

I wanted to fist-pump the air.

Travis withdrew from my body and got up on one elbow to look down on me. "I guess we should have waited to shower."

"Or we could just take another one together."

He grinned. "You read my mind."

TWENTY-TWO

TRAVIS

I PUSHED the sides of Sydney's robe apart as she stood in front of me. From my position on the toilet seat, I kissed her belly right above her underwear.

She dabbed something on my forehead. "Hold still. It's hard to do this when you're moving around so much."

Right now, she was trying to cover up my bruise with makeup. I'd told her it was fine, but she'd insisted.

I'd rather be doing other things.

I cupped her bra-covered breasts. "I don't want to hold still," I grumbled.

She laughed at me.

I ran my fingers over her navel. "I like the belly-button piercing."

She looked down as if she was surprised to see it there. "I struggled with my belly for almost my whole life—or as far back as I can remember. And it took me years to accept my body for the way it was, but I thought maybe, if I dressed up my stomach a little, it might make acceptance

even easier. It was my thirtieth birthday present to myself."
She smiled.

I looked at it a little closer. "It says, *90% Virgin?*"

She laughed. "Yeah. It's kind of a joke. One of my friends gave it to me."

"Do I get to be in on the joke?"

She laughed nervously. "In college, I didn't have sex until my senior year, but I would do everything else. My friends started calling me Virgin Whore as a joke, and the nickname stuck."

I laughed. "You ladies are funny."

"Or something like that," she said.

I reached up and brushed my fingers over the tattoo on the top inside of her left breast. "This looks like a heart-rate reading."

She smiled wistfully, her green eyes focused on the wall. "It is. It's an EKG reading from my mom before she passed away. I wanted her heartbeat to be over mine forever."

"Wow. I bet, if she could see it, she would love it."

Sydney laughed. "I did it before she died, and when I showed her, she about fainted from shock. But then she burst into tears and demanded that I get my ass over there and hug her."

"Can I ask what happened?"

"She got the flu, and it spread to her heart."

I kissed her belly again. A body part I found absolutely nothing wrong with. "I'm sorry you lost your mom."

She hugged me. "Me, too." She pushed my head back. "Now, can I finish?"

"I suppose."

"Are you this bad when you're having your picture

taken? I can just see the photographer getting everything lined up with lighting, and then he looks over to see that you've moved five feet."

"You think you're pretty funny. But, no, I'm very professional." I grinned. "Of course, it's easy when I don't want to fuck the photographer."

She looked at me like she was appalled. "We had sex, like, four times today. How many times do you need to do it?"

I lifted a shoulder. "A lot apparently." Plus, it had been a while for me. And, even before that, I'd forgotten how fun and amazing sex could be.

Even when I'd first started dating Christy, she'd never liked me seeing her naked. She had just started getting into being a personal trainer after losing weight. When I'd met her, she'd weighed more than she did when we broke up. But, ironically, the more weight she'd lost, the more self-conscious she became.

She would never have stood up and walked to the bathroom like Sydney had after I interrupted her time with Tripp. Christy would never have made out with me in the bathroom, letting me undress her. She would have complained that the lights were too bright or immediately covered herself back up.

But Sydney hadn't even batted an eye.

The other ironic thing was that Christy had a body that looked like it belonged on *Sports Illustrated: Swimsuit Issue*, whereas Sydney was softer in some places and didn't have the same proportions and curves.

But I found Sydney's confidence and body acceptance a

hundred times sexier than someone who had the "perfect" body.

I'd been trying to stay away from her—and all women really, I could admit now—after how things ended with Christy. I knew I didn't want to be alone forever, but I didn't know if I could trust someone again right now. It was why my last few dates had gone nowhere and why I'd kept myself and my interest away from Sydney.

My control had slipped briefly the night of the last book signing after we had dinner. Hearing her talk about herself and her not wanting me to judge her, I'd found myself in front of her with my lips on hers.

Thankfully, I'd gotten ahold of myself and my desire and been able to walk away. I had known I owed her some explanation, but I'd been putting it off. And I'd been shocked when she hadn't asked me about it or started stalking me.

I'd once met a woman on the road and shared a kiss with her—a kiss, nothing more—before I called a halt to going further. I found her attractive but felt nothing when our lips touched. After I went home, she liked and commented—multiple times—on every Instagram post I made. She would get mad when I didn't comment or like back. She started messaging me to tell me what an asshole I was for avoiding her. I'd had to unfollow her and eventually block her.

My friends had told me that the woman had done a number on me. I always shrugged it off as part of dating, but I was beginning to realize that the woman, someone I'd just met, really affected how I saw the opposite sex now.

Sydney stepped away from me. "I think I did it." She nodded toward the mirror. "Take a look."

I stood and looked at my reflection. I moved my head from side to side to get as much of a profile shot as I could.

She wrinkled her nose. "You can kind of see the bump still, but at least it's not purple."

I leaned back to get a wider view. "I'm just glad you could do it without putting makeup on my whole face." I shuddered.

"Because it's too girlie?"

"I couldn't care less about that. It's because it's too cakey. I feel like my skin is suffocating. I had to wear it once for a photo shoot, and I said never again." I turned and looked at her. "I like the natural look."

She blushed, and I cupped the back of her head and pulled her close to kiss her.

She really did that well. She put her whole being into her kisses. It made me want to get inside her all over again.

She'd had to go up on her tiptoes to reach my mouth, and she now put her heels back on the floor. "We should probably get ready."

I pulled on her robe. "Do we have to?"

She walked behind me and started pushing me out the door. "Yes. There are women waiting to meet your fine ass."

I turned once we were past the doorway. "What are you? My pimp?"

"Hmm." She tapped her chin and dropped her hand. "Yes. Yes, I think I am."

"Okay. But I'm not having sex with anyone, for you to charge them and keep all the money," I said as I started for my room.

"So, you're saying you want to split it?"

I did a one-eighty and walked backward. "Ha-ha. No." I spun back around and kept going. "But, if you did put a price on me, you'd have to charge them five hundred dollars."

"Five hundred dollars? Someone thinks mighty highly of himself." She yelled the last part because I was now in my room.

I stuck my head back into hers. "Did you or did you not come multiple times?"

She swallowed and lifted her chin. "I might have had an orgasm or two."

I laughed. "Liar. I should be charging you a thousand. You're lucky you got all this for free." I pointed to myself.

She rolled her eyes, but I caught a hint of a smile. "Go get dressed, Travis."

TWENTY-THREE

SYDNEY

TRAVIS and I walked into the back of the hotel restaurant that was reserved for parties and banquets. It was filled with people standing around, talking and drinking.

"Hello," a cheerful middle-aged woman greeted us at the door. "Can I get your names?"

"I'm Sydney Hart."

The woman, whose name tag said *Donna*, looked down at her clipboard and smile. "Here you are." She made a mark on her sheet of paper and then looked up at Travis. "And you, young man?"

"Travis Zehler."

Donna went through the same process. "I found you. You were in a different section." She made another mark and looked up at us. "We have authors, VIP readers, assistants, and models. It would have been easier to put everyone together." She threw her hands up. "But I didn't print the list."

I didn't know what to say, so I just smiled at her.

She pointed to the back of the room. "Anyway, you can go on back there to the table and pick up your name tags."

"Thank you," Travis and I both said.

"She said models. I wonder if there will be others besides you."

I had done my usual routine of checking out upcoming authors, but I hadn't even thought to look at the model list. Probably because I already knew the one I wanted to attend was coming with me.

Travis looked around. "Good question. It's always nice when I'm not the only one."

I shook my head in fake sadness. "But, if there are others, we're going to lose some money tonight. Especially if they charge less than five hundred bucks."

He put his arm around my neck and pulled me close. "I don't think I could do more than one round anyway. I only have so much stamina before my penis is begging for a break. You used me up today."

I grabbed on to the hand that was draped over my shoulder. "Damn it, this is what happens when you start sampling the merchandise."

We both laughed.

We reached the table, and Travis dropped his arm as we searched for our names in the pile of name tags.

I just found mine when I heard someone call my name.

"Sydney."

I looked around until I saw someone waving her hand at me. I grinned when I saw it was Vanessa. She was an author I had first become friends with through Facebook and then had met at a previous book signing in St. Louis.

I rushed over to her and gave her a hug. Vanessa lived in

Florida, so this was only the second time we'd ever seen each other in person.

"How are you?" she asked, her brown eyes shining when we pulled apart from one another.

"Good. Your hair is *so* cute."

She touched the back of her short black hair. "Thank you. It's a little cold for Chicago though."

I chuckled. "It's warmer here than back home for me."

She shuddered. "Remind me to never visit you."

I laughed. "Just make sure you come in the summer when it's hot." I looked around, trying to find a tall, good-looking black man in the group. "Is Trevon here with you?"

Vanessa's husband came with her to events and helped her. I thought it was so sweet, and I hoped to one day have a husband as supportive as hers.

Vanessa looked around. "He's here somewhere. He had to take a phone call for work, so who knows how far he wandered?" She looked back around to me and then behind me. She hit my arm. "Don't look now, but a nice piece of man meat is coming this way."

I glanced over my shoulder.

"I told you not to look."

I grinned. "That's just Travis. He's attending the event with me."

"That man is not *just* anything." She took a sip of her mixed drink and shook her head.

Travis reached us then and handed me a glass of white wine.

"Thank you." I was touched that he'd remembered what I'd had to drink from our dinner together even if he probably had a fifty-fifty chance of getting it right just by guessing.

"You're welcome."

"Travis, I'd like you to meet Vanessa. Vanessa, this is Travis." I made the introduction and took a sip of my wine.

"Are you two dating?" Vanessa asked,

Not wanting to spray wine all over the room, I forced it down my throat and, unfortunately, into the wrong tube.

I started coughing, and for a moment, I couldn't breathe.

Travis started pounding on my back. "You okay?"

I nodded, but then I changed my mind and shook my head. Everyone was starting to look at me, and I felt like an idiot.

"I'll…be…okay"—more coughing—"I…think."

Travis rubbed my back and looked at Vanessa. "I'm here to help Sydney."

I took a drink of my wine, which did help a little. "He's on the cover…of my new book."

Vanessa gasped, and her eyes widened. "That's you?" Her gaze drifted down to his name tag, which was a different color from my own. "You're a model."

He smiled a little shyly and dropped his arm. "I am."

"Where are you from?" Vanessa asked him.

"Minneapolis."

Vanessa's eyes lit up. "Did you two ride together?"

I nodded, still not quite confident to speak normally.

Vanessa gave me a look that said, *Tell me everything.*

I took another drink to clear my throat. I should have maybe gotten some water. "Travis and I met last year at a book signing, and we've become friends. Kind of."

He frowned, and I laughed.

"What do you mean, kind of?" He leaned close to my ear, put his arm around my waist, and whispered, "Do you let all your *kind of* friends fuck you the way you let me?" He pulled away, an amused smile on his face.

I tried to give him a look that said, *Not now*, despite the tingle I felt in my nether regions.

I turned to Vanessa. "We went to one other book signing and have communicated a few times. We haven't really hung out together."

I didn't know why I was trying to justify our relationship. Maybe because I didn't want to be disappointed when this weekend was over. I had no illusions that what we were having was a fling. I didn't want Travis to think that I was expecting roses and a ring after we went back home. I sure as hell wouldn't mind though.

I had no idea what Travis was going to say after that because a couple of readers approached Travis, looking timid and hesitant. I knew this because their name tags were also a different color.

I had gone to a few book events before I was a writer, and I remembered feeling nervous toward authors. In my head, I always put them on a pedestal.

But, now that I was an author, I knew that most of us were just as unsure as the reader. We wanted readers to like us as much as readers wanted authors to like them.

"Hello," I said so that they knew they were welcome.

Vanessa chimed in with a, "Hello."

But their eyes were all for Travis.

Join the club, ladies.

"Um…are you Travis Zehler?" a tall brunette named Giselle, as her name tag showed, said.

Travis stiffened.

It was kind of an odd response since I'd seen him now at two different signings. He'd never seemed to shy away from readers in the past.

I leaned around him. "He is," I said with a smile. "He gets nervous in front of fans," I joked.

The readers laughed, and I felt Travis relax.

The other reader, a short blonde called Rose, said, "I saw that you were going to be here, and I hope I'm not being too forward if I ask you a question."

Travis stiffened again.

What is up with him?

"Ask away," I answered for him.

Each of them pulled out two books from their big purses they carried.

"Will you sign our books?" Giselle asked and turned her novels, so we could see the covers.

I smacked Travis on the arm. "You're famous."

He hesitantly looked at me, so I smiled and waved him on.

"Do you have a pen?" Travis asked.

Rose dug around in her bag until she pulled out a Sharpie.

Travis took each book and signed them.

Giselle and Rose walked away with grins on their faces.

"No matter what else happens, they are going to be smiling all night. You totally made their day," I said.

Travis smiled shyly. He rubbed the back of his neck. "I don't know about that."

"I do." I leaned closer to him and lowered my voice. "You totally should make me your pimp. I would have charged them five bucks a book signing."

Travis laughed, and he finally relaxed completely. "That's mean."

"What did I miss?" a voice said.

I looked over to see Trevon approaching Vanessa.

He put his arm around his wife as she said, "Some readers just wanted autographs."

Trevon's dark eyes brightened. "Yours? That's great, babe."

Vanessa laughed. "No, not mine."

Trevon looked over at me. "Hey, Sydney."

"Hey, Trevon."

"Fans of yours?"

I shook my head. "Unfortunately, no." I pointed my thumb at Travis. "They're his fans."

I wasn't sure, but it looked like Travis blushed.

TWENTY-FOUR

SYDNEY

SEVERAL HOURS LATER, we walked into the already-busy nightclub. Vanessa had suggested we all go out after the meet-and-greet was over, and since we didn't have anything else on the schedule until the book signing at one the next afternoon, we'd decided to go.

I hadn't really planned to go out when I packed, but I managed to find a cute enough top that I had tossed in my bag. It was black with the shoulders cut out, so it showed a little skin, and then it dipped low in the front, letting me show off my two best assets. I only had a pair of jeans to wear with it, but I thought I looked pretty good.

Travis had pulled on a dark gray henley shirt that fit him perfectly. It wasn't too tight but snug enough that I could see his chest muscles. He'd paired it with a pair of dark jeans. He looked good enough to eat, but he could wear anything and look great.

The first thing we did was head to the bar to order drinks.

"What do you want?" Travis asked close to my ear since the music was so loud.

"A beer."

"No wine?"

I shook my head. "Nope. I'm in the mood for a beer."

He smiled. "Beer it is then."

When he finally got the attention of one of the bartenders, he ordered two.

With our drinks in hand, I looked around for Vanessa and Trevon. We'd lost them in our quest to get drinks.

"There they are." I pointed to the two of them sitting in a curved booth.

I headed in Vanessa and Trevon's direction, making my way through all the people like a human maze. I was concentrating on finding open holes in the crowd, so I didn't notice I'd lost Travis until I reached Vanessa and Trevon's table.

I turned around and saw him a few feet back, talking to a gorgeous blonde. They were only speaking, but I could tell that she was into Travis by the way she was leaning into him and playing with her necklace.

I was assaulted with many emotions upon seeing the two of them together. They looked great together, for one, and if someone got out a camera and Travis pulled her into his arms, they could be an awesome photo.

I was also sad. I had been real with myself about Travis and me only being a thing for the weekend, but apparently, I'd thought it would last the whole weekend. Foolish girl I was.

And, of course, I was jealous. I envied her beauty and the way she probably never had to wonder if a guy was into her. She had a butt I would kill to have instead of mine, which looked like a back with a crack in it.

I was also jealous because I knew that Travis and most anyone else would choose her over me. And, even though I couldn't make the feeling vanish, I could acknowledge it and work through it. I would not let my feelings control me or my actions. At least, not this feeling.

TRAVIS

I nodded at something Jenna was saying. I'd been surprised to run into someone I knew here, but then Jenna had reminded me that she lived there.

I had done a couple of photo shoots with Jenna in the past. There was one when I'd let Christy on set, and she had stormed off after seeing the two of us posing. It had been embarrassing and made me understand why some models didn't let their partners come on set.

"Who are you here with?" Jenna asked.

I pointed to the table where Sydney was just sitting down. "I'm here with a friend for a book signing."

"Sounds fun. I've been to a couple."

"You should come over and meet them."

"Sure."

We started for the table.

"Who are you here with?" I asked Jenna.

"A couple of friends. They're around here somewhere."

"Hey, Sydney," I said when they reached the table. "This is Jenna."

Sydney stood and shook Jenna's hand. "Nice to meet you. How do you two know each other?"

I studied her for any kind of unwanted reaction, but she seemed genuinely sincere in her greeting to Jenna. I probably shouldn't be surprised with how she'd acted around the readers who asked for my autograph earlier tonight. She'd been cool about it and even encouraged the readers. Despite having broken up with Christy months ago, she still obviously affected me. I'd been waiting for Sydney to be upset at the attention I was getting now that we'd slept together.

But it hadn't happened then, and it wasn't happening now.

"I've done a couple of shoots with Travis."

Sydney's eyebrow went up. "You're a model, too?"

Jenna smiled. "On the side. My day job is HR at a hospital."

"I think I've seen a couple of your photos," Sydney said. "And I think I've even seen you on a couple of books."

"Really?" Jenna asked. "I'm always in shock when someone actually recognizes me."

"Same here," Sydney said. "When I tell people I write books and they've read them, I want to jump up and down." She smiled. "Of course, I play it cool."

Jenna laughed. "Same here."

"You should stop by the book signing tomorrow," Sydney said. "I wish I had a book with you on the cover. You could totally come and sit with us."

"I might just do that," Jenna said.

"Awesome." Sydney looked behind her. "This is my friend and fellow author, Vanessa, and her husband, Trevon."

Vanessa and Trevon stood and shook Jenna's hand.

"What is your last name?" Jenna asked Vanessa.

"My author name is Vanessa Lane."

Jenna's eyes lit up. "I've read a book of yours."

It was Vanessa's turn for her eyes to shine. "Really? Which one?"

"*Love at a Distance.*"

"I just finished the sequel to that book. I heard Sydney invite you tomorrow. You should come, and I'll get you a copy of book two."

"That would be great," Jenna said. She looked at Sydney. "Would you mind if I dragged Travis out onto the dance floor?"

"Go for it. I can't wait to see his moves," she said.

"You don't want to. I can't dance," I told her.

Jenna took my arm. "He lies. He's a great dancer." She stepped back and took me with her. "We'll be back."

"I sure hope so," Sydney said. "I need his cute face to sell my books tomorrow."

Everyone laughed, except for me. I didn't really want to dance with Jenna. I'd rather hang out with Sydney. But, since she hadn't asked me to dance instead, I couldn't think of a nice way to tell Jenna no.

"Come rescue me in twenty minutes," I told Sydney.

She laughed and waved me away.

TWENTY-FIVE

SYDNEY

WHILE TRAVIS WENT OUT on the dance floor, I took the opportunity to talk to Vanessa and her husband for a bit. It was nice to have someone in the industry to discuss stuff—from the latest, crazy copyright fiasco to what the new rules were that we had to follow online. It was hard for people who weren't in the industry to get some of it sometimes.

It also helped me keep my mind off Travis dancing with beautiful Jenna. Beautiful *and* nice Jenna. Despite my jealousy, I really did like her and hoped she came to visit us tomorrow.

Vanessa raised her eyebrow and nodded her head toward the dance floor. "You'd better get out there."

I turned to see a couple more girls dancing with Travis and Jenna. I would guess they were friends of hers by how casually and easily Jenna was touching one of them.

I turned back to Vanessa. "And what would I do?"

"Go get your man."

I laughed. "He's not my man." I wished he were. But he wasn't.

"I can tell you like him."

I recoiled in horror. "Oh God. Is it that obvious?"

Trevon shrugged. "I didn't notice."

"Whew." I pretended to wipe sweat off my forehead. "Watch out, Vanessa. I'm about ready to kiss your husband."

Trevon laughed, and Vanessa continued on like I hadn't threatened to make out with her husband.

"It's not completely obvious, but I can tell."

For someone who mostly knew me through a computer screen, I wasn't exactly comforted by this.

Vanessa picked up her drink and finished the little bit that was left. "Let's go dance."

"Okay," Trevon said.

"Hey, you can't leave me here, all alone," I protested.

"You're coming with us."

I could see the determination in her eyes. She wanted me to go there because of Travis.

I stood up, so Vanessa could slide out. "Uh...okay. But I'm going to get another drink first. I'll meet you out there."

Trevon got out on the other side of the booth, and Vanessa took his arm.

"Okay. We won't wander too far in."

"Okay." I waved at them and headed back to the bar where I promptly took a seat at the first open stool. There was no way I was going to be a third wheel out of pity. And I wasn't going to dance with Travis and Jenna either.

A bartender came over, so I ordered another beer and took my phone out of my pocket.

I had a couple of messages from my niece and Harper. I hadn't told her anything that had been going on with Travis yet, except to yell at her for sneaking the condoms in my bag. I'd tell her about the weekend in person once we got back.

I slid my phone back in my pocket when the seat next to me opened up, and a nice-looking guy with light-brown hair and hazel eyes sat next to me. He was no male model, but he was the kind of guy I was much more comfortable around.

"Hey," he said.

"Hi."

He held out his hand. "I'm Owen."

I took his hand and shook it. "I'm Sydney."

"Is it okay if I sit here?"

"You already are," I pointed out.

Owen laughed. "I guess I am."

The bartender finally brought my beer and told me the amount.

I reached for my money, but Owen put his hand up.

"Do you mind if I get this for you?"

I thought about it and didn't want to give him the wrong impression by letting him buy me a drink. Even if something happened with Travis and Jenna tonight, I was not taking Owen back to the hotel or going to his place.

"Only if you let me get the next round," I told him. That way, I wouldn't owe him anything.

He grinned. "Deal."

Owen ended up being a pretty good guy. We talked for

about fifteen minutes, finishing our drinks, and he helped me keep my mind off Travis. A little.

I was ready to order us another round since it was my turn, but Owen asked, "Wanna dance?"

I looked behind me and didn't see any of the people I'd come with. "Sure," I told him.

We hopped off our stools, and I asked him, "Did you come alone?"

"No, I came with a friend, but he ditched me to dance with someone. What about you?"

"I came with some people. They're all supposed to be dancing, too, but I don't see any of them at the moment."

"We can make our way around the room," Owen offered, close to my ear now that the music was getting louder as we got closer to the dance floor. "Maybe we'll find them."

"Or they can come to us," I said.

Owen laughed. "I like you. You're smart."

I shrugged and smiled like I was clever but really didn't want to interrupt Vanessa and Trevon. Also, I really didn't want to watch Travis dance with other women.

Thankfully, the music was fast, and I caught the beat right away. I had gone out to dance all the time when I was in college. I thought that was how I'd burned off the drinks I'd consumed back then. But I rarely went out to nightclubs anymore, which was a shame. Getting older was nice, but it also sucked in some ways.

Owen and I danced and mingled with the couple around us. Pretty soon, I forgot about Travis and no longer wondered what he was doing.

Out of nowhere, two arms wrapped around my middle

and pulled me back against a tall, hard body. I was startled but only for a moment because I recognized Travis almost right away. I didn't know if it was his smell or the way he felt, but I knew it was him.

"You were supposed to come and rescue me," he said right next to my ear.

I tried to turn to look at him, but he had a tight hold on me. I leaned my head back on his shoulder. "I thought you were joking."

He met my eyes. "I wasn't. I came here to hang out with you, sexy. Not them."

His words caused a warmth in my belly that spread throughout my body. I reached up and cupped the back of his head and pulled it down, so I could kiss him. If I'd thought about my actions, I wouldn't have done it, afraid I was overstepping. So, I was glad I hadn't thought about it because he did not hold back. He didn't care if anyone saw us. His kiss made my toes curl.

"Travis," someone shouted his name.

He lifted his head and looked around. I also turned my gaze in front of me.

"Hey, Sydney," Jenna said. "We were wondering where you were."

I studied her for a moment to make sure she wasn't upset about me being in Travis's arms, but she seemed normal.

"Yeah. I went to the bar. And I met Owen." I looked around and saw Owen had moved away. Probably after Travis had approached. I motioned him over. "Hey, Owen, I found some of my friends." I introduced him to Jenna and Travis.

"Come on, Owen. Let's dance," Jenna said to him.

Owen looked starstruck but managed to nod.

Travis slipped his hand underneath my shirt as we danced. His hand was like a brand on my belly. It was hot, and the heat was traveling down to my pussy.

I could feel his erection pushing against my ass. He hadn't been hard when he first showed up, and I hoped that it was caused by his desire for me.

Travis put his mouth on my neck and kissed me there. His pecks turned into open-mouthed kisses that only made the need inside me get stronger. He felt so good; he could have taken me on the floor in front of all these people, and I would have gladly let him just to have him inside me again.

The song ended, and a slow ballad started. Travis spun me in his arms, and I wrapped my arms around his neck.

"I want to take you back to the hotel and fuck you. So badly."

"Why don't you take me then?"

TWENTY-SIX

SYDNEY

AFTER FINDING and saying goodbye to Vanessa and Trevon, Travis and I were now back at the hotel. I pulled him onto the elevator and hit the button for the second floor. It would be a quick ride up, but it felt like it took forever for the doors to close.

At the last second, a hand went in the middle of the doors to keep them open, and an extended family of seven crowded into the small space with us.

Travis pulled my back to his front, and my ass hit his hard-on. He sucked in a breath at our contact, maybe a little from pain and a little from pleasure.

I chuckled at his predicament. Thankfully, the family was too busy talking over each other to pay much attention to the two of us in the corner.

I rubbed my ass over his erection, and he groaned.

He nipped my ear. "You'd better be careful."

I tilted my head back to speak into his ear, "What are you going to do?" I wiggled my eyebrows. "Spank me?"

He smiled and shook his head. "I'm going to tease the fuck out of you."

I decided to call his bluff. I arched my pelvis forward and slipped a hand in between our bodies. I ran my thumb down his cock, and then I squeezed him with my fist.

Travis grabbed my hand as the doors opened. "In the back," he said to let the group know we were getting off.

He pushed me forward, and once in the hall, he grabbed my hand and pulled me down to our rooms. We stopped at his room where he quickly pulled out his key card and let us in.

As soon as the door shut behind us, Travis pushed me against the door and kissed me. Then, he slowly walked us backward toward the bed.

He stepped away from me. "Get naked and lie on the bed. I'll be right back."

He disappeared into my room for what I assumed was to get some condoms, so I did what the man had asked. I took off my clothes and got on the bed.

Travis came back with several condoms, a couple of things that looked like pillowcases, and my vibrator.

I gasped. "How did you find Tripp?"

He grinned. "I saw where you'd stashed him after you threw him at my head."

He tossed the toy and condoms down next to me on the bed and sat on the opposite side. He was very close to my head, and I didn't understand why until he lifted one of my arms above my head.

"What are you doing?" I asked.

He lifted one of the items that was indeed a pillowcase.

"I'm going to tie your hands to the headboard." He wrapped the pillowcase around one wrist.

"Okay." I'd never done anything like this, but I wasn't opposed to it. I was getting excited to see what he had in store for me.

Once he was done with one arm, he lifted the other and repeated his actions. Travis stood, and I tested my restraints. They weren't tight, and I could probably get out of them. I was kind of relieved that I wouldn't be trapped in here if Travis had a heart attack or something. Not that anything was going to happen, but it was still a comfort.

Travis walked to the end of the bed and pulled one of my legs, so I was no longer sitting halfway up. This way, my arms were stretched above me.

"I know you can easily get out of those," he said to me, "but I'm trusting you to keep your hands there." He raised an eyebrow.

I nodded in agreement.

He smiled. "Good." He put a knee on the bed and pushed my legs open. "Wow. Already wet. Someone likes being tied up?"

I shook my head. "Someone likes being with you."

He pushed a finger into me, and I moaned. "Great answer."

He pulled his hand away and got down on his stomach. He ran his nose along the inside of my thigh and then did the same with the other. He looked up at me and grinned. As he maintained eye contact with me, he put his mouth on my clit and sucked.

It was a very strong sensation so soon, and I threw my head back and bucked my hips.

Travis wrapped his hands around my legs to hold me still.

I closed my eyes and let myself feel as Travis licked my center and proceeded to give me the greatest head of my life. I always loved it when a guy liked going down on me. No woman ever wanted a guy to do it just because he felt like he had to.

Travis slowly built me up with every kiss, lick, and stroke. When he put his lips on my clit again and sucked, I was ready for the sensation. And I was also ready to come.

I rotated my hips across his face and was almost there when Travis pulled away.

I opened my eyes to see him sitting up. "Wha—wh— why'd you stop?"

He tilted his head to the side and pretended to look confused. "I'm sorry. In the elevator, I said I was going to tease you if you teased me. You went for it, so I thought this was what you wanted."

"Noooo," I whined.

He grinned. "Revenge is a dish best served hot and wet."

He picked up Tripp and turned it on. He studied it for a moment and then looked at me.

My eyes widened as I realized what he was going to do. He brought it down and put it directly on my sensitive clit.

I thrashed my head back and forth. I was so close.

He moved it away before I could come and pushed it into me. It didn't feel as good there, but I supposed that was the point. He fucked me with Tripp for a few minutes and pulled it out and held it up.

"Look how fucking wet you are. Amazing."

I would have blushed if I wasn't so turned on.

I thrust my hips. "Please."

He put the vibrator back between my legs. "Please what?"

He pushed it down on my clit again, and I knew I was going to orgasm in seconds.

He pulled it away.

"Noooo," I cried again. "This isn't fair. I'm sorry I teased you. Please let me come."

Travis grinned, turned off Tripp, and stood. I'd forgotten he was still completely dressed, except for his shoes. He pulled off his shirt and pushed off his boxers and jeans. I moved to touch him, as he was hard and beautiful, but I was stopped by the ties.

"I want to touch you."

He shook his head. "Not yet."

He reached for a condom, and I watched him slowly roll it down his impressive length. I wasn't sure, but I thought he was putting a show on for me.

It worked because I only wanted him more.

"You're mean." I pouted.

Travis just laughed.

He pushed my legs wide and knelt between them. He grabbed my vibrator again and turned it on. He thrust it in and out of me a couple of times and then pulled it out. "Are you ready?"

"I don't know." I didn't know what he was going to do next.

He laughed. "I'll take that as a yes."

He pressed the toy down on my clit again, and despite my being afraid that he was going to pull it away, my climax was barreling down on me.

And, like a moron, I yelled out, "Oh shit, I'm going to come."

"I know, sexy. Let it go."

And, right before my orgasm hit, he thrust into me.

I came so hard that I actually saw stars, and I didn't care if I passed out.

Thankfully, I didn't faint, and I rode my orgasm for what felt like a full minute. It was glorious.

When my body finally relaxed, I felt like a limp noodle. I opened my eyes to see Travis grinning down on me.

"Hey, sexy."

He untied my hands, and I used all my strength to run my fingers down his six-pack.

He twitched inside me, and I smiled.

"Your turn."

Travis leaned over and kissed me as he began to thrust into me. He pushed an arm under one leg, bringing it to my chest, giving him access to go even deeper.

I moaned as he rode me to his own climax. I held on tight to him and enjoyed the pleasure. Even if I couldn't come again, it still felt incredibly good.

And, as Travis came, I squeezed down on him in hopes that it would make his orgasm feel as amazing as mine had felt.

He collapsed on top of me, breathing hard and sweating.

I never wanted the weekend to end.

TWENTY-SEVEN

SYDNEY

TRAVIS GOT up to get rid of the condom in the bathroom, and I snuggled down under the covers.

I didn't know if I should stay or go to my own room, but I told myself to worry about it after a few minutes. Travis wouldn't mind me staying there and relaxing for a bit.

I heard the toilet flush and the sink turn on and off, and then Travis came out of the bathroom.

He smiled when he saw me. "You look comfortable."

I had the covers up to my nose and half of my face buried in the pillow. I smiled back at him. "I am."

He slid into bed on his side and picked up the remote. "Want to watch some TV?"

"Sure," I said as I let my eyes close. "If I fall asleep, feel free to wake me."

Travis grabbed my wrist and tugged on it. "Come over here."

I opened my eyes to see him pat his chest.

This was an invitation I'd be crazy to turn down.

I scooted over, and he slid an arm under my neck. I

pushed my body flush with his, resting my head on his shoulder.

He kissed my forehead. "Go ahead. Close your eyes."

And I did just that.

———

TRAVIS

I rubbed Sydney's back, enjoying her half-lying on me. But that wasn't the only thing I enjoyed. I'd had fun with her all night.

The more I was around her, the more I liked her, and I planned to see more of her when we got back home.

I remembered how she had said we were kind of friends. She thought we were barely friends. Obviously, she was unsure of where I stood, and I was probably to blame for that. I had kissed her and ran.

But maybe I could do something to start now, so she would know that I saw us as more than *kind of* anything.

Sydney's breathing had changed almost as soon as she lay down, so I could tell she was sleeping. Very gently, I used the arm that wasn't holding her to reach down to the floor for my jeans that I'd thrown to the side of the bed when I'd undressed. Once I found those, I felt around until I found my phone in my pocket and pulled it out.

I opened Instagram and hit the plus sign to add a new post. My photos opened, and I looked through the ones I'd taken tonight. I had a few of Sydney and a couple that we had taken together as selfies. I picked my favorite of each. I wrote a comment about having a great time that night with Sydney, but I couldn't find her.

I could have sworn that Sydney was on Instagram.

Going back to the home page, I used the search button to look for her.

I had to scroll through a few, but there she was.

Hmm. I could see that she'd followed me, but I'd never followed her back. I immediately hit the button to remedy that. Maybe that was part of why she'd thought we were only *kind of* friends.

I went back to posting the pictures of us from earlier that night and added, *Had a great time with this lady tonight.* I hit Share and set my phone down.

Hopefully, that would help to let her know how I felt.

SYDNEY

I awoke the next morning, disorientated. I didn't quite have a hangover, but I could feel the effects of the alcohol on my sleep.

I was going to need lots of coffee to get myself up and running for the day. Thank heavens the signing didn't start until one in the afternoon.

I reached for my phone that I'd been smart enough to put on the nightstand when I'd gotten undressed last night, but there was something hindering my movements.

I pulled up the covers to see Travis's arm around me.

I immediately smiled.

I'd fallen asleep in his bed, and apparently, he didn't mind me being there.

I went for my phone again, careful not to disturb Travis. I hit the button to wake up my screen to see that it was already almost eleven in the morning.

Crap. That meant I needed to get moving. I still had to set up for the book signing.

I was looking forward to it, as always, but right now, I was really enjoying lying in bed with Travis.

I decided going through my notifications was a good excuse to stay in bed for a few more minutes.

I checked my messages, my e-mails—both personal and author e-mails—and then Facebook. That took me a good ten minutes. I didn't have anything from Twitter, which wasn't a surprise because I wasn't on it very much. I did have a couple of notifications from Instagram.

I opened the app and saw that Travis had *finally* followed me, *and* he'd tagged me in a post.

I admitted it. I was giddy. Especially when I saw his caption. *Had a great time with this lady tonight.*

I had the sudden desire to see his face, but I didn't want to wake him. I pulled up the camera on my phone and flipped the screen around, so I could see the two of us.

The first thing I noticed was my red raccoon eyes and *eek* face upon seeing them. That was what happened when I fell asleep without washing the makeup off my face or taking out my contacts. I used my finger to get most of the black out from under my eyes.

Then, I lifted my phone, so I could see Travis. His face was buried in my neck, and he looked so peaceful. It made me wonder how I'd missed how close he was to me when I first woke up.

I lifted my phone and snapped a few pictures of us. I then swiped through them in hopes that I'd gotten a good one. I wanted one that I would be able to look at someday in the future and remember this weekend. I paused on my favorite and smiled.

"Did you just take a picture of me sleeping?"

I jumped, thinking Travis had still been asleep.

I held up my phone and showed him. "I did. But don't worry. I won't post it on social media or anything." As much as I would love to brag about whose bed I was in, that wasn't something I would do.

He chuckled and squeezed my waist. "What's with you taking pictures of me sleeping next to you?"

I frowned. "What do you mean? I only just did it now."

"What about the book signing in Iowa?" I could hear the smile in his voice.

I almost turned over to defend myself, but I remembered that I hadn't brushed my teeth last night. "That wasn't me. That was Harper. You were awake for that?"

He kissed the back of my head. "Not at first, but I woke up when you were arguing about taking the pictures."

"Ugh…how embarrassing. I apologize for my friend."

"Do you have the pictures?"

"Yes…I do," I reluctantly admitted.

"Let me see."

I swiped through my pictures until I got the ones that Harper had taken in Iowa of Travis sleeping on my hotel bed. I held my phone up to show him.

He took it from my hand.

"Hey," I said, but I didn't try to get it back. If he wanted to delete them, he had every right.

Travis rolled to his back, and so did I. I watched him as he looked at the pictures. It was taking him a while, but finally, he handed my phone back to me.

I looked through the images. "You didn't delete them."

"Why would I?"

I shrugged. "Because Harper took your picture without your permission."

Travis pulled me, so I was lying on his chest. "I thought it was funny. I actually sent them to myself."

My eyes widened. I hadn't expected that.

Travis rubbed his hand down my naked back, butt, and leg. "When do you have to get up?"

I kissed his neck. "Now, unfortunately."

"I was afraid of that." He released his arms, and I sat up. "I think I'm going to do a quick workout. You want to come?"

I looked over my shoulder to answer him but got side-tracked by the image of a tan, muscular, naked model in the middle of white sheets that barely covered his goods. I took a deep breath, wishing I could take a picture of him now. "Um…no, thanks. I have to go and set up."

Travis winced. "Oh. I should probably help you with that. I kind of forgot. Sorry, sexy."

"It's okay." I patted his leg. "I kind of like to set up by myself. Harper says I'm anal about how my table looks. Go and work out. We'll meet up when we're both done."

He sat up and pulled me toward him. He kissed me long and thoroughly, unbrushed teeth be damned. "It's a deal."

TWENTY-EIGHT

SYDNEY

AS ANOTHER READER left my table, I looked at Travis. "You're like female catnip." I tilted my head to the side. "Well, more like straight-female-slash-gay-male catnip."

Travis chuckled.

"You laugh, but I wish I could put you in my bag and take you to all my signings with me."

He grinned. "Why don't you then?"

Surely, he was joking. There was no way he wanted to come to every one of these events. He probably had bigger and better things to do. Rather than responding, I just laughed. But it did get me thinking that I needed to look into having other models who might be kind enough to join me for a book signing.

I always felt awkward about asking because it probably wasn't that much fun for them.

"Do you like going to book signings?" I asked.

"Heck yeah. They are usually a lot of fun."

"I know I joked about you being catnip, but does it ever get old?"

"Only when someone starts stalking me on social media and doesn't understand the word *no*."

My face heated. I turned to look away from him. I had totally stalked him on social media.

Travis leaned forward. "Are you blushing?"

"Hmm? What? No," I said, shaking my head.

He nudged me with his shoulder. "What did you do?"

"I might or might not have stalked you on social media after meeting you." I kept facing forward, so he couldn't see all of my humiliation.

Travis laughed and put his hand on my knee. "Don't fret, sexy. I stalked you a little, too."

I turned to look at him, mouth agape, but his attention was caught by someone yelling his name.

"*Travis.*"

He stood as Jenna approached our table. Wow. When I'd invited her to show up, I hadn't thought she'd actually come. To me, she was so beautiful and majestic that it seemed like she would have so many other things to do.

Travis kissed her on the cheek when she reached us.

"Hey, Sydney," she said with a wave.

I smiled and waved back. "How's it going?"

"Good." She looked behind her. "I stopped and said hello to Vanessa on the way over here." She held out her hands, showing two books she'd bought from Vanessa. "I had to buy the books and have her sign them since I'm here."

"I bet Vanessa loved that."

Jenna smiled and picked up a copy of my book with Travis on the cover. "Very nice."

"Thank you," we both said.

The three of us laughed.

"I guess it depends on what you're complimenting," I said.

"The whole thing. Nice picture, Travis. Great book design, Sydney." She handed me the book. "How much?"

"Ten dollars."

I opened the cover and grabbed my marker to sign it. After I was done, I gave it to Travis to sign. He finished up and handed it back to Jenna.

"Hey, I'm going to run to the restroom. You want to sit here with Sydney for a minute and help her?" Travis asked Jenna.

"Sure." She looked at me. "If that's okay with you?"

"Of course. But I don't really need that much help. You can just sit and relax."

"Thanks," she said as she took Travis's seat. "How's today going so far?"

"Good. I woke up late, so I was rushing to get set up before the event started."

Jenna smiled. "Stayed out too late?"

"Yeah. I'm not as young as I used to be."

"You know, I think Travis really likes you."

That had kind of come out of nowhere.

"Really?"

"Yeah, he was looking for you last night. He was disappointed that you hadn't come to get him."

"I thought he was joking about the whole twenty-minutes thing."

"He wasn't. You should have seen his face when he found you." She smiled. "He was pretty happy."

My face flushed but for a different reason. I loved

hearing that he had been excited to see me. Now, I wanted to find Travis and leave the book signing, so I could take him upstairs.

I suddenly decided I needed to take advantage of my time with him. Even if it meant taking a break from my own event.

"I need to use the restroom, too. Do you mind sitting here until Travis gets back?" *Please say yes. Please say yes.*

"Sure."

I jumped from my chair.

"What do I have to do?" Jenna asked.

Ah, crap. I hadn't thought about that. *Screw it.* I was going anyway. "Books are ten dollars each. If someone wants me to sign it, I'll be back as soon as I can." I started walking away but stopped and remembered to be polite. "Thank you," I said as I made a quick turn.

Jenna laughed. "You're welcome."

TRAVIS

I was standing outside the restrooms, talking to Trevon, when the door burst open, and Sydney walked out.

I smiled immediately, and her eyes lit up when she saw me.

She approached Trevon and me. "Hey, Trevon, do you mind if I steal Travis for a minute?"

Trevon looked at his watch. "Not at all. I'd better get back to Vanessa anyway."

"Talk to you later," I said to him.

"Later," Trevon said with a smile as he walked away.

I turned to Sydney. "Do you need me to go back in, too? Sorry, I got sidetracked."

"No, that's okay," she said as she looked around.

I frowned. She seemed to be looking for something.

She walked away from me, down the hall to another door. She opened it, peeked inside, and walked back to me with a sneaky grin on her face.

"What's going on?" I asked her when she reached me again.

She grabbed me hand and pulled me toward the door. "Come on. You'll see."

When we reached the door and opened it, it was dark. The light from the hall gave off enough illumination for me to see it was an empty banquet room, smaller than the one the book signing was in.

Sydney tugged me inside and pushed me against the wall as the door closed with a click. We were surrounded by complete darkness.

Sydney arched up and kissed me, and I quickly decided I didn't mind my lack of sight so much. I put my arms around her and cupped her little ass. I loved how tiny it was.

Sydney ran her fingers down my stomach to my jeans and squeezed my dick through the outside of my pants.

I groaned into her mouth and felt her smile.

She kissed me again and began attacking my fly.

I was instantly pulled in two different mental directions. I liked what she was doing—a lot—but I was also worried I would get caught with my pants down—literally.

Sydney pulled my jeans down just enough for my cock to spring free, and then she was gone from my arms.

"Wha—" was all I got out before she wrapped her lips around me and sucked my shaft into her hot mouth. I threaded my fingers in her hair. "*Holy shit.*"

I forgot all about getting caught.

Sydney traced her tongue around the head of my dick and sucked on the tip as she played with my balls. I wanted it to go on forever. There was something about getting head that felt incredible. And there was something about getting head from someone you liked that felt unbelievable.

Sydney worked me over, and I knew I wasn't going to last long. I was disappointed that it had to end, but it was for the best. I didn't want to get caught before I came, and I knew Sydney had to get back to her event.

Since I wouldn't last much longer, I decided to see how far Sydney would go. I slid my hands from her hair. Grabbing her wrist, I pulled it away from my body, and she let me.

I dropped her hands and heard them fall down to her sides.

Not being able to see anything really did heighten my other senses. Both of us were breathing hard, and mine got more ragged as I pictured what I was going to do next.

I cradled the sides of her face and stroked her cheeks with my thumbs. She nodded as if she knew what I was asking.

It was all the permission I needed before I gently pushed my cock into her mouth. She didn't gag or stop me, so I did it again. And again and again.

I always felt a little like a pervert when I fucked a woman's face, but I fucking loved it. I never forced anyone to do it, but if a woman was willing, she was a keeper in my mind.

Of course, since this explicit act was my kryptonite, it wasn't long before I was right on the edge. "*Shit.*"

I dropped Sydney's face, and her hands touched me again. She cupped my testicles once more as she wrapped her other hand around my base. She pumped me twice as she sucked me back into her throat, and that was when I exploded.

My head fell back against the wall with a thump, but I barely felt it. My orgasm was coursing through my body, causing me to feel like I was floating.

When I became too sensitive for Sydney to touch me any longer, I put my hand on the top of her hair.

She released me, and with a little help from me, she tucked my cock into my jeans. Then, she kissed my belly and stood.

I drew her into my arms and held her close.

Thankfully, we looked like we were cuddling because that was when a hotel employee pushed the door open. She looked more startled to see the two of us than we were to see her.

"Oh my God," she said.

I smiled reassuringly, and Sydney stepped out of my arms.

"It's okay. We were just leaving."

I heard a sniffle and turned to see Sydney pretending to wipe her eyes.

I went with it. "She just needed a few minutes alone," I told the employee.

The woman nodded. "It's okay."

I grabbed Sydney's hand and pulled her from the room. "We should get back."

Sydney gave a loud sniffle as we walked by the employee, but once we were past her, she burst out laughing. "That was fricking close."

"Tell me about it."

We stopped at the doors to the book signing, and I kissed her. "Thank you for the spectacular head."

She grinned up at me. "You're very welcome. I suppose we'd better get inside and rescue Jenna."

TWENTY-NINE

SYDNEY

I GLANCED over at Travis as we turned onto my street. My weekend with him was finally over, and I sighed at the thought.

He looked my way. "You okay?"

I mustered up a smile. "Yeah. Just not ready to go home and get back to work tomorrow." Even though I got to do what I loved, it was still work.

"I was hoping you weren't too tired from last night."

I laughed. "No."

We had gone to dinner after the book signing and gotten back to the hotel early. We'd had a few rounds of sex, but I thought we had gone to bed around ten thirty.

"I do wish we could have slept in a little more." We had gotten up at seven that morning. "But it's nice to get back to Minnesota at a decent time." I was going to bed early and hopefully sleeping all night long.

Travis pulled into my driveway, and I was impressed that he'd remembered where I lived. As soon as he put his SUV in park, I jumped out.

"I just have to open my garage door, and then I'll get all my stuff out."

I used the garage code on the doorframe to open the big door. I spun around and started back to the SUV where I saw that Travis already had the back open.

"Hey, you don't have to help me," I told him.

"What kind of gentleman would I be if I sat and watched you bring in all your books and materials?"

"That's a good point," I said as I grabbed my suitcase and my banner while Travis carried my big cart full of books and other materials. "You can just set them in the garage."

"Are you sure? I can bring them in the house."

"I leave them out here until I'm done with book signings for the season. Then, I bring it all into my basement."

We set our items down toward the back of the garage, and then we turned to each other. I didn't know what we were supposed to do now. We weren't in Chicago anymore, and the weekend was pretty much over, so I wasn't sure if I should kiss him or shake his hand.

Travis took a step toward me when the door to my house opened.

"Hey, Syd. I thought I'd heard the garage open."

Travis stepped back.

"Hey, Lexie," I said to my niece. I was disappointed she'd interrupted us, but it could be for the best. No weird goodbyes. "I didn't know you were here." I hadn't seen her car.

"Rose dropped me off. Brendan's picking me up later."

"Hi, Lexie," Travis said.

"Hey, Travis. How's it going? How was Chicago?"

Travis looked at me. "Great. It was great."

I cleared my throat and looked up at Lexie. "It was good." I frowned. "How long have you been here?" I asked suspiciously in a tone that was only slightly joking.

Lexie rolled her eyes. "I've only been here for an hour or so. I knew you were coming back today. I didn't throw a party." She stuck her tongue out at me.

"Well, I'd better get going." Travis said.

"Oh, yes." *He probably has plans tonight.* "Thank you again for coming. I really did have a lot of fun."

He smiled at me, and I knew what he was thinking when I'd said *fun* even though that hadn't been my intention.

My thoughts turned to the blow job I'd given him. I was still amazed at my braveness to do that in a public place. And poor Jenna had looked lost when we returned. But she'd said I'd only missed a couple of readers. It had been completely worth it.

Travis moved closer and kissed my cheek and hugged me. I held on tight for a few seconds, breathing in his Travis scent and enjoying how good he felt one last time.

"See ya later, sexy," he said in my ear.

"Bye, Travis." I wish I had a good nickname to call him.

He released me and walked back to his vehicle. He waved goodbye from behind the wheel and pulled away.

I sighed wistfully.

"That bad, huh?"

I looked at Lexie. "What?"

She smiled. "Nothing." She went back into the house.

I glanced down the street one more time, but Travis was gone.

It was getting late. Lexie's boyfriend had picked her up a couple of hours ago, and I had talked to Harper on the phone for over an hour, telling her about the weekend and she telling me about hers. It was time to head to bed

I grabbed my phone from my coffee table and headed upstairs.

I scanned through my notifications, as I always did before bed. I saw Facebook notifications that reminded me that I had meant to message Vanessa.

I pulled up my Messenger app because that was the way the two of us always communicated with each other. I didn't even have her phone number, and I'd never given her mine.

> Me: Hey, Vanessa. It was really good to see you again. Sorry we didn't get to hang out much yesterday. I hope you made it home safely.

The three dots appeared, telling me she was typing.

> Vanessa: We made it back safe and sound. Do not fret about us not seeing each other much yesterday. I know how busy it gets.

> Me: Keep me posted on your next book signing. Hopefully, we'll get to meet up again.

> Vanessa: Will do! Have a good night.

> Me: Night!

I reached my room and bit my lip.

I really wanted to message Travis, but I didn't want to come across as needy.

I set my phone down on my nightstand but picked it back up again. Maleficent followed me into the bedroom and jumped on my bed. I stared at her feline face and thought about what she would do if she were a human. If it were anyone else, I wouldn't hesitate to send a message. I should just do it and not worry about it so much.

I found his name.

> Me: Heading to bed, and I just wanted to thank you again for taking the time out of your busy life to come with me this weekend. I really did have fun. I hope you're having a good night, and have a great week, too.

I hit Send before I reread what I had written a million times. I set my phone down again and walked away from it to get ready for bed.

I finished my nightly routine and turned on the TV as I walked past to get into bed. As soon as I slid under the covers, I picked up my phone to see no return messages.

I couldn't help the disappointment, and rather than focusing on what to watch on television, I opened up Instagram. On top of my feed, I saw that Travis had new stories to share.

The first story was a video he had taken of me sleeping in the car on our drive home. It was hard to see my face, but I knew it was me.

I could hear the sound of the road, and Travis said, "This is my travel buddy. She fell asleep ten minutes after we left, leaving me to stay up all on my own." He quickly turned the camera around to face himself and grinned before sticking his tongue out.

I was embarrassed but happy that he'd shared the video of me even if he called me his buddy.

The story was a picture of him in front of his house with the caption, IT'S GOOD TO BE HOME.

But the next video was of Travis scanning the room of what looked like a restaurant or bar and grill of some sort. There was a bar area, but there was also a table in front of the camera with food on it. The next video, someone had tagged him and the group he was sitting with. There were at least six of them, and Travis was laughing at the camera, but he was leaning toward a woman with red hair.

And that was the last story.

Emotions bombarded me. I felt left out that he had gone out tonight without me even though, rationally, I knew that we weren't that close, I wasn't part of his friend group, and he'd probably had these plans before this weekend. I was still sad.

And, of course, I was jealous of whoever the redheaded woman was. Even though there were no signs they were romantic, I couldn't help how I felt. And I knew I had no right to feel that way. He was not my boyfriend, and he'd made no indication he wanted to start a relationship.

Maleficent came over and curled up at my side, and I sank my hands in her fur.

I sure did regret sending him the message that I was going to bed. He probably thought I was a loser. Or maybe I just wasn't in my twenties anymore, and I'd lost a lot of my desire to party like when I was young. I needed to stop worrying about what Travis thought.

I threw my phone onto the other side of my bed.

I needed to just take a step back from him and maybe even forget about him for a while. Like all crushes, it would pass if I just gave it time.

———

Travis

I set my fork on my plate and picked up my napkin from my lap. After wiping my face, I threw it on the table. I'd eaten too much, but it was worth it.

I pulled out my phone from my pocket and saw that Sydney had messaged me. My grin was so big it almost split my face.

"Whatcha looking at?" my sister, Sloan, said as she looked over my shoulder. "Ooh…is that the author you went to Chicago with?"

"Yes," I said as I put the cursor in the response box.

"Do you like her?"

I looked at Sloan. "I think I do."

Her face got serious. "Is she anything like Christy?"

I shook my head and smiled at my big sister's overprotectiveness. "Far from it."

"Okay then. I say go for it."

"Wasn't looking for your permission, but thanks, sis." I went back to my phone and started typing.

THIRTY

SYDNEY

THERE WAS something about mornings and the new light of day. It made the things that you'd worried about the night before seem not as big of a deal.

I thought about the things that had upset me before I went to bed, and while they still bothered me, I knew I would get past it, and life would go on easily. So easily that I didn't even pick up my phone before or after I got out of bed.

I had learned that I got my best writing done in the morning and that the best way to do that was to stay off social media. I could get so caught up with looking at funny memes and reading news articles that I would see hours of good writing time go down the drain.

I went downstairs and grabbed a cup of coffee. About a year ago, I'd made it a habit to set my coffee to auto-brew, so I wouldn't have to wait for it in the morning. I filled up my favorite mug and headed back upstairs to my office.

I hit Ctrl+S on my computer and stretched my arms over my head. I'd done some good writing.

I looked down at the clock in the corner. *Dang.* I'd been working for almost three hours straight. I needed a break. Maybe a shower.

I was really into my story, so I wasn't surprised that I'd worked that long without stopping.

I was writing a story about an FBI team of a man and a woman who had been together for years and saw each other as more than coworkers. After working long hours together, they'd also become best friends. To the point where they told each other everything, including when they'd had sex even if it was bad.

My main characters had to go undercover and pretend to be a romantic couple. It was nothing unusual. They'd done it a half-dozen times or so before this, but in this case, they were staying with the person they were investigating, and the room was wired. There would be no one sleeping on the couch this time around without the bad guy getting suspicious.

My favorite part, which I'd just finished writing, was an awesome sex scene. In the beginning of the book, my heroine had complained to the hero about how she'd gone on several dates with a guy but called it off when he gave her lousy head.

Fast-forward to the scene I'd just written, and the hero spread the heroine's legs and told her, "This is how you eat pussy."

Just thinking about it had me rubbing my hands together and giggling on the way to my room. Sometimes, I had to work hard to make everything fit, and sometimes, things just magically fell into place.

I went into my bathroom and turned on the shower since it always took a million years for the water to get warm. I stripped off my clothes and threw them in my laundry basket in my walk-in closet. On my way back to my bathroom, I saw my phone and figured I'd better check it.

I had quite a few notifications, most of them nothing important, and a couple of messages. Lexie had messaged me before school, and Travis had messaged me, too. Last night. I hadn't heard it because I put my phone on silent after a certain time. I hated being woken up by stupid social media notifications.

I couldn't believe he'd messaged me.

> Travis: I wish I were there with you. You can stop thanking me. I had fun. At a late dinner with some friends. Talk tomorrow? BTW, my sister says she approves of you. LOL.

I reread the message a couple of times. *He wishes he were with me? As in, in my bed with me? And his sister approves of me? What the hell does that mean?*

So, that pretty redhead in the video might be his sister.

I got excited all over again.

Slow your roll, Sydney. Let's take this one step at a time.

I took a calming breath and started to type my response, only to realize I had no idea what to say. And steam was starting to come out of my bathroom.

Just send him a quick message and go shower.

> Me: Hey. Sorry, I just saw that you'd responded. My phone goes on silent at night, and I got up and went straight to the computer this morning. Hope you had fun with your friends…

I bit my lip, unsure if I should finish the message the way I wanted.

If Travis were anyone else who I hadn't put on a pedestal, I would flirt with him.

Just do it.

> Me: Wish you'd been here, too.

I hit Send. Quickly, I threw my phone back on my bed and ran for the shower.

I refused to wait around for him to message me back like some lovesick schoolgirl. I wanted to think I was strong like that, but in reality, I showered with record speed and raced back to my phone.

Really smooth, Sydney. Way to be strong.

I suddenly realized I had been talking to myself a lot in my head this morning.

"Maleficent," I called out. This was why I had a cat after all—to talk to. "Maleficent."

I heard a meow, and my cat crawled out from under my bed. She looked at me like I was the lowest form of dirt.

I patted the top of my bed. "Come here. I need someone to talk to."

She turned around and walked down the hall.

I should have gotten a dog.

Ding.

I lasted all of a second before snatching my phone up.

> Travis: I had a good time. Maybe not as much fun as I'd had with you.

> Me: You mean, none of them took off their clothes and let you have sex with them?

> Travis: LOL. No. And I didn't want them to either.

> Me: That's too bad.

> Travis: Nah. I'd rather have you take your clothes off for me.

> Me: Maybe that can happen again sometime.

I was a little nervous about my last message. I was flirting, but I was kind of putting myself out there, too.

> Travis: I wish that sometime could be tonight.

I fist-pumped the air.

> Travis: But I work until 8 p.m., and then I have to help a friend with something after work.

I dropped my hand. It had been too good to be true. And I couldn't help but wonder if he'd picked tonight so that he had a reason to say no.

Either way, I refused to look desperate, and I wasn't going to ask him again.

Me: Hey, I get it. I hogged you enough over the weekend. You have to make some money, and your friends need you, too.

Me: I have a lot of writing I need to do today since I took three whole days off and only worked a little bit in the car on Thursday.

I'd had to add the second message, so he knew that I had a life, too.

Travis: What about later this week?

Me: Sure.

Travis: You don't sound very excited.

Me: I'll be excited when I see you. How about that? :-)

Travis: Sounds good because you will see me.

THIRTY-ONE

SYDNEY

"SO, you and Travis keep planning on seeing each other, but it hasn't happened yet?" Harper asked.

I laughed. "How long have you been waiting to ask that?"

She rolled her eyes. "All night."

It was Saturday, and Harper and I were having a night out, just the two of us. Her mother-in-law was in town, and Harper always needed to get away for a bit when she came to visit. We'd gone shopping and had dinner, and we were waiting in line to buy popcorn at the movie theater. Then, after this, we were going to have an adult sleepover. It was something we tried to do every few months.

"So, spill it. Does he keep making excuses?"

"No, it's not like that. He said he wanted to see me later this week, but he hasn't brought it up again."

"Have you?"

"No," I answered.

"Why?"

"Because I already said I wanted to see him. And he has

plans, like, every night. He is always on the go. Honestly, the more we talk, the more I think that, if we really did date, I'd be exhausted."

Harper laughed. "Haven't you ever heard that opposites attract?"

"If we ever see each other again."

"So, what is he doing tonight?"

"Going out with friends again."

"Why didn't he invite you?"

And that question was probably the only thing that bothered me. He could have included me in whatever he was doing, but he never asked. I was glad that Harper and I had made our own plans tonight.

"I honestly don't know. And I'm not about to ask because I don't want him to know I care."

Harper wrinkled her nose. "You going to keep talking to him?"

I shrugged. "I suppose. I'm not going to pencil in our wedding date or anything though."

Harper nodded. "That's my girl."

It was our turn to reach the counter and order, and the subject was dropped.

———

We got back to my house and dropped our stuff by the back door.

"I'm going to call Ian and see how it's going at home," Harper said. "And then I'm going to rub it in that he missed a great movie."

"You're the best wife."

She grinned. "I know." She took her phone from her purse and walked toward the living room.

"Wine?" I asked as she left.

"Always."

I grabbed two wineglasses from the cupboard and poured us each a glass. I drank my first glass because I was in for the night and because I could, and then I went to find my own phone. It was buried deep in my purse. I had driven us to the movies and back, and I was making a conscious effort to stay off my phone while driving. And, to do that, I either listened to an audiobook or a podcast or I buried it so that it wouldn't be lying on top of my things, taunting me.

I unlocked my screen to see that Travis had messaged me a couple of times.

> Travis: Whatcha doin'?

> Travis: I'm sitting here, thinking I had more fun last Saturday.

I laughed. "Serves you right," I said to my phone. I also didn't know where *here* was, and I was proud of myself for not memorizing his schedule.

I opened my camera to take a rare selfie. I put my glass to my lips and held the camera high. *Click.*

> Me: I'm at home where I just opened a bottle of wine.

And Send.

> Travis: I want to be that wine.

187

Ooh, he was flirting again. The man was such a tease.

I downed the rest of my wine exactly like I'd been taught not to do and took a picture of the empty glass.

> Me: Too late. It's all inside me now.

> Travis: Now, I really want to be that wine.

> Travis: BTW, thanks for giving me a fricking hard-on at my aunt's wedding.

I burst out laughing. That was right. His aunt was getting married for, like, the fourth time or something like that, and Travis did not want to be there.

> Me: #sorrynotsorry

> Me: I've been wet for almost a week, so I don't feel bad for you.

Clearly, the wine had already gone straight to my head.

> Travis: Send me another picture. This time, naked.

> Me: Ha. Never going to happen. If you want to see me naked, you're going to have to do it in person.

> Travis: Hold that thought.

Harper came back into the kitchen. "What'd I miss?" she asked as she picked up her wine.

I scrolled to the top of my messages and handed her my phone. "Come on. Let's go relax on the couch."

I grabbed the bottle of wine and took it with me as Harper slowly walked and read behind me. I set the bottle on the coffee table and dropped down onto the couch.

Harper plopped down next to me and gave me back my phone. "Wow."

"You think so?"

She took a sip of her wine. "Now, you know why he didn't invite you."

"Yeah, way too early for a wedding date, especially a family wedding."

"Has he texted you back yet?"

I checked my phone. "Nope."

"What do you think he meant by *hold that thought?*"

I shrugged. "Beats the hell out of me."

Harper gasped and sat forward. "You don't think he's going to send you a naked pic first?" Her eyes rounded. "He's going to send you a dick pic."

I took a drink of my wine and shook my head. "Please, no. I really like him, and I want him to be smart enough to know that women don't want pictures of penises." I held up a finger. "However, I wouldn't turn down a full nude. But it doesn't mean I'm sending him anything in return."

An hour passed without anything else from Travis. But, by then, Harper and I were on our second bottle of wine, and I didn't care too much that he hadn't gotten back to me. I was tipsy, and he was with his family.

It was just after eleven when Harper yawned. "Maybe it's time for us to put our pajamas on."

"What? No way. We have to stay up and party."

"This from the girl who, earlier tonight, said that it sounded like Travis had an exhausting social life."

"That's before I turned my bloodstream into an alcohol-stream."

"How soon you forget that you party until you crash, and then it's lights out for you for the rest of the night."

I took a sip of my wine. "I beg to differ."

"Your twenty-second birthday. You made it up the stairs where you sat down and promptly fell asleep with your head on the top stair."

"Okay, you might have a point."

Harper pursed her lips. "There is no *might* about it."

"Okay, let's go change. We can party in our pajamas."

Harper stood. "A party with just the two of us?"

"Three of us," I corrected. "We have Maleficent, too."

Harper looked over at my cat, who was sleeping upside down on my chair.

I shrugged and laughed. I pushed myself off the couch to go upstairs where the two of us could change when the doorbell rang.

Our eyes met.

"Who would be at your house this late at night?"

"I don't know." I gasped. "It's a rapist. A murder. A murdering rapist. Or would it be a raping murderer?"

"You watch too much TV."

"Scoff all you want, but I saw an episode of *Forensic Files* where a guy knocked on a woman's door in the middle of the night, left, came back, raped her, and left her for dead. And that shit is real life."

"I'm going to go and peek out the window."

I grabbed Harper's arm. "No. What if he sees you?"

"What if it's a she?"

I straightened my spine. "You think a woman wants to rape and murder us?"

Harper rolled her eyes and pushed my hand off her. The second she went to go to the window, my phone rang.

I screeched and jumped.

I picked it up from where it sat on the couch, and Harper and I both said, "It's Travis," at the same time.

I looked up. "How did you know Travis was calling me?"

She pointed out the window and grinned. "I didn't. Travis is outside."

THIRTY-TWO

SYDNEY

"WHAT'S TRAVIS DOING HERE?"

"I don't know," Harper said. "Why don't you answer the door and ask him?" She pointed to my ringing cell. "Or at least answer the phone."

I rushed to the door and yanked it open.

Travis grinned and lowered his phone from his ear. "Hey. I was beginning to doubt you were home even though your lights were on."

Harper came up behind me. "She thought you were a serial killer."

"Actually, I said murdering rapist."

Travis laughed.

"Well, I'm going to go," Harper said as she squeezed past me. She already had her purse and her overnight bag on her shoulder.

"What?" I said.

"Nice to see you again, Travis," she said as she passed him.

"You, too." He looked back at me.

Harper walked down the steps and turned around. She made an O with one hand and repeatedly stuck the finger of her opposite hand through the O, making the universal sign for sex.

I put my hand over my mouth as I burst out laughing. Sometimes, I felt like I was getting old, and other times, like now, I wondered if I would ever truly grow up.

Travis spun around, but Harper quickly dropped one hand and turned the other into a wave.

"Have fun, you two."

"Wait. You can't drive. You've been drinking."

A car pulled up in front of my place.

"I already called an Uber," she said as she walked to the end of the drive.

"That's not an Uber. That's your husband," I shouted at her.

"Yeah, but Uber sounds cooler." She opened the car door. "Hey, baby," I heard her say to Ian. "Let's go park and make out since your mom's with the baby." She got in and shut her door, and Ian drove off.

I took a step back. "Would you like to come in?"

Travis smiled, his green eyes ablaze, as he stalked toward me.

"Do you want some wine?" I asked as my back hit the wall.

Travis reached me, circled my wrists with his hands, and pushed them over my head. "I think you misread my text. I said I wanted to *be* the wine. Not that I wanted to taste the wine."

I studied his face. I had missed seeing it the last six days. I was in so much trouble. "Then, taste me already."

Pushing his pelvis into mine, Travis kissed me. His tongue slipped past my lips, and I opened my mouth to let him in.

I lifted a leg over his hip to try to bring him closer, but it wasn't going to happen with our clothes still on. I pressed against Travis's hands, and he let go. His fingers moved to my waist while I attacked the fly of his pants.

Travis kissed down my neck while I pushed his khakis off his hips. I pulled at my own pants, which thankfully had an elastic waistband. They fell to the floor, and I once again put my leg over his hip and sank down on him, pushing his cock into my body.

My eyes rolled back as my head hit the wall.

"Holy shit, Sydney." Travis gripped my hips and started thrusting into me. "You feel fucking amazing."

I lifted my head. "So do you."

He kissed me again. "You know, I was planning to take my time with you. Give you lots of good foreplay."

I giggled. "Alcohol makes me horny."

He groaned. "Please tell me you're going to remember this tomorrow."

I wrapped my arms around his neck. "I'm not wasted, just a little drunk."

"Thank God."

I laughed. "I don't know if it's appropriate to thank God while fucking."

Travis grabbed my thighs, lifting my leg that had still been on the floor around his waist. "I think it's very appropriate. He gave us these bodies to enjoy."

"Mmm," was all I said in agreement as he drove into me.

"I can't get over how incredible you feel."

Uh-oh.

"I think we forgot a condom." Or maybe it was me who'd forgotten the condom since I was the one who pulled him inside me without a second thought. "My bad."

Travis thrust into me and then stopped. His head dropped against mine. "Fuck me. I knew it was too good to be true. I also knew I'd forgotten something on my race over here."

I grinned. "You raced over here?"

"Shh. I have a reputation to uphold."

"I have condoms upstairs."

Travis sighed with relief. "That was close. I was going to cry if you didn't."

He pulled me away from the wall, and I held on tight to him as he carried me toward the stairs.

I kissed his neck. "You wouldn't need to cry. There are other ways to finish."

He took the first step up the stairs, and I whimpered as it caused him to move inside me again.

"But I want to finish right where I am."

I didn't know what it was about the stairs, but each step brought me closer to orgasm. "I think you need to pull out," I said breathlessly.

"You're going to come?"

I nodded.

"Fuck yeah. I want to feel that."

"Do you think that's wise?" We almost reached the top of the stairs when I felt the first spasm hit. "Too late," I was barely able to say before my climax hit me hard.

I cried out, and Travis swore.

He fell to his knees, and I landed on my back on the top step in the middle of the hall.

The force of our fall sent him deeper into me.

"I can't—" Travis started before I watched his body give in to its pleasure.

His hips bucked into mine, and I held on to him through his orgasm.

When his breath caught and his body relaxed, he said, "Oh shit."

I chuckled. "I'm clean and on birth control."

He kissed my neck. "Me, too, sexy."

"I've never had the no-condom conversation so early in a relationship before." I sucked in a breath. The words had just come out of my mouth without me thinking.

Stupid wine. Now, I didn't know if I should backtrack or just hope he hadn't heard me, except that I noticed that his body was stiff.

Great.

"Don't mind me. My brain has no filter when I have alcohol in me. I didn't mean relationship—"

Travis lifted his upper body off of me. "What did you mean?"

I felt like a deer in the headlights. *Why is he questioning me? Just let me take it back, damn it.*

"I don't know," I whined. I put an arm over my eyes. "Just forget I said anything."

I felt Travis withdraw from my body—probably for the last time—and move away from me.

I squeaked when he yanked me up, put his shoulder to my belly, and lifted me over his shoulder.

"Ooh…nice ass," I said.

He slapped mine, and I jumped. "Where's your room?"

"End of the hall."

He walked into my room, threw me on my bed, and lay down next to me. He pushed my hair off my shoulder. "It's a little premature, but I would like to think we're heading toward a relationship."

I raised my eyebrows. "You're not just saying that so you can have sex with me without a condom again, are you?"

Travis pulled me into his arms and laughed. "My little skeptic. I'm saying that, so I get to hang out and spend time with you. Because that's what people in relationships do."

THIRTY-THREE

TRAVIS

I LOOKED AWAY from my phone as I heard Sydney move on the bed. She rolled toward me and put her head on my shoulder. Her brown hair was messy, and her eyes were puffy from sleep.

She looked adorable.

"Mmm...good morning," she said, her voice hoarse from sleep.

"Good morning." I kissed her forehead and slid an arm under her head.

She brushed her hand down my chest and abdomen and back up. "Mmm...it's been a long time since I woke up to a man in my bed."

"Are you forgetting last weekend?"

She smiled up at me, her eyes half-closed. "That was the hotel bed. I'm talking about *my* bed."

"Ah...got it. And I'm glad I could break your dry spell."

She looked to my phone, which I was holding up. "What are you doing?"

"Just scrolling through Instagram."

She continued to rub my torso. "That's your app of choice, isn't it?"

"Yeah. I used to be on Facebook, but it got to be too much. My personal page, my professional page, groups…"

"I forget how young you are sometimes."

I wrinkled my forehead. "I'm not that young."

She kissed my chest and smiled. "Young enough that you're in the group of twenty-something-year-olds that make me feel old for using Facebook."

"I never said you were old."

She laughed. "I know. You should hear my niece."

I smiled. "I can imagine." I opened up my messages and scanned through them. At the same time, I noticed that Sydney looked away. I assumed it was to respect my privacy.

The woman was a keeper.

I went through them, saving some to reply to later and replying to a few right away. "Oh my God." The next one, though, I hadn't been prepared for. I should have been, but those kinds of messages still surprised me every time.

Of course, Sydney looked up at my exclamation.

My first instinct was to hide the image on my phone, but I was innocent.

"Is that…hold on." She reached over and put her glasses on. "Holy crap." She burst out laughing. "Those are some huge boobs." She grabbed my cell out of my hand and zoomed in and out. "Wow. Those babies are impressive." She handed me back the phone. "Do you know who sent the pic?"

I just stared at Sydney. She'd *laughed*. She hadn't gotten mad or upset. She thought it was funny.

I cleared my throat. "Uh, no. It's some random fan."

"You, too, huh?"

"What do you mean, *you, too?*"

She rolled her eyes. "I've gotten my fair share of dick pics."

"You have?" I was surprised.

"Yeah. I guess it's because I write romance. Apparently, the conclusion is, I write about sex, so I must want pictures of strangers' dicks. When are men going to learn that women don't ever want that, and if they do, they'll ask for it?"

I laughed. "Do you keep any of them?"

She looked away from him. "Do you?"

"Don't judge, but sometimes, I show some of my friends before I delete them."

"You perv. I can't believe you," she said, her voice full of sarcasm.

My eyes widened. "You do it, too."

"Duh. Of course."

"So, do you have any on your phone right now?"

"Uh…no." She looked up at the ceiling.

"You liar."

"Okay, I have one because I've never seen anything like it."

I made a come-here motion. "Show me."

"Okay. But it's your turn not to judge me." She grabbed her phone from her nightstand, did a couple of moves on her phone, and passed it over to him.

"Holy shit." Instinctively, I reached down and cupped my dick.

"Right? It's a Jacob's Ladder. Ribbed…for her plea-sure." Sydney laughed at her joke.

I was horrified. "That looks so painful."

"I suppose it is." She took her phone back. "I've always thought it would be cool to have sex with a guy with a penis piercing, but this is just too much."

This caught my attention. "You want to have sex with a guy with a penis piercing?"

"Technically, I said it'd be cool. I want to know if it feels good or if it feels weird."

I took her phone out of her hand and threw it on the bed as I rolled Sydney under me. "How about I show you what feels good, right now?"

She grinned up at me and spread her thighs.

I pushed into her, groaning at the sensation of her wet, slick heat surrounding me.

I kissed her neck and drove into her over and over. Sydney moaned as she lifted both legs and sank her nails into my back. I thrust into her until I brought both of us to completion, whereupon I collapsed on top of her.

I quickly fell to her side, so I didn't suffocate her, and then I pulled her against me.

"Feel good?" I asked.

"Yeah," she said, panting on my chest.

"And I did it all without a cock piercing."

Sydney laughed and kissed my sweaty chest. "What are you doing today?"

"I'm hoping you have a gym nearby I can go to."

"You can go to mine. Do you go every day?"

"Yep. I might take a day off, but it's usually only once a week. Or, if I can't go, I do something else to get exercise in."

She groaned.

"What? You don't go every day?"

"Hell no. I do three to four days a week." She looked up at me. "Does this mean you're going to break it off with me?" Her eyes widened, and she shook her head. "There I go again, opening my big mouth. And, this morning, I can't even blame the wine." She got up on an elbow. "Feel free to ignore me."

I laughed. I liked that she saw us together. The best part was, I wasn't scared, nor did I feel the need to push her away.

I pulled her back down. "I'll forget what you said if you go work out with me."

She rolled away and jumped up from the bed.

I sucked in a breath at her sexy, naked body.

"I take it back," she said as she walked toward her bathroom. "You can remember me sticking my foot in my mouth."

I laughed.

Five minutes later, I joined her in the shower.

An hour later, she joined me at the gym.

Two hours later, we met up in the shower again.

THIRTY-FOUR

SYDNEY

I ENJOYED SPENDING the day with Travis so much that I didn't realize how late it had gotten.

The doorbell rang, and my front door was pushed open. My dad came through the doorway and stopped when he saw Travis in my living room. "Oh."

"Dad, what are you doing here?"

"Dinner."

I looked at the clock on my wall. It was just after five. "Dinner?"

"Yeah, you said you were making dinner tonight."

Crap. "I completely forgot. I don't even have anything to make."

Travis and I had just been talking about going out to eat.

My father shrugged. "That's okay. We can order pizza."

"Dad."

He looked at me, and I darted my eyes toward Travis, hoping he'd get the hint to leave.

My dad stepped forward. "I'm sorry. I didn't introduce myself. I'm Doug Harting."

Wrong hint, Dad.

Travis took my father's outstretched hand. "I'm Travis Zehler."

My dad gave him the side-eye.

Please don't question him on his intentions, I telepathically begged.

"Are you a Vikings fan?"

Travis smiled. "Yes, sir."

"Twins?"

"Yes."

"Wild?"

"Yes."

"Timberwolves?"

"I'm not really much of a basketball fan, but I suppose so."

My father continued his narrow gaze toward Travis for two more seconds, and then he grinned. "Good man." He slapped Travis on the upper arm and sat down on the recliner.

And that was all it had taken to win the approval of my father.

"Dad, Travis and I were thinking of going out for dinner." *Alone.*

My dad grabbed the remote and turned on the TV. "Nah, let's stay home and order pizza."

I threw my hands up in the air. I angled my body toward Travis. "I'm sorry. If you want to leave, you can. I know you didn't sign on to meet my father tonight. Or ever."

He smiled at me. "It's cool. I like pizza."

My front door opened again, and Ryan, Grace, Lexie,

Ben, Gretchen, and Lexie's boyfriend, Brendan, came barreling into my house.

I looked at Travis again and raised my brow. "You still think it's cool?"

He grinned at me and shrugged.

———

"Pizza's here," Lexie yelled after the doorbell sounded through the house.

Travis and I were upstairs in my office where, upon the arrival of my family, I had quickly whisked him off.

"I'm giving you one last chance," I told him. "I will smuggle you out of here."

Travis, who was leaning against my desk, pulled me into his arms and kissed me, which was hard to do because he was also laughing. "I'll be fine. I have to meet them sooner or later, right? Might as well be tonight."

He stood, and I backed up, stunned at his comment. It was exciting to think he'd planned to meet my family, no matter what.

"We'd better go down."

I sighed. "Yeah."

I wasn't looking forward to the twenty-one questions Travis was going to get. It was times like this that I missed my mom. She would have loved Travis. And she would have shut down any questioning or ribbing of him she felt had gone too far or gone on too long.

That reminded me. "Travis."

He stopped at the top of the stairs. "Yeah?"

"Don't mention my mother. My dad still struggles with her passing."

Travis put his hand on my cheek. "I'm sorry, Syd."

"Thanks. It's hard. It's only been four years. I still miss her." I stood on my tiptoes and brushed my lips against his. "I just wanted you to know, so you didn't bring her up. If you had, everyone probably would have stared at you like you'd run over the family dog. I didn't think you'd really have a reason to, but better safe than sorry."

Travis chuckled. "Thanks for watching out for me."

We headed downstairs where everyone was getting situated around my dining room table. Someone had brought out paper plates and plasticware, and my brother was bringing in a couple of folding chairs from the garage, so we'd have enough seats for everyone.

"Who ordered the salad?" Lexie asked with her nose wrinkled up.

"Oh, that's me," Travis said.

Lexie handed it to Travis as he sat down next to me at the table.

"Why are you having salad on pizza night?" Lexie asked him.

"I like to balance my meals out. It helps me stay in shape."

Ryan and Grace sat across from Travis and me, and I saw both of them study Travis at his words.

Grace pointed her fork at Travis. "You're the cover model, right? On Sydney's book?"

Travis blushed, and I thought it was adorable that he was embarrassed.

"That's me," he said.

"So, is that all you do?" my brother asked.

"Ryan, don't be rude."

Ugh. Sometimes, my brother was a snob.

Travis cleared his throat. "Uh, no. I am also a personal trainer. Someday, I'd love to own my own gym, but that won't happen for a long time."

I hadn't realized Travis wanted to be his own boss. Of course, we hadn't known each other that long.

I put my hand on his leg. "You'll do it."

"It's hard work," my brother said.

"I'm sure Travis knows that, Ryan."

Ryan shrugged. "I'm just sayin'."

I looked at Travis. "Ignore my brother. He's a pompous asshole who thinks his shit don't stink."

"Sydney," my father said.

"What?"

"We don't swear at the table."

I laughed. "Don't swear, but I can call Ryan names?"

"Only if they're true." My dad winked at me.

The table laughed, and Ryan threw wadded-up napkins at our dad and me. "I'm just looking out for my sister. Knowing you, you only made sure he followed your favorite sports teams."

My father shrugged. "So?" he said and shoved a big bite of pizza in his mouth.

"Thank you, Ryan, but I can take care of myself. Besides, Travis and I just started dating." I quickly glanced at Travis out of the corner of my eye to see if there was any reaction to my dating comment. He didn't look uncomfortable, and I was pleased. "It's not like we're getting married. You can lay off the third degree."

Grace patted my brother's arm. "Syd's a big girl."

My brother rolled his eyes. "Fine. I'm sorry," he said, sounding only half-sincere.

Travis smiled. "I understand. I have a sister."

"Oh?" Grace said. "Younger?"

"No. Older. But I still like to look out for her."

"That's so sweet," I said.

Ryan set his pizza down. "Wait. So, Travis is sweet, but I'm a pompous asshole?"

"Ryan, language," our dad said.

"Yes," I told my brother with a grin.

"That's not fair."

"Dad, you always say life's not fair," eleven-year-old Gretchen said from the end of the table.

"It's true, Dad; you do," Ben added.

Lexie laughed. "Ha-ha. She got you there."

Ryan went for Lexie's head to ruffle her hair, something he'd done a thousand times, but she dodged him.

"What do you do to work out?" Brendan asked as he looked at Travis's arms and then his own.

"I'll tell you after we eat, so we don't bore the whole table with gym talk."

Brendan grinned. "Thanks, man."

"No problem."

THIRTY-FIVE

SYDNEY

THE FOLLOWING FRIDAY, I went to Travis's gym where he worked.

"How can I help you?" the buff young guy behind the counter asked.

"I'm here to meet Travis Zehler."

The man looked down at his big book and slid his finger over to Travis's name and down the bottom of the page. He looked up at me with an uncertain expression on his face. "I'm sorry, but it looks like Travis is off here in a few minutes. Perhaps he gave you the wrong day?"

"Oh, no, I'm not a client. I'm here to meet him, so we can go to dinner."

The guy breathed a sigh of relief. "You had me worried there for a second. Travis is probably back in the office. Let me call him for you." He picked up the phone.

"That's okay. I can take her back."

I turned to see a young blonde woman behind me. She was fit and had on workout clothing.

I smiled. "Thank you."

She didn't smile back. "This way." She was all business.

"Thanks, Christy," the guy behind the desk said.

Feeling uncomfortable, I quickly followed her. Even though she had offered to take me, I felt like I was putting her out.

"So, how do you know Travis?" the woman, apparently named Christy, asked after we walked through the main part of the gym.

We were now past the locker rooms in an empty hallway.

I didn't know how to answer. Christy was Travis's coworker and not a client, but I didn't know how well he knew her. And I had no idea how much personal stuff Travis liked to share with the people he worked with. But I also didn't want to be rude.

"I'm an author, and I met him at a book signing."

Christy stopped so quickly that I almost ran into her. She turned to me. "But you're dating him now?"

"Uh…" was all I managed to say at first, having been caught off guard. "I don't know if that's any of your business."

"Word of advice: the modeling thing is sexy in the beginning, but it gets old after a while. You might as well get out now because Travis isn't going to change."

An uneasy feeling went through me. It sounded like this woman had dated Travis at one point, and I looked at her through a whole new set of lenses. She was stunning in a way I never would be. Even though she was dressed for exercise, her hair was up in a cute ponytail, and her makeup was on point. Her clothes were tight and stylish. My workout clothes were baggy and comfortable and forget about the makeup. I went to the gym to sweat.

I didn't like the way I felt *less than* around her. But her beauty seemed to be only skin deep, and I wasn't going to let her make me feel like I wasn't as good as her.

I also didn't like the way she'd put down Travis. I didn't feel comfortable talking about him without him present, but I also couldn't let her mean comments go.

I straightened my back. "I don't want Travis to change. And I think he can do whatever he wants to. His body is his business, and his career is his business."

"You say that now when you can brag that you're dating a cover model. But you just wait until you get sick of seeing him in intimate poses with other women. And the way they all drool over him when they meet him in person. And, when you ask him to quit, he won't. He likes that attention too much."

I put my hand up. "I'm going to have you stop right there."

I had seen Travis at book signings, and even as a single man, he'd never given me the impression of an attention-seeker, so I highly doubted he was worse when he was in a relationship. And, yes, readers liked him, but Christy was being very disrespectful to his fans.

"I am proud of Travis for doing what he does, and that is all I'm going to say on the subject. I don't feel comfortable talking about him behind his back. Now, will you please take me to him?"

TRAVIS

I had been about to come out of the office to meet Sydney at the front when I heard Christy talking in the hall. I should've gone out there and called a halt to the conversation, but my feet had lost their will to move as I froze up.

Hearing Christy talk about all the things she didn't like about me had brought up some ugly memories. But, when Sydney had stood up for me, I'd felt humbled and awed. And that gave me the kick in the ass I needed to get my feet working again.

I marched out of the office to see the two women facing each other.

"Christy, that's enough."

Sydney turned when she heard my voice. Her face was a mixture of happy and guilty. I needed to make sure to let her know that she'd done nothing wrong.

I held out my hand to her. "Hey, sexy."

Sydney stepped toward me and took my hand.

I hauled her close and kissed her deep. Not because I was showing off or trying to prove anything to Christy, but because I plain old wanted to.

"What was that for?" Sydney asked, breathless.

"I'll tell you later."

"You two make me sick," Christy said and stomped away.

"I take it, that's your ex?" Sydney asked.

"Unfortunately. I apologize for the way she talked to you."

Sydney put a hand on my chest. "Don't be. You have no control over others' actions, and she obviously has a lot going on with herself, inside." She arched up and kissed me. "I don't know what you heard, but I hope she didn't make you feel bad. It seems like she has issues she needs to deal with."

I was in awe of the woman in front of me. I was the one who was supposed to be telling her not to feel bad. "She used to make me feel guilty and like crap, but that's over now."

"Good. You deserve better than her."

I grinned. "Someone like you."

She snorted. "I don't know about that." She tried to play off my compliment, but her cheeks turned pink.

"I do." I was lucky to have found her. "You ready to go to dinner?"

"Yes. I'm starving."

I took her hand and led her back toward the locker rooms, so I could grab my bag. "Didn't you eat lunch?"

"I did but not much."

It was probably because we'd just gotten done talking about Christy, but alarm bells began to go off in my head. I remembered the first time Christy had begun to drastically cut her calories. It had been the beginning of the end of our relationship. The less she'd eaten, the more she'd become obsessed with what she ate or didn't eat.

"Why's that?" I asked carefully.

"Don't judge, but I haven't made it to the grocery store yet."

I chuckled with relief. "You still haven't gone?"

"No. I keep saying I'm going to go every day, but I start working and don't stop. I've been eating a lot of mismatched meals. But I've gotten a lot of writing done."

213

We stopped in front of the men's locker room.

"We're going out to dinner, and then we're going grocery shopping."

"Ugh. You need to work on your dating skills."

I laughed and pushed open the locker room door.

THIRTY-SIX

SYDNEY

I KNOCKED and pushed open the door to Travis's townhome. We'd been dating a little over a month, and we were to the point where we walked into each other's homes.

"Travis?" I called out when I didn't see him right away.

He didn't answer, but I heard him talking in his main-floor bedroom. I walked in there to see he was on the phone. He smiled when he saw me and held up a finger.

"Yes." He nodded. "Yes, that sounds good."

I stepped away and went to the kitchen. From the way he had been talking, I could tell he was not on a personal call.

I'd stayed at Travis's last night, but this morning, I had gotten up to go to my monthly writer group meetup. Then, I had stopped at the store on the way back to Travis's. I put my bag of groceries on the counter and unpacked them.

After I was finished, I pulled my phone out of my purse and curled up on the recliner to do what most people did when they were bored. I checked my social media. Since dating Travis, I had started to use Instagram more, so I went there first. I clicked on Travis's stories before even checking my notifications.

The first was an inspirational quote. But the next was a picture of me sleeping with the caption, *This girl*. I had my mouth halfway open, and my hair looked like a wild animal had had its way with it. Only half of my face was buried in the pillow, so you couldn't see it was me. Except the man had tagged me in it.

"Okay. I will see you then. goodbye," I heard Travis say from the other room.

When he walked into the living room, I turned my phone around to show him the screenshot I'd taken and said, "I'm never spending the night with you again."

He had the audacity to laugh. "Come on. You looked so cute. I couldn't resist." He strode over to me, picked me up so that he could sit down, and set me on his lap.

"You'd better hope no one else took a screenshot of that."

He kissed my neck. "Or what?" He kissed it again and sucked on my skin.

A shiver went through me. "Stop trying to distract me."

He cupped the other side of my face and drew me closer as he pulled the top of my shirt off my shoulder. "I can't help it. You taste so good." More kissing and sucking and licking ensued.

"You're too good at that," I whined but didn't stop him because I loved when he kissed and touched me.

"Let's get naked."

"No way."

He pulled back to look at me. "What do you mean, no way?"

"That's your punishment."

His brow furrowed. "You're not really mad, are you? That wasn't my intention."

I ran my fingers through his hair. "No, I'm not really mad. A little embarrassed but not mad."

"I'm sorry, sexy."

I kissed him. "Apology accepted."

He grinned, and I knew he was going to kiss my neck again.

"Who was on the phone?" I quickly asked before he could make his move.

"Do you know who Robert Hahn is?"

"Does a bear shit in the woods? Of course I know who he is."

"That was him on the phone. He asked if I would fly out to do a photo shoot."

My mouth dropped open. "Shut up. That is awesome."

Travis grinned. "I take it, you're a fan?"

"Yes. He takes stunning photos. I love his work."

TRAVIS

I was overcome by the joy in Sydney's face that I opened my mouth and said, "Do you want to come with and watch?" before I actually thought about what I said. I usually had a better brain-to-mouth filter.

But, when she jumped off my lap and shouted, "Are you fricking kidding me? I will clear my calendar to go with you.

I don't care if it's someone's wedding. I will be there," I really couldn't regret asking her.

I laughed. "Okay then. I'll make sure to book you a ticket."

"Ooh, we're flying? Where are we going? California? Florida? New York?"

I laughed. "Sorry to burst your bubble. We're going to Denver."

"Colorado? I guess that works." She sat back down in my lap and threw her arms around me. "I'm still excited. Thank you for asking me."

I squeezed her tight. "You're welcome. But you're going to have to put up with me while I prepare for my shoot."

Sydney leaned back. "What does that mean?"

"Working out every day for longer than I do now. And eating a lot of boring food. No cheat days from now until then."

She ran her hands over my chest and stomach. "I think you look great now, but I understand. When is then?"

"The end of July." It was June, so I had a little over a month to prepare.

"I'll make sure and eat the yummy food for you."

I chuckled. "Thanks."

"I can't wait. It'll be fun."

I hoped so.

Later, as Sydney lay beside me, fast asleep, I couldn't help but remember the last time I'd let someone I dated go with me. I really hated how my mind always went back to the time I'd dated Christy, but I'd been told it was natural since we'd dated for some time. She'd obviously left an impact on me.

I'd taken my ex to a local photo shoot, thinking she would have fun and enjoy watching me work. She pouted and acted bored the whole time I took my solo shots. And then, when I teamed up with another model to take a couple of pictures, Christy freaked out. She yelled at the photographer for even suggesting I pose with someone. And then she yelled at me for not refusing to do the couple photos. The photographer ended up kicking her out, and I had been embarrassed and felt guilty for bringing her along.

Later, after the shoot was over, Christy apologized. She explained that she had been jealous. I understood where she was coming from. Everyone got jealous of something or someone sometime. It was a natural human emotion, and emotions couldn't be controlled. Otherwise, everyone would be happy all the time. But what Christy had chosen to do with that emotion was something she could have controlled.

So far, Sydney had been nothing but supportive of my career. Maybe because, as an author, she understood the business a little. But, more likely, it was because she was a completely different person than Christy.

I rolled over and gently pulled Sydney into my arms. "You're not going to disappoint me, right?"

She hummed in her sleep, and I took it as a promise that she wouldn't.

THIRTY-SEVEN

TRAVIS

I PULLED into a parking spot at the bar where we were meeting my friends for the Fourth of July. Since the holiday was on a Thursday, Lilah had suggested that we go to Stillwater for the day. It was a scenic town east of the Cities on the St. Croix River. It had bars that were in walking distance to each other and a fireworks show to watch after dark.

It was hopefully going to be a fun and relaxing day. Sydney had yet to meet my friends, so I was excited and nervous for them all to meet. Broderick had told me, as long as I didn't bring Christy, he approved, so maybe I was worrying too much.

The first stop was the Freight House. It had a lot of deck space and was a perfect place to sit outside to eat and drink.

I pulled out my phone and checked my messages. "They're already here."

Sydney took a deep breath. "Great." She sounded like she didn't quite mean it.

"Are you nervous?"

She smiled. "Maybe a little."

I took her hand. "Come on, let's go."

It was mid-afternoon, and despite it being a holiday, the bar wasn't too busy. I led Sydney through the establishment to the back where the deck was. When I spotted Broderick, Dan, and Lilah, I waved.

They all smiled at Sydney and me, and I saw it as a positive sign that they were going to be open to meeting her.

"Hey, everyone, this is Sydney. Sydney, this is Broderick, Lilah, and Dan. Dan and Lilah are married."

Lilah wiggled her left ring finger.

"And Broderick is hopelessly single."

"Uh-uh-uh...I brought a date," Broderick corrected.

I looked around. "Is she invisible?"

"You think you're funny, but she's in the restroom."

"Or she ran away," Dan said. "Did either of you see a blonde running away when you came in?"

"You guys are dicks," Broderick said.

I looked over to see Sydney laughing, and I couldn't help but smile.

"Let's sit." I left the seat next to Broderick open, pulled out the next one for Sydney, and then sat next to Dan.

The server came over as soon as they were both seated. "What can I get for you?" he asked.

"I'll have a beer." I was taking one cheat day in the middle of my training for my next shoot since it was a holiday. I looked over at Sydney. "Wine?" She always drank wine, so I figured it would be a yes.

"No...I think I'll have a beer, too."

My eyebrows rose. "Really?"

She held up her hands. "Yeah, this feels like a beer day."

"Okay." Travis turned back to the server. "Two beers."

221

"And cheese curds," Sydney said.

I turned to see that she had one of the menus on the table open. We'd only been here for a couple of minutes, and I loved that about her. I liked that she ate.

"Okay, two beers and cheese curds," the attendant said. "Anyone else need a refill?"

Broderick raised his glass.

The server jotted down Broderick's request and took off.

Two seconds later, a short blonde walked toward the table. This had to be Broderick's date.

"Hey, Alice. I'd like you to meet my friend Travis and his date, Sydney."

"You're the model?" she asked me as she took her seat. She had that look in her eyes that some women got, like I was an exciting new toy.

"I am." Sometimes, I got annoyed that this was what people first thought of me.

Why did Broderick have to tell her that?

"But he's also a personal trainer," Sydney said with a stern voice.

And I could've kissed her. I didn't need her to stick up for me, but it sure was sweet.

"Oh. That's...nice," Alice said.

Sydney smiled as if she'd won a competition with the other woman. "It is nice."

I threw my head back and laughed.

"I have to go use the ladies' room," Sydney said when we got to the next bar.

"Me, too," Alice said.

Despite the rocky start, the two women had been getting along well for the rest of the afternoon.

As soon as they were out of sight, Lilah said, "Oh my God, I love her."

I chuckled. "How does Dan feel about that?"

Dan shrugged. "Fine with me. She's great."

"Yeah, she's a hundred times better than Christy, dude," Broderick said. "Where did you find her again?"

"At a book signing."

"The very thing Christy didn't want you to do," Lilah said. "Is that like irony or something?"

"Beats the hell out of me," I said. "But I'm glad you guys like her. I really like her, too."

"How old is she?" Broderick asked.

"Not that it's any of your business, but she's thirty-four."

"You stud. An older woman," Broderick said and smacked me on the arm.

"Broderick, we're not in high school anymore. So she happens to be a few years older. Big deal."

Lilah nodded her head. "Way to be mature about it, Travis." She looked at Broderick. "Sometimes, I don't know why we keep you around."

"It's so you have someone to marry when Dan keels over."

Lilah raised her brow. "I would never marry you. You're lucky I'm your friend."

"The woman has a point," Dan said.

"You're just siding with her because she's your wife."

Dan put his arm around Lilah. "Only a fool wouldn't."

"Hey, what's going on?" Alice asked from behind them.

"We're just talking about your date," Lilah told Alice.

I put my arm around Sydney. "Everything go okay in there?"

She frowned and laughed. "Yeah, why?"

"Just making sure." I raised my voice to the group. "Let's go find a table, and we can tell Alice all the things wrong with Broderick."

"You guys are dicks."

"They're just jealous because you're the best-looking," Alice told her date.

A chorus of, "Ooh," sounded through the group of us.

Broderick grabbed Alice's hand and kissed it. "You, milady, will be rewarded later."

"Ew," we all said at the same time.

"Did you have fun today?" I asked Sydney as we cuddled on the blanket in front of the river.

The sun had gone down, and we were waiting for the fireworks to start.

"I did. Thanks for bringing me."

I kissed her on the head. "It was my pleasure."

"Do you think they like me?"

"Does it matter what they think?"

"Well, they are your friends," she pointed out.

I grinned. "Yeah, they like you."

"Sweet. Because I like them, too."

The next moment, a big burst of light went through the sky, and I held Sydney close as we watched the show.

THIRTY-EIGHT

SYDNEY

THE UBER DRIVER pulled up to an old building in downtown Denver. "We're here."

I looked out the window. "This is it?"

"This is the address you gave, ma'am."

"Ugh. Don't call me ma'am. I'm not that old," I said under my breath.

Travis laughed and opened his door while I got out on my side.

We met on the sidewalk.

"I'm excited. Are you excited?"

"I'm excited to eat again. The only good thing I've had to eat the last month and a half is your pussy. I'm buying dessert tonight, and I can't wait."

A couple passed us on the street, hearing Travis's declaration. The woman's eyes widened, and the man tried to stifle his laugh. My cheeks felt hot.

"*Travis*," I said, putting my hand on his arm.

He looked at me. "What? I'm hungry."

225

I laughed. He seriously didn't even realize that the couple had heard what he said.

I shook my head. "Never mind. You deserve to eat all the dessert you want."

We headed into the building, and it was as old inside as it was outside. It was a renovator's dream. The floor was hardwood that had probably been there since the place opened, and the walls were made of brick.

There was a hallway on the right and stairs on the left.

"We're supposed to go upstairs." Travis pointed up.

"I'm glad you know."

There was no one around to tell us where to go.

"Oftentimes, these things are informal. Professional but informal."

After we walked up the stairs, there was another hallway and a door right in front of us. It was open, and there was music coming from the room. On the main level, I had thought it was Muzak, but now that we'd reached the second floor, I saw a stereo in the corner, sending out the tunes.

"In here, I think," Travis said.

The front area looked like a little reception area, but when I looked up at the ceiling, I could see none of the walls were attached. They were makeshift walls of a large, open space.

A silver fox of a man with a camera in his hand walked into the area and smiled. I froze in place. He strode over to us with a confidence that shone off of him. When he reached us, he and Travis clasped hands and pulled each other into a hug.

He slapped Travis on the back. "Good to see you." The

two separated as the man stroked his face where his beard would be if he had one. "I like the fur."

Travis touched his short beard. "Oh, yeah. I wasn't sure if you'd have me shave it off today."

"I think we should keep it." He tilted his head toward me. "Who'd you bring with you?"

"Sydney, I'd like you to meet Robert Hahn."

I didn't move. I couldn't.

Travis chuckled. "Robert, this is Sydney. She's a romance author and a huge fan of yours."

Robert grinned at me and held out his hand.

I slowly raised mine to shake.

"Nice to meet you, Sydney."

"Same here. I mean, it's nice to meet you, too. Huge fan." *Idiot. Travis already said that.*

"Come on through here, so you can meet everyone."

We followed him into the next room, which had different things along the walls for various backgrounds. There was a metal wall, an old wooden barn door, and some of the exposed brick, to name a few. There was also another doorway that looked like it led to another picture-taking area.

There were several people standing around. A very handsome black man, who I thought I had seen on social media before, was the first person I noticed.

"Travis, have you met Leon?" Robert asked.

"No." Travis held out his hand, and Leon took it. "How's it going?"

"Good." Leon smiled, and I noticed his eyes were a beautiful hazel color. "Nice to meet you."

There were also two attractive women in the room, who stepped forward.

Robert held out his hand toward the woman closest to him. A tall, thin blonde. "This is Trish. And this is Michelle," he said, pointing to a shorter, thinner Asian woman.

I smiled at them while Robert continued on, "If it's okay with everyone, I'd like to take some single shots of each one of you and then couples shots with all of you. Maybe a few with threesome shots." Robert smiled. "I have some requests from authors."

His eyes darted toward me, and I held up my hands.

"Not me." I laughed. "Not that I'm against those books. I have been known to read them. I just haven't written one. Yet."

"If you haven't guessed, Sydney is a romance author. Maybe we'll get her to purchase one of our photos."

"I've actually bought two from you in the past."

Robert grinned and held out his fist. "All right."

I pounded my fist against his.

"You'll have to show me your covers when you have a chance. Sometimes, my assistant gets behind on adding them to the website."

"Will do," I told him.

"Shall we get started?"

Everyone nodded.

"Sydney, you can take a seat over there. That's where the girlfriends and boyfriends sit." Robert pointed to the corner where another man was sitting. He smiled at me.

I looked over at Travis. I didn't know if we were

boyfriend/girlfriend yet, but he had no reaction to Robert calling me that.

"We'll take standing shots first," Robert continued as I went over and sat down on one of the chairs against the wall. "Then, we'll move to the other room and do some shots of you all sitting and lying on furniture."

I got comfortable as I watched Robert and the models do their magic. I was amazed at the number of pictures taken, and it showed how much work it took to get a good shot. It explained why over half the pictures on my phone were subpar.

When it was Travis's turn, I couldn't tear my eyes away. It was almost like he became a different person. He was totally in a zone, and he looked so hot that I thought my underwear was going to combust.

When Robert called Michelle over, Travis and she nodded their heads as Robert gave them directions. As soon as the camera went up, their bodies came together, and if I didn't know any better, I would think they were a couple.

I could finally understand where Christy had been coming from, and I supposed I could see myself going down the same path as Travis's ex, but I didn't let myself do it. I saw what they were doing as art, and I knew he'd be in my bed tonight. I'd never been a person interested in paintings. But photographs were a different story. Whether it was scenery or people, I thought they were beautiful.

I also found it very hot, watching Travis pose with Michelle and then Trish. Trish stood in front of Travis and his bare torso, and he put his hand on her stomach, pushing her shirt up. His pinkie slipped underneath the waistband of her pants, and I felt a twinge in my gut.

But it wasn't jealousy or an uneasy feeling. It felt like a cramp.

Uh-oh.

I grabbed my phone and pulled up my period app. It confirmed what I'd thought. My period wasn't due for three more days. Being on the pill, I was a twenty-eight-day girl.

I looked around the room, trying to figure out how I was going to escape without having everyone's eyes on me.

There was no way that was going to happen, so I did the only thing I could do. I quickly slipped out of the room. I walked down the hall and didn't see a restroom. I was also beginning to feel like I was trespassing, the farther away I got from the studio. I should have asked where the bathroom was before I left the room.

I walked back down the hall and down the stairs. No one was around, and I debated on what to do. All the buildings outside were other businesses. Not a convenience store or gas station in sight.

I headed into the main-floor hallway, feeling like a full-fledged intruder now. I was, however, rewarded because at the end was a restroom.

"Finally," I said out loud.

Once in the restroom, I discovered that I had indeed gotten an early visit from Aunt Flo.

"Really, body? You just had to do this today?"

I pictured my brain shrugging at me without a care in the world.

I had brought my purse with me when I fled the studio, but as I pawed through each pocket, my panic began to rise.

I always kept feminine products in my purse. Always. For reasons like this. Even though I was on a schedule, sometimes, I would forget. Plus, I could be out with friends, and they might need something. But I couldn't find anything.

And the only other two women I had seen were the models upstairs. The thought of asking them if I could borrow a tampon sounded horrific. I did not want to have to pull them aside and ask them something so personal.

I went through my pockets again, as if something had changed in the last few minutes. I had cleaned out my purse before we left Minnesota, and for some reason, I must have forgotten to put my period stuff back.

Part of me wanted to cry.

I looked around, and there was a cupboard in front of me and under the sink. I was going to go from trespassing to snooping, but I was desperate.

I looked in the cupboard across from me, only to find cleaning supplies. My shoulders sank.

Next, I pulled open the door under the sink, keeping one eye closed because part of me didn't want to see if it was empty of the thing I needed.

I gasped. *Success.*

"Whoever put tampons in here, thank you. And I owe you one."

THIRTY-NINE

TRAVIS

I WAS BEGINNING to worry about Sydney. She had taken off in a hurry. I had tried to keep my eyes on the camera, but the few times I'd looked over at her, she'd seemed to be fine. She'd actually appeared to be into my job.

But then she'd taken off. At the same moment I'd gotten very close to Trish.

A hot flash went through my body as the memory of Christy storming out of the photo shoot took over my brain. I couldn't go through that again. Not in front of Robert Hahn.

Trish stepped away from me, and I realized I had zoned out.

"Why don't we take a break? Go get some air," Robert said.

I couldn't get a read on the photographer's face, and I was starting to get anxious about why Sydney had left.

"Thanks," I said and took off for the stairs so quickly that I didn't even bother to put on a shirt.

When I reached the bottom, she was just coming from

the end of the hall and looked up when she heard me. She looked like she might be guilty, and an uneasy feeling went through me.

"Hey," she said.

"What happened to you?" I really liked Sydney, but I wasn't going to beat around the bush.

She looked up behind me as the other models started coming down the stairs.

She blushed and stepped closer to me. "I don't want to tell you here."

I grabbed her hand to lead her upstairs. Whatever it was, she was embarrassed for others to hear.

I kept walking past the main area and past the area where we'd just been taking pictures to the third area that had a chair, a twin bed, and a couch.

I pulled us to the corner where it felt more private. "Okay, tell me what's going on."

Sydney put her hands on my chest. "Hey. You look really worried." She reached up and smoothed her thumbs over my eyebrows. "It's not a huge deal." She dropped her hands and looked around. "I got my period," she whispered. "And I wasn't prepared," she added in her normal voice. "I had to search this whole damn building for a restroom, and then I couldn't find a stupid tampon in my purse." She wrinkled her nose. "I'm not grossing you out, am I?"

I pulled her into my arms as relief overcame me. She hadn't been jealous. She'd just gotten her period.

I started laughing.

Sydney pulled away. "What's so funny?"

"I thought you were jealous and ran off."

She frowned. "Uh…no. Watching you pose for pictures

was hot. I just had to hightail it out of there before I ruined my clothes." She stuck out her tongue as if she'd tasted something bad. "Trust me; that wouldn't have been pretty."

I was still focused on her calling my pictures hot. I leaned down and kissed her neck. I loved her neck. She was so soft there and always smelled good. Plus, I knew she liked it, and I also loved getting a response out of her.

"You think I'm hot."

She hummed and laughed as she pushed a couple of fingers through my belt loops. "I think you already know that. At this point, it would be easier to list the women who didn't think you were sexy."

"Hmm…that's nice, but I only care about one woman's opinion," I said behind her ear.

"Stop getting me all worked up. We can't have sex tonight."

Kiss. "Why"—kiss, suck—"not?"

"Hello? Stupid Mother Nature."

I bit her earlobe. "There's always the shower." It didn't really bother me, but I knew that it sometimes bothered the woman, so a shower was always a great solution.

She looped her hands around my neck. "I like the way you think."

I put my forehead against hers. "It's a date then."

She grinned. "Is this before or after you have dessert?"

I smiled. "I really love having sex with you, but I'm eating dessert first."

She laughed, and I heard a noise off to the side. I figured it was everyone coming back, but when we looked over, it was Robert with his camera up.

The camera was lowered, and Robert looked sheepish.

"Sorry. I should have asked permission first, but I didn't want to ruin the moment." He wiggled the camera back and forth. "I can delete them if you want."

I looked to Sydney with a raised brow, putting the decision in her hands.

"Do they look good?" she asked.

Robert scoffed. "Of course."

"Then, keep them. But I want to see them."

Robert grinned. "Deal. I'll send them to you once I go through them." His eyes moved to me. "Everything okay?"

"Everything's great."

"I think everyone is coming back. You ready to get started?"

"Yep."

"How would you feel about taking some photos with Leon?"

"You mean, some male-on-male pictures?" Sydney asked, her eyes wide.

"As long as they're both okay with it."

"Sure." I'd done them before, and the hardest part was me and the guy I was posing with not laughing too much. For me, it was always easier to fake intimacy with women, but I was constantly impressed with how my pictures with other men had turned out. It probably had more to do with the person behind the camera though.

"Yes," Sydney said. "I can't wait. Note to self: write MM novel ASAP."

SYDNEY

Travis collapsed against me as he pinned me to the cold shower wall. It felt good against the heat of his body and the warm water pelting down on us.

"That was amazing," I told him.

Travis grinned at me while he slowly withdrew from my body and set me on my feet. "It kind of was, wasn't it?"

I playfully socked him in the stomach. "*Kind of?* In that case, I want you to know I was fantasizing about Leon while we were doing it."

Travis gasped mockingly and put his hand on his chest.

I rolled my eyes as I grabbed the body wash, but he took it out of my hand.

He poured a big glob in his hand and began washing my front. He turned me toward the water and began scrubbing my back. "You weren't really thinking about Leon, were you?"

I grinned and had to bite my lip from laughing out loud. "No."

I heard his breath release.

"But, to be honest, when I watched the two of you taking pictures together, I did get worked up. It is so hot, seeing two guys together. Until you both ruined it by laughing."

Travis chuckled. "Sorry, sexy. Sometimes, it's hard to fake it for long periods of time. Laughing and joking take some of the pressure off."

I thought about what it would be like to intimately pose with a woman. While I found women beautiful and I could definitely see their attraction, I wasn't attracted to them. It would be hard, but I assumed it would be harder for a heterosexual man. Women were naturally more intimate with their friends. Harper and I had shared a bed before when there was nowhere else to sleep. It wasn't a big deal. I bet, if two straight guys ran into that problem, one of them would sleep on the floor. Not all men, but a lot that I knew.

"I understand. I think you both did an excellent job today. I'm hoping to buy one of your pictures for a book cover."

He wrapped his arms around my middle, and I leaned my head against his chest.

"You know I'm not going to oppose that." He kissed my cheek. "I just need to quickly wash my hair, and then I'll get out of your way, so you can have the shower to yourself."

"Sounds good." I liked sharing a shower, but it was hard to actually get clean sometimes.

When I got out of the shower, I could hear Travis talking on the phone through the door.

"It went great. Much better than last time. I'll have to tell you about it when I get home." Pause. "Really? When?" Pause. "Okay. That would be nice. I'll have to warn her."

I wondered if I was the *her* that he was talking about and what he had to warn me about.

I dried off, slipped on my robe, and stepped out of the bathroom as he was finishing up his call.

"Our plane gets in at five thirty." Pause. "Okay. See you then." Pause. "Bye, sis." He hit End on his phone and threw it on the bed. "Sloan is going to pick us up from the airport tomorrow."

"Oh."

His friend Broderick had driven us, so I'd assumed he'd take us home. I had yet to meet his family, and we actually hadn't really talked about it, so I was a little surprised. But it was also exciting that he was inviting me to meet his sister.

He studied me. "Is that okay?"

"Of course." I smiled. "I would love to meet your sister. I just hope she likes me."

Travis pulled me into his arms. "She's going to love you."

FORTY

SYDNEY

TRAVIS'S SISTER didn't love me. Don't get me wrong; she didn't hate me. But I did not feel any love coming from her when she met us at the airport.

Sloan ran up to Travis and threw her arms around him. I was a little envious because, even though my brother and I saw each other often, I could never picture either of us running up and hugging each other. We simply weren't that close.

When they separated, Travis introduced us, and Sloan held out her hand to me. I shook it as she studied me. I hoped she wasn't wondering what a guy like her brother was doing with a woman like me. She nodded politely after her assessment, but I felt an *I don't know if I can trust you yet* vibe.

"Nice to meet you," I said to her despite her reservations. I was looking forward to seeing another side of Travis.

"Same here," she said, her voice cool and her face devoid of an expression. She didn't sound like it was especially nice to meet me.

Sloan had red hair and the same green eyes. She was

pretty but not as good-looking as Travis. But I could be biased.

"Do you need to grab any luggage?" she asked us.

"Nope, we both brought carry-ons," Travis said.

"Great. Let's go then."

I trailed behind Travis and his sister as we walked to her car. They were talking about someone they apparently both knew, so I just followed them, eavesdropping on their conversation about someone who had gotten into trouble with the law again.

When we got to Sloan's car and loaded our bags in the back, Travis turned to me. "Sorry. We were talking about our cousin."

I shrugged and smiled. "No big deal."

I'd had him all weekend. His sister could certainly have his attention for a while.

I moved to get in the backseat behind Sloan, so I could see Travis in the passenger seat. It took a few minutes to get out of the airport parking ramp, but soon, we were on our way. Seeing as it was the weekend, the traffic was pretty thin compared to a weekday, and I hoped we would quickly get to Travis's place.

"Last-minute family dinner tonight. How does Cowboy Jack's sound? Mom and Dad are going to meet us there," Sloan asked.

"Sounds delicious. But, surprise or not, you should have warned us." He looked down at his T-shirt and shorts. "I would have dressed better." He looked back at me and grinned. "I hope I look okay."

I smiled back, but it took a little effort. I had thought we were hanging out the rest of the evening. Usually, if I went to his place on Sunday, I wouldn't go home until Monday morning or afternoon when he went to work. But, apparently, he was having dinner with his family. And brushing me off. Although maybe I shouldn't have assumed we would be hanging out all night.

Travis must have noticed my discomfort. "Hey, is that okay about dinner?"

I reminded myself that I couldn't be a Travis hog. I was disappointed, but there were things I could take care of at home, too. I didn't need to be with him all the time.

"Yes, it's fine. I'm sure your family wants to hang out with you as much as I do."

He smiled at me and looked at his sister. They exchanged a look, but I didn't have the slightest clue what it could mean.

"Where is Cowboy Jack's?" I asked. I had never been there.

"Bloomington."

Uh-oh. Bloomington was on the way to Travis's house in Minnetonka. It would be out of the way to go to his house and then turn around and go back to the restaurant. It would add at least an extra half hour to the trip.

"Are you planning to go to Travis's first?" I asked.

Sloan looked into the rearview mirror and met my eyes. "It doesn't make much sense to go to his house and drive back to the restaurant. Travis said you lived in Bloomington. Did you need something at his house?"

Just my car. And I don't live in Bloomington. I live in Shakopee.

I looked at Travis to see if he'd tell her that I needed to get my vehicle, but he kept his mouth shut as he stared out the front window, oblivious to my situation.

241

I pulled my phone out from my purse. "I left my car at Travis's, but I can ask someone to come and get me from the restaurant. I live in Shakopee, so you'd have to go out of your way to drop me off at my house or Travis's place."

"Sorry, I must have heard wrong," Sloan said.

I blew out a big breath. We should have discussed tonight's plans while we were still at the airport. I could've had someone pick me up from there. Then, I could have told Sloan that she didn't have to take me home since I didn't live in the city she thought I did.

But at least the restaurant would be closer to home and to Travis's house, so it would be less driving for whoever picked me up.

I saw Travis turn in his seat as I dialed Lexie. As I put the phone to my ear and listened to it ring, I looked up to see him frowning.

I wasn't surprised when she didn't answer. She rarely used her phone for talking to people, as with most teenagers. And I didn't bother leaving her a message, as her voice mail was never listened to. I'd have to send her a text to call me back.

I brought the phone down from my ear and sighed as I hit End.

"What are you doing?" Travis asked.

"Trying to get ahold of Lexie."

"Why?"

I shrugged. "I don't know. Because she's young and single." I snorted. "I'd rather bug her to give me a ride than Harper."

Travis chuckled. "No, I mean, why are you trying to find a ride in the first place?"

242

My eyes darted to Sloan and back to Travis. "Because you're going to dinner with your family, and I don't want your sister to have to drive out of the way to your place or my place."

I looked away. I was getting crabby with the whole situation. Another joy of having my period. I suddenly wanted to be home and have this night be over, so I could hopefully wake up in a better mood.

Stupid hormones.

I quickly sent Lexie a text to call me right away, but I was probably going to have to bother someone else. I didn't want to wait outside like a loser while his family was eating inside. It felt weird.

"Syd," Travis said.

I looked up from my phone. "Yeah?"

"You're going to dinner with us, you know."

My eyes shifted to Sloan again. I was pretty sure Travis had that wrong. Nowhere in that conversation had I been invited to eat with them.

Sloan looked in her rearview mirror to meet my eyes again. "Oh, yeah, you're going. You and Travis have been dating a while, and we thought it was time to meet his girlfriend."

I looked at Travis, and he laughed.

"You should see your face."

I could only imagine the look I was sporting at the moment. That was the second time someone had called me his girlfriend.

Does he really see me that way? And why didn't they just say we were all going out to eat?

I was feeling feisty now. I crossed my arms over my chest. "It's not like you said anything."

He leaned over and put his hand on my knee. "We've been talking about going to dinner since we got in the car."

"Yeah, well, I didn't know I was invited."

He squeezed my leg. "You're always invited, Sydney."

I narrowed my eyes at him, but it didn't last. A smile broke through my mean look.

But I was still a little frustrated, so I stuck my tongue out at him, too.

Travis laughed, and I picked up my phone to tell Lexie never mind.

FORTY-ONE

SYDNEY

TRAVIS'S PARENTS were both nice, regular-looking people. I'd always pictured two supermodels giving birth to someone like Travis, but they were an everyday, average couple.

"Sydney, these are my parents, Chad and Bonnie. Mom, Dad, this is Sydney, the woman I've been dating."

Travis's father had a full head of hair that was completely gray, and he had a little bit of a belly. In my head, I'd thought he'd be as fit as Travis.

His mother was short and blonde with crow's-feet. Her smile was bright and sincere.

"Nice to meet you both," I said. "I'm sorry I'm not better dressed."

Travis wasn't the only one wearing comfortable travel clothes.

"That's okay, dear. We know that you two just got off a plane."

"Zehler," someone from the hostess stand called out.

"That was fast," Chad said.

We were brought back to a long table with three chairs on each side. I made sure to sit by Travis while the rest of his family sat on the other side.

"So, you're an author?" Bonnie asked.

"Yes. I write romance."

I waited to see their responses. Some people insulted romance novels even though it was the highest-selling fiction genre. There was still stigma around it that it was smut or mommy porn.

"Oh, I love romance." Bonnie leaned toward me. "It's a bit weird to read a novel with my son on the cover though."

"Tell me about it," Sloan said. "It kind of creeps me out."

I laughed. "I never really thought about it, but it makes sense."

"Do you have any sons, dear?" Bonnie asked.

"No. But I do have a brother and a nephew." *Yikes.* "I think I would have to ignore the front of the book and just keep reading."

Bonnie winked at me. "That's what I usually do." After the server came over and took our drink orders, Bonnie asked me, "So, how long have you been writing?"

I had to think about that. "For about six years now. But it was only about a year and a half ago that I was able to quit my day job and write full-time."

"Oh, what did you do before you were a writer?" Chad asked.

"I was a buyer for Target. I like my job now much better."

"Good for you for doing something you love," Bonnie said. "Are your parents proud of you?"

"Well, my mom passed away four years ago, so I had only just gotten started with my writing career."

"I'm so sorry, sweetheart," Bonnie said.

Travis put his arm around the back of my chair and kissed the side of my head.

I smiled. "Thank you. It makes me sad, but I like talking about her. And, as for my dad, as long as I can support myself and I don't start rooting for the Packers, he stands behind whatever I do."

Travis laughed. "Your dad is funny."

"You've only met him once."

"Yeah, but all he cared about was if I watched sports. Nothing about his daughter."

I rolled my eyes. "You noticed that, huh? Yeah, he's a real peach."

Dinner went by fast, and before I knew it, we were done eating and picking at our plates. Or more like, Travis was still picking at my plate when the server brought over the bill. His parents wouldn't let me pay, so I insisted they let me leave the tip.

We walked out to the front of the restaurant, and Chad said, "Son, can you stop over a minute and help me move the couch?"

"Sure. I'll come over after Sloan drops us off."

"Just ride with Mom and Dad. Sydney can ride with me. I have to stop and pick up a prescription, and we'll meet you there." Sloan put her arm through mine. "We can have some one-on-one girl time."

247

Travis looked at me, and I wanted to say no, but I hated to sound rude. I couldn't say that I was scared to be alone with his sister out loud.

"Sure. That works."

At his sister's car, he pulled me into his arms and kissed me. "Text me if she starts getting mean."

"*Hey*," his sister said from the other side of the vehicle.

"I'm joking," he told Sloan. He looked back at me and shook his head. "Seriously, text me."

I put my hand on his chest. "I will." I wouldn't because I didn't want to come between siblings, but I loved that he was worried about me.

We all said goodbye, and I got in the car with Sloan. We took off, and neither of us said anything for about five minutes.

"Travis said the photo session went well. What did you think?" she asked me.

I felt my body relax. This was an easy question. I hadn't even realized I was tense. "Yes, it was fun. I loved seeing the things the photographer had the models do to get certain shots. I'm excited to see the finished products."

She nodded in understanding or in approval. I didn't know which one.

"So, nothing about it bothered you?"

I had a feeling this had to do with Travis's ex after the comment Christy had made to me at the gym. And I decided to be honest with her. "Truth be told, there were a few moments I did get a little bored. Because they do the same pose with just little adjustments over and over. I almost pulled out my phone a couple of times, but I didn't want to hurt Travis's feelings."

Sloan smiled. "That's good to hear."

"Does this have to do with Christy?"

Sloan's head whipped toward me. "What do you know about Christy?"

"I had the *pleasure* of meeting her one night at the gym. I only talked to her for a few minutes, but I got the impression she has low self-esteem and some issues she needs to address."

Travis's sister snorted. "*Some* issues? Try *a lot*. She was very…normal when she and Travis started dating, and she seemed proud that Travis was a cover model. But then she started getting increasingly jealous of his work. In the beginning, it was minor, but then she began working out a ton and lost a lot of weight. I think she felt like she wasn't pretty enough for Travis, but her insecurities got worse, the more weight she lost."

"I can kind of understand the part about not feeling pretty enough. I know he's your brother, but there is just something amazing about him. He has this aura that he puts off that makes every straight woman's heart beat faster. He's good-looking, he's charming, he's nice, and to top it off, he's a model. It can be intimidating."

"But you're not?"

"Intimidated?" I had to think about that. "Definitely not now. In the beginning, maybe a little. But I think it was more a girl falling in lust with a hot guy." I laughed. "I remember being worried that I would say something stupid in front of him. But he isn't the first guy I've been that way around."

Sloan glanced at me, so I kept going, "But, if you're wondering if I'll end up like Christy, the answer is no. I spent many years of my late teens and early twenties striving for the perfect body. But that will never happen, and I'm okay with that. I might not love my body, but I like my body. And, more importantly, I like food. I refuse to starve myself for anyone, even me. I'm at that point in my life where I really want to be healthy more than anything."

"How old are you?"

"Thirty-four."

Her eyebrows went up. "Wow."

"I know; I'm a lot older than your brother."

"Maybe that's a good thing. I'm twenty-nine, and I understand a little of where you're coming from."

"I don't know everything that happened between Travis and Christy, but I can tell she really hurt him. There are times when I feel like he's holding back."

Sloan blew out a deep breath. "Her jealousy got so bad that she started forbidding Travis from doing photo shoots or going to book signings. He actually stopped for about six months. But it didn't help. She hacked into his phone and put some sort of parent-watch program on it. She would read his e-mails and his messages." She looked at me. "Has Travis ever said anything about unsolicited messages?"

I laughed. "Oh, yeah. We've laughed at some of them."

"Well, Christy would be furious even though Travis had no control over who sent him stuff. She called him out about a particular message. That was how he found out about the spyware. He was pissed."

"I bet."

"But I think he was more hurt than anything."

Oh, Travis. My heart went out to him.

"The final straw was when Angela asked him to go to a book signing last year. Travis had known her for a long time, and he didn't want to tell her no. Christy freaked out and said it was over. The next day, she went back to Travis and begged him to forgive her. But, in between those eight hours, she'd slept with someone else. She was so convinced that Travis would cheat on her that she felt like she had to have sex with someone else first. I guess, technically, one could say they were broken up, but Travis felt like he'd been cheated on."

"Wow. I had no idea."

"I don't know if I should have told you all that. It was probably my brother's place to open up to you, but I love him, and I don't want him to get hurt again. So, if you're going to start acting crazy, please tell me now."

"No crazy plans. I swear. But, in full disclosure, I stalked him on social media after I met him."

Sloan laughed. "I think we've all Facebook-stalked someone."

And that was when I finally felt like Sloan might actually love me…someday.

FORTY-TWO

SYDNEY

LATER THAT NIGHT, I walked out of Travis's bathroom and toward his bed. He was sitting up in bed with his shirt off, looking sexier than anyone had the right to. I wanted to attack him, but I knew we needed to talk first.

I stopped at the end of the bed, so I blocked the TV.

His eyes moved from the screen to me. "What's up, sexy?"

"Can I ask you something?"

"Of course."

I put a knee on the bed and crawled toward him. I lay down next to him and put my head on my hand to prop it up. "Did something bad happen at a photo shoot when you were dating Christy?"

He stiffened. I was immediately worried I'd stepped too far, but then his body relaxed.

"Have you been talking to my sister about me?"

"Duh. Of course," I joked. "But, seriously, she's worried about you. And she's worried about me. And I already knew

Christy had hurt you. I just never knew if I should bring it up."

Travis cleared his throat and turned down the volume on the television. "I took her to one shoot with me. She threw a fit and walked out. I was so embarrassed. Modeling is not my main source of income, but it's still my job. Could you imagine if I had an office job and she did that?"

I put my free hand on his arm. "I'm sorry she did that to you. Is that why you were tense about the photo shoot?"

He looked at me. "You could tell I was tense?"

"Yes."

"Wow. Um, yeah, that was why. Not that I thought you would ever really act that way, but I can't just forget about it either."

I rolled onto my back. "I understand. I had a boyfriend many years ago who would always make negative comments about my friends. I stopped hanging out with them at first to keep him from saying stuff until I realized how toxic he was. But, even after we broke up, the next guy I dated, I felt like I was always waiting for him to make a remark. It took a long time for me to stop expecting something to happen."

"I hate that you dated a jerk like that."

"Hey, me, too, but it wasn't for very long." I raised my eyebrows. "Your sister did tell me some stuff, but I was wondering if you wanted to tell me yourself. I feel bad that I heard it from Sloan first."

Travis sighed.

"Hey. You don't have to tell me anything right now." I was a little hurt by this.

The Chicago trip had been at the beginning of May, and it was now the end of July. He'd met my family, and now, I'd met his, but I understood if he still had reservations. It didn't help the wounded feelings at the moment, but I didn't want to push him.

"Despite me being called your girlfriend twice this weekend, we've never discussed it. You can tell me when you're ready." I was giving him time to talk to me, but I was also letting him know that I expected him to talk to me at some point if this relationship was going to continue.

Travis picked up my hand and started playing with my fingers. "Did my sister tell you how paranoid Christy got?"

"She mentioned how Christy put something on your phone, so she could monitor you. That's not cool."

"Yeah. In the beginning, we were like a normal couple, but as time progressed, she started being jealous of everything. She didn't even like my female clients."

"But I'm guessing she had male ones?"

"Yes. But that's different, you know," he said, his voice laced with sarcasm. "She got so paranoid that she made me paranoid. I would keep my phone on silent and only check it when she wasn't around because she would freak out if I talked to anyone else." He smiled. "The morning when you saw the unsolicited pic in my message, I had a flashback of being with Christy. But then you laughed. That was like a gift, babe."

"Aw, and I wasn't even trying."

He met my eyes. "That's the best part. You don't get jealous, you don't spy on me, and you trust me."

"Well, the relationship is still young."

Travis's eyes widened.

"I'm joking. Life's too short for those things. If you don't trust your partner, then why are you even with them?

Although, to be fair, I think Christy might be that way with everyone. She needs to talk to someone about her insecurities. But I don't want to lie to you. I have felt jealous before. It's a feeling that I think everyone experiences. But it's what a person does with it that matters."

"What did you feel jealous about?"

"This is embarrassing, but I was jealous of your relationship with Angela."

Travis frowned.

"I know that Christy was jealous of that, too, but I don't feel the same way," I quickly reassured him. "I don't want you to stop being friends with Angela. I was just jealous that you two were close because I wanted to be friends with you, too. I hope that makes sense."

He nodded. "It's not a *you or them* thing. It's a *you also* thing."

I smiled. "Exactly. I would never stop you from being friends with someone unless I really felt like they were a threat. Like, if someone were truly trying to come between us. But I'm not worried, and I'm not going to spy on you. If I were worried, I would talk to you about it. I wouldn't go behind your back."

Travis scooted down on the bed, and we rolled toward each other.

"You're too good to be true."

I busted out laughing. "We both know that's not true. You sometimes have to drag me to the gym with you and to do outdoor activities."

He grinned, and his dimples showed. "I'll reform you yet."

I put my thumb over one of his adorable marks. "Ha. You wish."

He put his arm around me, pulling me close. "The important thing is that I trust my girlfriend, and she trusts me."

"So, you're saying that I'm your girlfriend?"

"Aren't you?"

I snuggled into him. "I'd like to think so."

He kissed the top of my head. "Good. Just no more talking to my sister. Next time, she'll tell you embarrassing stories of when I was a kid."

"I don't know if I can promise you that. Your sister and I have something in common now."

"What's that?"

"We both care about you."

Travis kissed me. "I care about you, too."

It wasn't quite love yet, but I had no doubt that we were headed in that direction. I rested my head against his chest and enjoyed the feeling of being grateful.

FORTY-THREE

SYDNEY

TUESDAY MORNING, I was deep in the writing zone when my phone notified me that I had a message from Travis. I had set a specific ringtone for when he messaged me. It was someone whistling. Whenever I heard it, it made me smile.

Travis: Three things.

Me: Okay.

Travis: Dan and Lilah invited the two of us to go to their place on Friday. You up for that?

Me: Yes.

Travis: I'll let them know that my *girlfriend* and I will be there.

Me: You're such a cheeseball.

Travis: LOL. You love it.

Me: I do. What's the second thing?

Travis: When is the book signing in Iowa?

Me: The second weekend in September.

It was the same signing we'd met at a year ago. I couldn't believe it had been a whole year.

Travis: Okay, good. Because the third thing is, I was invited to go to another photo shoot next weekend, and since I already prepared for the last one, I figured it was a good time to go. It's in North Carolina with David Wayne.

Me: So, this weekend, we hang out with your friends, and next weekend, you go to NC?

I wanted to be sure I had my dates correct.

Travis: Yes.

Me: Sad face. I can't go with you even though I would love to. Next weekend is the weekend I'm watching my brother's kids because they're going to New York.

I had promised to take the weekend, and my dad was going to take the week. I couldn't back out now. I wasn't as big of a fan of David Wayne, but I would still love to meet him.

Travis: Crap. That's right.

Me: I would way rather go with you, but I promised my brother months ago. Just make sure you bring me home a souvenir. I've never been there.

Travis: You don't mind if I go without you?

Me: Not at all. I'm jealous because we both know you'll have more fun than me. But, really, you don't want to stay here and help me babysit. Bor-ing.

Travis: LOL. You're the best, babe.

Me: LOL. I try.

On Friday, Travis and I headed over to Lilah and Dan's house for dinner. I hadn't spent a lot of time with Travis's friends, but I liked them. We'd had fun on the Fourth of July, and all we had done was barhop all day.

Travis parked in the driveway of their house, and after getting out, we went to the back of his SUV to get the food and drinks we'd brought with us. I had made a simple pie for dessert, which I grabbed while Travis picked up the beer and wine we'd bought to drink.

As he was closing the door, his phone flew out of his hand and landed on the hard pavement.

I gasped, and we both froze for a moment.

"Oh no," I said.

"Shit." Travis pushed the wine toward me. "Here. Hold this a second."

I took the paper bag, and he went over to his phone to pick it up. He turned it around to show me the screen, which was cracked in several places.

"Shit is right," I said. "Does it work at all?"

Travis pushed the Home button, and the screen lit up. Unfortunately, he couldn't read a single thing on it. "Damn it."

We started for the front door.

"Sorry, babe. That sucks."

"I just bought this a few months ago. I can't afford a new phone."

"Do you have insurance?"

"No. I should probably look into that with my next one."

"Take it to the place you bought it. If it lights up, hopefully, it's only the screen that is ruined. It's a lot cheaper to replace that than the whole phone."

We reached the door, and Travis hit the doorbell.

"I hope that's the case. I'll have to take it in tomorrow, so it can be done by next weekend. I don't want to go out of town without a phone."

"Yikes, that would be bad," I said as the door opened.

"Hey, how's it going, you two?" Lilah said.

"Travis dropped his phone in your driveway and cracked the screen," I said as we walked in the house.

"Oh, that sucks," Lilah said.

"Yeah, it does, especially since I'm going to sue you because it happened on your property," Travis joked.

"Go for it. We live paycheck to paycheck."

Travis laughed as he carried the beer into the kitchen. I was glad that he wasn't going to let his phone ruin his night.

I handed Lilah the pie. "I brought a little something for dessert. I hope that's okay."

She smiled. "No, that's great. Is that wine?" She nodded toward the paper bag I was holding.

"Yes."

Her eyes lit up. "Let's crack that baby open, shall we?"

"Let's."

About ten minutes later, Broderick showed up, all alone.

"Where's Alice?" Travis asked.

"Who?"

"Broderick," Lilah scolded.

"I'm kidding. We broke up."

Lilah rolled her eyes. "I'm not surprised. The guy can't date someone for more than a month," she said to me.

"I heard that, and I can, too. I just choose not to."

"Yeah, I'm not sure that's much of a distinction," Dan said.

Broderick stuck out his lower lip. "Why is everyone always picking on me?"

"Because you make it so easy, dude," Travis said.

I went over to Broderick and looped my arm with his. "It's just because they're all jealous of you."

Broderick's mouth dropped open, and he smirked as he pointed to me. "See, she gets it. FYI, Travis, I'm stealing your girl."

"Over my dead body," Travis said with a dimpled grin.

"Okay, everyone, it's time to eat," Lilah called out.

We all sat down to dinner, and everything was going well, but after a while, I noticed Travis looked bummed.

"What's up?" I asked him.

"It's stupid, but I wish my phone worked so that I could take pics of everyone and share it."

I knew that Travis had over fifty-five thousand followers on Instagram, and he liked to let them know what was going on in his life. There were quite a few male cover models who had more followers than some of the actors I followed. It always astounded me that male models could be so popular.

"Do you want to use my phone? It's easy to add another account and switch back and forth." I used to have a Sydney Hart Author profile and a Sydney Harting for my personal stuff, but it had gotten to be too much. I'd pretty much stopped using my personal one even though I never closed the account and was still signed into it.

"Really? Thanks, babe."

I handed over my phone. "The passcode is zero-eight-one-five."

"You trust me with your passcode?"

I shrugged. "Yeah." I didn't think it was that big of a deal. "I'm not giving you the password to my bank account though. Just don't forget to sign out of it. I don't want your five million notifications crowding up my phone," I said with a smile.

"Ha. I don't get that many. But I'll make sure to do that."

Travis laughed and opened my Instagram app, and he proceeded to share the entire night with his fans while I wondered if I'd ever get my phone back.

FORTY-FOUR

SYDNEY

ON SATURDAY, we took Travis's phone into the shop to get the screen fixed, and they gave him a loaner phone to use while he waited to get his back. But he wasn't supposed to download any apps, so he used mine all weekend.

If he hadn't already called me his girlfriend, I would say that we were officially a couple because non-couples didn't share phones. I complained that he had my cell more than I did, but I secretly loved it. I trusted him with my phone, and he trusted me with his Instagram account.

If I wanted to, I could have taken a picture of him on Sunday morning, sleeping with his mouth open, and posted it for all his fans. To be clear, I didn't. But I could have. I was really tempted, so I ended up posting it to my account instead with the caption, *This guy*.

Thankfully, Travis laughed.

I spent all week deep in the writing zone because I had another deadline coming up, and I had gotten behind for various reasons, but one of them was going to Denver. That'd really set me back, and I knew I wouldn't get much done the coming weekend since I would be watching my nieces and nephew.

I spent Monday night with my dad, Tuesday with Harper, and Wednesday and Thursday with Travis. Thankfully, he'd gotten his phone back on Wednesday, so he was ready for his trip, and we wouldn't be out of touch.

On Friday morning, I drove him to the airport.

"I'm going to miss you like crazy," he said when I pulled up to his airline check-in.

"Me, too. Quick, kiss me before I get in trouble for sitting here too long."

Travis put a hand behind my neck and pulled me close. He took my mouth in a deep, soul-searching kiss. It was one that should lead to us taking our clothes off, not us saying goodbye.

"Come back quick," I told him when he released me.

"I will. Good luck this weekend."

"Thanks. I'm sure they'll be like this all weekend." I pretended to look down at an electronic device and let my mouth hang open.

He laughed.

"Please let me know when you've landed, okay?"

"Will do." He kissed me one more time. "See ya later, sexy."

"See ya."

Travis got out of my car and grabbed his bag from my trunk. Then, he was gone.

I was going to miss him.

After leaving the airport, I went home and did some more writing before I packed up my stuff and went to Ryan and Grace's for the weekend. It was easier for me to go there than for the three kids to come to me. Plus, I lived close. I could always run home if I needed something.

I picked up Ryan and Grace, and for the second time that day, I went to the airport. I should have tried to have Travis coordinate his takeoff with my brother and sister-in-law's. Thankfully, Ryan and Grace weren't coming back until next Friday, and Travis was coming back on Sunday.

When I got back to my brother's, the kids were all where I'd expected to find them. On the couch or in their rooms, doing stuff on their phones.

"Hey, guys, your favorite aunt is here. Let's hang out."

Gretchen looked up from the couch. "We are hanging out."

"No. You're on your phone while I stare at you."

Gretchen shrugged. "Then, why don't you get on your phone, too?"

I threw my hands up. "Okay, what do you want for dinner? Pizza?"

She looked up from her phone at me. "Yes."

"Ben, Lexie," I yelled. "Do you want pizza for dinner?"

"Yes," Ben yelled back.

A minute later, Lexie walked out of her room. "I'm going out with Brendan tonight."

"Really? You were supposed to keep me company tonight."

Lexie laughed. "You'll be fine. Put your feet up. Watch a movie."

"I suppose I can try."

My brother did have a big television with every channel imaginable. I only had Netflix and Hulu at my house.

Lexie left, and I ordered pizza. While we were waiting, I got a text from Travis.

> **Travis:** Made it here safely.

> **Me:** I'm glad.

> **Travis:** I'm catching an Uber now. I'll call you later.

> **Me:** Okay. Miss you.

Travis must have already put his phone away because he didn't answer.

A couple of hours later, I was deep into a *Law & Order: SVU* marathon when my phone rang. I turned down the TV and answered the video-chat request Travis had sent me.

Once our sound and video connected, I was surprised to see that he wasn't at his hotel room. For some reason, that was where I'd expected him to be. Instead, he was at a loud and crowded restaurant or bar. I couldn't tell exactly what it was.

"Hey, sexy," he said as he walked outside. The sound of the establishment dimmed as the door closed behind him.

"Hey. Sounds like you're having fun."

"Yeah." He shrugged a shoulder. "Just hanging out with the photographer and some friends."

"I'm a little jealous. Here's my entertainment for the night." I turned my phone, so he could see my niece and nephew buried in their phones and the TV. I spun it back to me. "Pretty boring here."

"I'd rather be there."

The door opened behind him, and at least two people shouted his name. Two women appeared, one on either side of him.

"Travis, what are you doing? We're supposed to go," the blonde on the left said.

"I'm talking to my girlfriend," Travis told them, and I could have reached through the phone and kissed him.

"Hi, girlfriend," the brunette on the right said and waved at the phone.

"Hey," I said with a laugh. I thought they were both drunk.

"I'm Nina, and this is Joy," the blonde said.

"I'm Sydney."

Joy threw her arm around Travis. "You are one lucky woman." She pinched his cheek. "This guy is a gem."

"Don't I know it?"

Travis shook them off. "Okay, ladies, let me say goodbye."

"Bye," they said into the phone.

"Joy," a guy behind Travis said. I saw him briefly come into view and throw Joy over his shoulder.

She giggled. "I'm just saying hi to Travis's girlfriend."

The guy leaned right into the phone. "Hi, girlfriend. Bye, girlfriend."

I laughed as they all walked away.

"That was George."

"They all seem like fun."

"They are." He looked behind him. "Listen, I'd better

go, or they're going to leave me." He turned back to me. "I'll call you later."

"Okay. I'll be here."

"Bye, sexy."

"Bye, Travis."

I hung up with him, feeling down that I couldn't be there with him. They'd looked like they were having a great time.

I swiped my finger down to look at my notifications. Maybe some happy social media would make me feel better. But, when I saw the number of notifications I had, I cringed.

I had fallen behind in my social media this week. I'd barely been in my reader group, and that was about it. I had notifications from Facebook, Instagram, Twitter, and a thousand and one e-mails.

I hit clear on my phone. It was too late for me to start going through them now. It would be a rabbit hole I would fall into, and I wouldn't come up for air for hours. Besides, I really should do most of them on my computer. It sometimes got to be too much to check everything on my phone.

I looked over at my niece and nephew. I had a feeling I would have plenty of free time tomorrow to go through my stuff.

Besides, I wanted to be ready for when Travis called later. Maybe I could convince him to have a little phone sex.

I smiled at my idea and turned the volume back up on the TV.

FORTY-FIVE

SYDNEY

THE NEXT MORNING, I took Ben and Gretchen to soccer practice.

I took a seat off to the side to wait. My brother had told me that I could drop the kids off and come back later, but since I was the babysitter, I was worried something would happen on my watch, so I was sticking around.

I pulled up my phone because I hadn't been smart enough to think to bring a book. But also because I wanted to make sure I hadn't missed any messages or calls from Travis.

I hadn't heard from him again last night, and I hoped he was okay. I'd sent him one text when I got up to tell him good morning, but I still hadn't gotten a response, so I assumed he was still sleeping.

I went through my e-mails and notifications, and I addressed the things I could on my phone. We didn't have any plans that afternoon, so I could do some of the other things on my computer when I got home.

After clearing off some of my stuff, I noticed I had a

message on Instagram, and I got excited. Most of my readers either responded to my newsletters or commented on my posts. If I got messages, it always seemed to be on Facebook. Probably because that was where I had the most presence. In my whole career, I thought I'd had about five messages on Twitter and maybe one on Instagram.

It was a lot of work to keep up with everything. I knew I'd have to hire a personal assistant someday, but getting messages on different platforms meant my reach and followers were growing. I absolutely loved knowing that people connected with my stories.

I opened the message and saw a picture of a woman in the little profile picture. I wasn't surprised. I had yet to hear from a male reader.

NIN_LOVE_MOD

I had a great time last night.

I frowned. *Last night?* I looked at the top of the message. It had been sent only about a half hour ago. I was so confused. I continued reading.

I bet you didn't know you were going to have so much fun in NC.

I sucked in a breath and turned my phone away as a nasty feeling clenched my gut.

It wasn't my message. It was Travis's. He'd forgotten to sign out of my phone, and I'd forgotten to remind him.

And, now, I didn't know what the hell to do.

The message could be innocent, but it sure didn't sound that way.

Did he cheat on me?

But, if he hadn't cheated on me and I'd read his message, that would make me no better than Christy. I didn't want to break his trust.

My heart was racing at this point. I felt like I was going to puke.

I got up from my seat and walked away from the crowd for more privacy, and I quickly dialed Harper.

"Hello?"

"I need your advice."

"What's wrong?"

"Remember how Travis broke his phone, and I complained that he was using mine?"

"Yeah?"

"He never signed out of his Instagram account on my phone, and he got a message this morning."

"Okay…"

"It's from a woman, I'm pretty sure, and she said she had a great time last night."

Harper gasped. "It could be innocent. People become friends with the opposite sex all the time."

"I know."

"Is that all it said?"

"No, but I'm afraid to look. I don't want to spy on him." I had explained to Harper a little of Travis's past, so she knew exactly what my problem was. "But, if I don't look …"

"He might be hiding something from you?"

"Yes. Especially since he never called or messaged last night. What if he was"—I swallowed—"with her?"

"Oh shit, babe, I don't know what to tell you." Harper's voice was very sympathetic, but it didn't help me make a decision.

"What would you do if it were Ian?"

"I'd read the fucker in a heartbeat."

"So, you're saying that I should read it?"

"Sydney, I can't make that choice for you, but I think you know what you want to do."

"I want to know what it says. I could give myself anxiety, wondering, and it might be nothing. I almost feel like not knowing is worse than if it were something bad."

"I'm not going to tell you what to do, but it sounds like you've made your decision."

"I'm scared, Harper."

"Whatever happens, I'm here for you."

"Thank you."

"Call me back."

I hung up the phone, opened up the app again, and started from the top.

NIN_LOVE_MOD:

I had a great time last night. I bet you didn't know you were going to have so much fun in NC.

BTW, I took a picture and a video for you to remember your night here. (I didn't want to post it and give your girlfriend the wrong impression.)

Have fun at your photo shoot today. I hope, when you get in the shower this morning, you think of me. I think I left my impression all over you. LOL!

When you're in NC again, promise to look me up! We'll have to do it again.

I felt sick. Everything about that message sounded bad. I clicked on the profile, and I saw that it was the blonde, Nina, from last night. She had a lot of professional photos taken of her. Just my luck. She was a model.

I hit the back button and saw that Travis had responded to her. Of course he had. The notification had popped up on his phone, too.

TRAVIS:

Ha-ha. Yes, I had quite the surprise this morning. Remind me to never drink that much again. And, yes, it took a while to wash all of your handiwork off of me. Thank you for that.

Thanks for not posting the picture or the video. I need to talk to Sydney before the whole world finds out what a fool I am.

My heart was breaking for various reasons, but the one at the top of my mind was that Travis had messaged Nina, yet he hadn't called or texted me.

I took screenshots, and then, without a second thought, I signed out of Travis's account. Knowing what the message said did not make me feel better, and I didn't want to see any more of what they had to say to each other.

I sent screenshots of the messages and nin_love_mod's profile to Harper with a message.

Me: I have no idea what this means, but all I can think of is that they had sex, and she left herself all over him. Barf. I want to throw up. And he wants to talk to me before the whole world knows what a fool he is? Again, my mind thinks he wants to tell me before the whole world knows he cheated on me. I don't know what to do, and I am freaking out.

Harper: Don't panic. Take a deep breath. It still might be nothing. But I'm on my way over. I'll meet you at your brother's.

FORTY-SIX

SYDNEY

MY WONDERFUL FRIEND talked me off a ledge on Saturday and helped me keep the rest of the weekend full, so I wouldn't keep thinking about Travis. He'd texted me about ten minutes after I sent the screenshots to Harper. Thankfully, I was driving home by then, so I didn't respond with a nice, *Fuck you.*

And, later that night, when he called to video-chat again, I was at a movie with the kids and Harper, so I had an excuse not to answer. I was afraid that, if I saw his face, I would blurt out what I knew. Harper had convinced me to let him tell me about his weekend first before I made any accusations.

If it were all a big misunderstanding, I would feel like a dumbass if I accused him of something.

I almost asked one of his friends to pick him up from the airport, but then I decided it was best that I did it. He would know something was wrong if I didn't come, and we would have the whole drive back to his place to talk about what had happened. And maybe, if I kept my eyes on the road, I wouldn't be tempted to shake him until he spilled his guts.

I pulled up in front of the airport fifteen minutes after Travis's flight landed. I didn't want to park and walk in, and I wanted to give him plenty of time to get off the plane and get to the exit doors.

I saw him standing outside, waiting for me a few doors down, and I drank in the sight of him. He was wearing shorts and a T-shirt. Nothing fancy, but he looked great, and I was struck with how much I'd missed him.

I inched my way forward, and when he saw me, his face lit up. I wanted to cry because he was happy to see me.

He rushed over to my car, put his suitcase in the back, and got in the front. He pulled me straight toward him and kissed me like his life depended on it. Despite my uncertainty, I didn't stop him. I wanted to remember this kiss in case it was our last.

An airport employee knocked on the passenger window to tell us to get moving, and Travis let me go. "Hey, sexy."

"Hey."

"I missed you."

"I missed you, too." I put the car in drive and pulled away.

"So, how was your weekend?" he asked.

"Good." Minus the message I'd read. "We had pizza on Friday night and hung out. Soccer practice Saturday morning, Sky Zone Saturday afternoon, and a movie Saturday night. And, this morning, I slept in, and now, I'm here with you."

Travis grabbed my hand. "I'm glad you had a good weekend."

"How was yours?" I asked as nonchalantly as possible as my heart raced in my chest.

"Good. After I talked to you on Friday, I got drunk."

And possibly had sex with someone, I said in my head. *Sydney, you promised to give him a chance.*

"The photo shoot was good. I'm excited for you to see the pics. Last night, I laid low. I didn't know if I could take another night of partying."

That's it?

"Sounds like you had...fun," I said.

"Yeah. I missed you though."

I turned away and narrowed my eyes. *Don't try and butter me up, bud. I'm on to you.* I looked back at him and smiled. "Me, too. I wish I'd gone with you." *Then, you wouldn't have made any stupid mistakes.*

Travis's phone rang. "Oh, it's my mom. You care if I take it?"

"Nope."

As he talked to his mom, I tried to control my runaway thoughts, but by the time we got to his home, I was pretty worked up.

In all the scenarios I had run in my head about what it would be like when we saw each other again, he'd always come out and told me about his Friday night. Not once had I practiced how I would go about bringing it up.

I needed to find an excuse to call Harper in private. She'd know what to do.

I was sitting on his couch, tapping my foot on the floor, when Travis walked out of his bedroom. He'd gone to put away his suitcase, and I noticed the look on his face. He looked nervous.

I sucked in a breath. Here it was. He was going to tell me what had happened. And it couldn't be good if he looked scared.

"I need to show you something."

My eyes widened. I didn't want to see any naked pictures of Travis and some other chick. But I couldn't tell him that. "Okay," I said.

He sat beside me on the couch and thrust his phone into my hands. "This isn't the way I wanted to tell you, but I figure, I'd better show you before it leaks on social media."

On the screen was a video. My hand shook as I hit play.

Travis was the first thing I saw. He was in a busy bar at a table.

"Travis," a female voice said from behind the camera, "can you say that again? Except, this time, into my phone."

There were giggles from others around them, and I heard someone say, "He is so drunk."

"Say what?" Travis said.

"Tell us what you just told that girl who hit on you."

"Oh." Travis grinned. "I told her no way in hell would I go home with her."

The person behind the camera sighed. "Why?"

"Oh. Because I love my girlfriend."

I sucked in my breath.

"I love her so much," Travis continued. "She's perfect. And the best part is, she doesn't even know it." He leaned closer, as if he were telling a secret, except he forgot to lower his voice. "I think she's the one."

"Now, do the song," someone told him.

Travis started singing. Badly. It was so bad that I couldn't even tell what song he was singing. All I knew was, it had something to do with love.

I held my hand to my mouth as I laughed and cried at the same time. *He loves me.*

The video ended, and Travis took the phone. "I have one more thing to show you."

He scrolled to a picture of him lying on a bed, passed out, with his shirt off. All over his whole body, someone—or several someones—had written, *Travis loves Sydney.*

"Oh my God," I said.

"Yeah. That was my new friend, Nina. She thought it was funny to write all over me the night before a photo shoot. It took me twenty minutes to wash that shit off in the shower."

I started laughing again, and I fell into him. "Oh my God, I'm so relieved."

He put his arm around me. "So relieved? About what?"

I buried my nose in his neck. "You didn't call me back on Friday night, and then, when I read the messages between you and Nina the next morning, all I could think was that something had happened between the two of you. But, instead, you'd told everyone you loved me." I kissed his neck, oblivious to the fact that Travis had gone as stiff as a statue. "I love you, too."

He didn't respond, and so I backed away to look at him. "What's wrong?"

Travis swallowed. "What do you mean, you read the messages between me and Nina?"

Oh shit.

I had never meant to keep it a secret that I'd seen the messages, but I sure as hell hadn't meant to blurt it out either. I'd known that I would have to explain it after what he'd gone through with Christy.

"About that." I chuckled, but Travis didn't crack a smile. "Remember how you borrowed my phone last weekend?"

"Yeah?"

"You kind of forgot to sign out of your account, and I happened to read Nina's message to you."

"You *happened* to read her message to me?" His voice was full of doubt.

"Yes. When I got the notification, I thought it was for me. I didn't look at whose account it was."

"But you said messages."

"What?" I was confused.

"You said messages between me and Nina. So, not only did you read the one message, but then you also went and read what I had written her, too."

He was clearly upset, and I didn't blame him. He had every right to be very sensitive to this sort of thing after his ex had invaded his privacy.

"Yes, but then I signed out."

He threw his hands up. "Oh, so that makes it okay. You only read two messages before you signed out." He stood. "And you were worried this whole weekend that I'd cheated on you, but you didn't talk to me about it."

I got up from the couch, too. "I was going to. But not over the phone. Harper and I both agreed it would be better to discuss it in person."

"Harper?" Travis clenched his jaw shut and sucked in a deep breath. "You shared my messages with Harper?"

I didn't want to answer. "Yes." I stepped toward him.

"You have to understand; I was freaking out. You were half a country away, and I didn't know what to do."

He backed up. "You should have talked to me. You shouldn't have gone behind my back and read my messages. You shouldn't have gone behind my back and talked to your friend instead of me."

"Travis, wait. You're making it sound worse than it is."

He looked away from me. "I think it's time for you to go, Sydney."

"What? No. We can't end the conversation like this."

He slowly met my eyes. "Yes, we can. It's over." He pointed to the door. "Now, please leave."

Travis was clearly too upset to talk, so I picked up my purse and left.

Unfortunately, I couldn't get his words out of my head.

Is the conversation over, or is the relationship over?

FORTY-SEVEN

SYDNEY

TWO WEEKS LATER

"WHO'S GOING to the book signing in Iowa next month?" Derek asked the monthly writer group.

My head whipped up from where I had been taking notes. "Oh crap."

Derek laughed. "Did you forget about it?"

I had completely forgotten about it. Since my breakup with Travis, I hadn't thought much about anything. I was behind on my next book's schedule due to barely writing, and I couldn't seem to find my concentration. I was a mess. I'd missed two takeovers and neglected my reader group.

I was trying, but it was like someone had taken over my brain and put it on the Travis channel twenty-four/seven. Every time I tried to change it, it went back to him.

"Are you still going to go?" another author asked me.

"I don't know."

It was the same author event I had met Travis at, and I knew he was going to be there with Angela. Angela and I had decided to split Travis's expenses and have him split up the time between our tables. But, in light of our breakup, I didn't think Travis wanted to be anywhere near me. And I honestly didn't know if I could go there and see him in person.

I hadn't even opened my Instagram in the last thirteen days because I was afraid I would burst into tears. I had no idea if he'd told the world about our split, and I really didn't want to know.

"I need to recheck my schedule. Some stuff has come up," I told the group.

While we were friendly, these people were still my professional peers. I wasn't going to tell them about my personal life.

The group called it a day, and I headed for home as I debated on what to do about the September signing. I could cancel, or I could still go and ask the event planners to put my table as far away from Angela's as possible.

Once I got home, I got on my computer and messaged the event hosts to see if there was a wait list. I would be very surprised if there wasn't one.

I got a response five minutes later, telling me there was a wait list. A huge sense of relief went through me. I put in notice that I was no longer going to attend. Then, I e-mailed Angela to let her know I would still split the costs with her. When attending a book signing, there was a table fee, an assistant fee, and a model fee, so it was nice to be able to share what one could.

HEY, ANGELA.

I'M NO LONGER ABLE TO ATTEND THE BOOK SIGNING NEXT MONTH IN IOWA. I KNOW WE AGREED TO SPLIT TRAVIS'S COSTS,

AND I WILL STILL HONOR THAT. E-MAIL ME THE RECEIPTS, AND I WILL SEND THE MONEY OVER TO YOU RIGHT AWAY.

I'M SAD I WON'T BE SEEING YOU AGAIN THIS YEAR, BUT I HOPE YOU HAVE FUN.

LET ME KNOW IF YOU NEED ANYTHING ELSE.

SYDNEY

I didn't explain much more since I figured that Angela already knew about Travis and me. He was pretty close to her, so I was sure he'd told her by now.

I texted Harper.

> **Me:** I'm not going to the book signing next month. I'm sorry. I know you were looking forward to it.

> **Harper:** Ha-ha. I figured you'd backed out a long time ago. No worries, Syd. I wasn't expecting you to go.

> **Me:** I'll find another one for us to go to.

> **Harper:** Sounds good to me.

I did a search for some other book signings. I knew it would be hard to get in, but I'd snuck in at the last minute before.

I found one in Wisconsin for the weekend following the Iowa event. It was a smaller, more intimate event, and it sounded perfect. I quickly filled out the form and messaged the coordinators to let them know I wanted to be put on the wait list.

Next, I went to my reader group and apologized for not being around much lately, and I told them the bad news about the book signing. I added that I was in the process of finding a new one to attend.

After that, I updated my website and actually wrote a thousand words without any breaks. It wasn't my usual amount, but it was a start.

I was feeling very good about myself for taking charge of my life and moving forward even if they were little things, and I thought I deserved a break.

Maleficent jumped up onto my desk as I went to see if Angela had responded to my e-mail. She hadn't, but I did get something from Robert Hahn.

I had no idea why the famous photographer would be e-mailing me, but it put a grin on my face.

But, the second I opened the e-mail, my smile fell.

GREETINGS, SYDNEY.

HERE ARE THE PICTURES I TOOK OF YOU AND TRAVIS THAT I PROMISED TO SEND TO YOU. APOLOGIES FOR THE WAIT. I HOPE IT WAS WORTH IT.

ROBERT HAHN

I knew I shouldn't, but I clicked on the link to his cloud drive.

And I immediately started crying.

The pictures of Travis and me were beautiful. The looks we were giving each other showed how much we liked each other. And I had thrown it all away.

I had tried to apologize to Travis several times after I left his house that awful night. But he'd told me that he couldn't trust me anymore. It wasn't so much that I'd read the messages, but it was the fact that I had done it behind his back. And because I had thought he'd cheated on me. I had really messed up.

I flipped through each picture, crying harder as I looked at them. I could barely see through my tears toward the end.

I couldn't look at them anymore.

I shut down my computer and walked downstairs. I went straight to my freezer and my carton of ice cream.

So much for moving forward with my life.

After a night of fitful sleep, dreaming about Travis and feeling like crap, I knew there was more I needed to do to move on from him.

And I had a plan.

I was going to do something I had never done in my career before, but I had to follow my instincts and my heart.

I e-mailed my editor and asked her to fit me in at the last minute and that I was putting my current project on hold. Next, I e-mailed Robert Hahn and asked him for permission to use one of the pictures of Travis and me on a book cover. With a yes from both my editor and the photographer, I contacted my cover designer and told her what I wanted.

And then I sat down and started typing, and I didn't stop.

I wrote *The One That Got Away: An Unconventional Love Story* in twelve days. It was the fastest I had ever written a book, but the second I typed *The End*, I felt like a weight had been lifted off my shoulders.

Love didn't always work out the way we wanted, but life went on, and my book represented that.

It wasn't a normal romance novel, and there was a chance that I would receive a lot of backlash for what I'd written, but sometimes, as a writer, you had to let the words out of your head before you went crazy.

I set the release date as the day of the Iowa book signing but didn't make a big deal out of it. No release blitz, no blog tour, no announcements. If people found it, great, but if they didn't, that was okay, too. I had written the book for myself and my journey to healing

The last step in my plan was asking Derek to do a favor for me. Now that *The One That Got Away* was finished, I regretted giving up my spot to someone else at the book signing. But such was life. I knew Derek would deliver my message, and hopefully, Travis would heal a little bit from my book, too.

FORTY-EIGHT

TRAVIS

I LOOKED around the lobby of the hotel until I spotted Angela.

"Hey, Ang," I said and kissed her on the cheek.

"Hey, stranger," she said as she hugged me.

"It's been a while, huh?"

"Can you believe it's been a whole year?"

I shook my head. We always kept in contact, but we hadn't seen each other in person since last year at this time.

Angela reached into her back pocket and pulled out a room key. "Here's your key. Room 335. Why don't you go upstairs and drop your luggage off, and then meet me back down here?" She looked over her shoulder and pointed to a room. "I'll be right over there. That's where the meet-and-greet is."

"I'll be right back," I told Angela and headed for the elevators.

I was torn between taking my time and rushing back down. I hadn't wanted to come to the event this weekend, but I'd missed Angela, and I'd promised her.

Also, deep down, whether I wanted to admit it or not, I wanted to see Sydney. I hadn't seen her for over a month, and try as I might, I missed her. This weekend was the perfect excuse to see her again.

I'd tried to catch glimpses of her online, but she hadn't posted much on social media. My sister was in her fan group and told me that Sydney was working on something and hadn't been on there much either. I hoped she was okay. I still cared about her and worried about her.

Truthfully, I still loved her, and the more time that passed, the less upset I was with her. And that scared me because I'd taken Christy's apologies over and over again, and nothing had changed. I couldn't do that again.

I had no idea how this weekend was going to go. I wasn't going to avoid her table, but I could only imagine how stiff the conversations were going to be.

I put away my things and went back down to the room off the lobby. I introduced myself at the door, got my name tag, and walked in. I saw Angela again but continued to look around.

"Hey, who are you looking for?" Angela asked when she walked up to me.

"Sydney," I admitted.

Angela looked at me sympathetically. "Honey, Sydney's not coming."

My head swung back to my friend. "What?"

"Yeah, she contacted me sometime ago and told me she wasn't attending. I figured you knew."

I shook my head. "No." My jaw clenched. She wasn't there and hadn't told me she wasn't coming. I knew I probably didn't have a right to be upset, but I was. At least from

289

a business perspective. "So, now, you have to pay for everything? I will help you out."

Angela shook her head. "Oh, no, Sydney's still paying for half. She didn't want to back out on our agreement. I thought it was very nice because I would have paid for you to be here." She smiled. "I am going to tell her to keep her money, by the way. I wouldn't feel right, taking it."

I smiled back.

"Travis?"

I turned around to see a guy standing behind me. "That's me."

The guy looked relieved. "Oh, good. I was just going by your picture. I know you were here last year, but we didn't talk." He held out his hand. "I'm Derek. I'm in an author group with Sydney, and she asked me to give this to you." He held out a book to me.

I took it. "Thank you."

Derek nodded. "You're welcome," he said and walked away.

The book was back side up, so I turned it around, and my breath caught.

"Is that you and Sydney?" Angela asked, looking at the cover with awe.

"Um...yeah."

"You two look beautiful together."

We really did. It hurt to look at the book because it reminded me of what I was missing. Our foreheads were touching, and her arms were around me. And the feelings we had for each other were painted all over our faces.

"When was this taken?"

"Robert Hahn took it when we were there."

"Well, that explains it. *The One That Got Away: An Unconventional Love Story*," she read the title and nudged my arm. "Turn it over. What's the book about?"

Average women know they shouldn't fall for handsome men, but sometimes they take the risk.

As a TV Show writer, Jane Platt knows falling for a beautiful man will not end the same way her television shows do. So when she meets insanely actor Colin Butler, her inner alarm system warns her to stay away from a situation that will be sure to end in heartache.

But she fails to resist temptation.

When she falls into bed with Colin, she knows she could easily fall in love, but nothing is ever that simple. He's a man who has learned to keep his guard up, and while they can't keep our hands off of each other, that's as far as he's willing to go.

Either this is the beginning of her own happily ever after, or she's about to learn that those are only for the characters in her TV shows.

"Is that supposed to be the two of you?" Angela asked. "Swap out author for television writer and model for actor."

I shrugged. I had no idea what to think.

I flipped it back over and opened the cover. The dedication made me stop breathing.

To Travis.
The one who got away.
There will always be a special place in my heart for you. Always.

I sucked in a breath and looked up at Angela.

Angela smiled understandingly and nodded toward the entryway. "Go."

"What?"

"I know you want to read it. Go."

I looked behind me at the door and back at my friend. "Are you sure?"

"Yes. Now, go."

I took my book and sprinted out the door.

I looked up at the clock. It was after three in the morning. I'd been reading for hours.

I'd been unable to put the book down.

There were some differences in the book, like the main characters lived in California and they were closer in age to each other. But there were also so many similarities in the book that I knew it had to be about Sydney and me. Her author profession had become a TV show writer, and my modeling had become acting. And the things that happened to the main characters had happened to Sydney and me.

Some parts of the book broke my heart.

While the character Jane never came out and said it word for word, she implied that she wasn't pretty enough for Colin. That she wasn't good enough for him. I'd just finished the part where the couple broke up, and my heart ached.

When I read what had happened, how Jane had come to read Colin's messages, it didn't seem so sneaky. The part that broke my heart wasn't that Jane thought Colin was unfaithful. It was that she didn't think she was worthy enough for Colin to stay faithful to.

I rubbed my chest as if the pain I felt wasn't just in my head. I'd been so angry; I'd never thought about things from Sydney's point of view. She always seemed so strong and confident, but I should know that everyone had insecurities. No one was immune to them. Look at my own with Christy —who happened to be named Krissy in the book.

It made me smile that she purposely hadn't changed the name too much, like she was calling Christy out for her actions. Not that Christy would ever read Sydney's book, but it would be funny to see my ex's reaction. She probably still wouldn't get the damage she'd done to me. Reading the situation from an outside perspective, it was clear to me that Christy had issues and truly needed help and that many of her actions were a reflection of her, not me.

I held the book up and saw the amount I had left wasn't very thick. I was excited and anxious to see how Sydney had brought the couple back together. That was the only part of the book that hadn't happened to us in real life.

I turned the page to see the next chapter was the Epilogue. *What?* I flipped back to the previous page just to make sure I wasn't missing something. It was the breakup and then the Epilogue. It didn't feel right, but I started reading anyway.

FORTY-NINE

THE ONE THAT GOT AWAY

The One That Got Away:
An Unconventional Love Story

EPILOGUE

"HONEY, HAVE YOU SEEN MY CLUTCH?" I called out to Gabe from the bedroom. After two years of marriage, he always seemed to know where I'd left stuff.

"It's in the kitchen."

Whew. I was worried I'd lost it.

I left the bedroom, putting my earrings in my ears as I went.

As I entered the kitchen, my dear husband whistled at me. "You look beautiful."

I curtsied. "Thank you, kind sir. You look dashing yourself."

Gabe had let me style his blond hair for the night, and he'd gotten new glasses for the event. He pulled at the collar of his bow tie. "I feel like I'm choking. This is why I don't wear ties to work." He smiled at me. "But it's worth it."

"Only if we win."

Gabe smiled. "Even if you don't win. It's not every day your show gets nominated for an Emmy."

I grinned. He was right.

After my breakup with Colin, I'd had to quit the show. Not because Colin had made me, but because the relationship and split had affected my writing. I could no longer be objective to the character he played.

But it'd ended up being a good thing because I pitched an idea for a show I'd come up with to a couple of networks, and I'd gotten a deal. I'd become the head writer of my own TV show, which was up for an Emmy tonight.

I knew everyone said it was an honor just to be nominated, and others scoffed at them, but at this point in my career, it really was an honor. It had already boosted ratings for the show.

Butterflies filled my stomach the entire drive to the show, and it only intensified as we got on the red carpet. Being as I wasn't an actress, not many people paid attention to me and Gabe, which was fine with me.

As I met up with the others from my show, I saw Colin and his wife out of the corner of my eye and sucked in a breath. I had seen him on television, of course, but I hadn't seen him in person since I left the show, and a little pang pierced my heart.

I slipped my arm around Gabe, and his went around my shoulders. He was deep in conversation with someone, so he didn't know what was going on inside me, but he instinctively held me close anyway, and I loved him for that.

Gabe wouldn't win any beauty contests, nor was he in the business. He was simply a regular accountant at a bank. No one ever questioned why he had married me, and he wasn't even on social media.

Colin turned, and his eyes met mine. I waved at him, and he

smiled. He looked like he didn't know what to do, but he eventually started walking toward me with his wife on his arm.

His wife was a famous actress and absolutely beautiful. She had long blonde hair that was in perfect contrast to Colin's dark locks. The two of them looked flawless together.

"Hello, Jane."

I let go of Gabe, so I could shake hands. "Hi, Colin. How's it going?"

"Good. This is my wife, Camila Grey."

I laughed. "I think the whole world knows who Camila Grey is."

Camila blushed, her porcelain cheeks turning pink.

I held out my hand. "Nice to meet you, Camila. I used to work with Colin on his show. I was one of the writers."

Camila shook my hand as Colin said, "Now, she's the writer of her own show, and it's up for an award."

It was my turn to blush at the pride in Colin's voice. "Thank you."

He smiled. "I always knew you could do it."

"Thank you again." I pulled on Gabe's bicep. "Honey?"

"Let's talk again sometime," he said to the man he had been talking to, and then he turned to me.

"I'd like you to meet Colin Butler and Camila Grey." I looked at the couple. "This is my husband, Gabe."

My husband put his arm around me while holding the other hand out for Colin to shake. "Nice to meet you both."

We talked to the couple for a few minutes and then said goodbye.

"Are you okay?" Gabe asked me. He knew that I had dated Colin and that the breakup had been hard on me.

I smiled up at my husband. "Yeah, I am."

It had hurt to see my ex at first, but after a few minutes, I realized that we were with the people we were meant to be with. I was with an ordinary person, just like me, and Colin was with someone whose beauty matched his.

Sometimes, love stories didn't end in happily ever afters. At least, not with Colin and me. I had found mine with Gabe, and it looked like Colin had found his with Camila. And I was happy for the both of us.

I kissed Gabe on the lips. "I love you."

"I love you, too." He squeezed my side. "Now, let's go in there and win you an award."

TRAVIS

I threw the book on the bed and got up to pace the hotel room. My mind was all over the place.

The couple in the book didn't end up together. That was the last thing I'd expected.

I wanted to call up Sydney and ask her what the book was supposed to mean. I wanted to ask her why Jane and Colin hadn't made up and gotten married.

Why did she write the ending that way?

I needed someone else's perspective. I needed someone else to read the book.

I swiped it up off the bed to take it to Angela's room, but I stopped when I reached the door.

Angela wouldn't have time to read it, and she had a full schedule of book signing things to do the next day. I looked at the clock. Correction: in a few hours. Besides, Angela didn't quite know everything that had happened when I dated Christy or Sydney.

I turned, went to the dresser, and grabbed my phone. After doing a quick search on my Kindle app, I called my sister.

"Hello?" Sloan's voice was heavy with sleep.

"Sloan, I need your help."

"If you need bail money, call Mom and Dad."

I sighed. "No, I'm in Iowa, remember?"

"Okay. Good night then."

"Sloan, I'm serious. I need you to wake up."

After a few seconds, I heard her moving around.

"Travis, it's four in the morning on a Saturday. This'd better be fucking good, or I will make you pay."

"I need you to buy Sydney's latest book and read it."

"What?"

"Please. She wrote a book about the two of us, and I need you to read it."

"What?" Sloan's voice was finally clear. That had woken her up.

"Yeah. It's not exactly our story, but I know it's about the two of us. She had someone hand-deliver me a copy. I've been up all night, reading it."

"What happens in it?"

I groaned. "Just read the damn thing, will you? I can't tell you. I mean, I could, but you need to read it yourself."

Silence.

"Please. I really need my big sister's opinion."

Sloan had never fully agreed with me about breaking up with Sydney. She had supported me, but she felt like there was more to the story and that I should give Sydney a further chance to explain. That was why I wanted her to read the book.

"Okay, okay. Quit trying to butter me up. I'm awake. I'll start reading the book."

"Thank you."

"You're welcome."

"Love you, sis."

"Love you, too, you big turd. Now, tell me what book I'm supposed to buy."

FIFTY

SYDNEY

AT THE BOOK signing in Wisconsin, I opened the book the reader had set in front of me and started to sign. It was a copy of my new one.

"I cried when I read it."

I looked up. "Oh no. I cried when I wrote it, and I wanted to make my readers feel, but I didn't want you to cry."

The woman laughed. "No, it's a good thing. I'm one of those people who likes when books make me cry."

I laughed, too, and pretended to wipe my forehead. "Whew." After signing the book, I gave it back to the reader. "Thank you for reading it."

The reader hugged it and walked away.

As soon as she was gone, Harper said, "Your book really was amazing, but I still think Colin and Jane should have ended up together."

I rolled my eyes. We'd had this conversation more than once. "Travis is my Levi."

Levi was a guitarist in a band. Harper had fallen madly in love with him, but in the end, things hadn't worked out for them. She'd been heartbroken for months but eventually moved on, found Ian, and gotten married.

"He's not my Ian. My Ian is still out there."

Harper shook her head. "Travis is not your Levi. Travis is maturer than Levi, not a partier who will never settle down."

"Okay, you have a point. But he's not my Ian either."

"He is. You'll see."

I doubted that.

I hadn't heard from Travis at all. Derek had texted me to say that he had given the book to Travis last weekend, but it had been crickets since. I didn't really know what I'd expected Travis to say in response, but I'd thought he would have said something. Even just a simple thank-you would have been nice. I had hoped that he would at least give the story a chance and maybe forgive me. I didn't expect him to take me back, but it would be nice to not have him hate me, too.

Two readers came up to my table, and one of them picked up *Beautifully Broken* with Travis on the cover. One of them started whispering to the other, and all I could hope was that they'd buy it. I had ordered extra copies with the intention of going to the Iowa book signing with Travis to sign them. I had a buttload that I would love to get rid of, so I didn't have to look at his face every time I opened the case where I kept all my paperbacks.

I almost regretted putting him on the cover, except that I had to admit that it was still one of my favorites.

"Is this Travis Zehler?" one of the ladies asked.

"Yep, that's him."

The two looked at each other and squealed. "We just saw him."

They must have been at the Iowa book signing the prior weekend. It wasn't unusual for readers to go to more than one, especially if they lived in a central location.

"You two are lucky," I said, hoping that would shut the conversation down. I didn't want to talk about him.

"He's super nice," one of them said.

"He is," Harper said, so I didn't have to comment.

"Too bad he's taken," the other reader said.

My breath caught in my throat, and Harper clutched my hand under the table.

"Are you sure about that?" she asked.

The first one shrugged. "That's what he said when people asked him."

Tears stung my eyes. *He's moved on already?*

It had been over a month, but he already had a *girlfriend*.

I pushed my chair back. "Excuse me. I need some fresh air."

I ran out of the room, not caring if anyone was looking at me, and out of the hotel. I walked around to the side of the building, away from everyone coming and going, and let myself cry.

I pounded my fist against the wall. *Damn it*. I'd thought I was done crying over this guy.

I let the tears flow because I couldn't go back in there with my emotions all bottled up. After a few minutes, I felt a little more like myself. I took a couple of deep breaths and went back inside, straight toward the restroom. I blew my nose and cleaned up my makeup. My eyes and nose were still a little red, but hopefully, that would calm down soon.

With my head held high, I went back to the room where the book signing was. When I got to my table, Harper was still there with sympathy-filled eyes.

"What did you tell the readers after I bolted? I'm guessing they aren't going to come back and buy the book," I joked.

Harper raised her eyebrows. "Oh no, they both bought a copy. They said they were going to come back to have you sign them later."

"Huh, maybe I need to have an emotional breakdown more often. Did I miss anyone else?" I asked.

"A couple of others stopped by and said they'd come back around." Harper put her hand on my arm. "Are you doing okay?"

I shrugged. "As to be expected. I knew he'd move on. I just didn't know it would be so soon. And I didn't know I'd have to hear about it."

"Have you seen anything on social media? Because I feel like I haven't."

I shook my head. "I have avoided going on Instagram. I post a few things for my readers, but I avoid scrolling at all costs. I haven't even gone to his page to unfollow because I'm worried about what I might see." And because a part of me didn't want to completely let him go. I knew, soon, I'd be torturing myself by looking at everything he'd posted. "I guess it's good you haven't seen anything. I wonder who she is."

"Do you really want to know?"

"Yes, and no." I put my head on Harper's shoulder. "Life sucks."

She put her arm around me. "I know, babe."

"Can I go home now?"

"No."

I stuck out my lower lip. "Boo." I sat up. "I'll be fine as long as I don't have to hear any more about Travis."

Harper nodded. "You can do this."

A whole gaggle of young girls came up to my table. They looked to be around eighteen. I envied their carefree attitudes and happy smiles.

I was surprised when they all went for *Beautifully Broken*. Usually, a group picked up a variety of my books and didn't all go for the same one.

"Here it is," one of them said, holding it up for the others to see. "It's the one with the guy on it."

Another one picked up *The One That Got Away*. "Here's the other book." She showed her friends.

I looked at Harper. "What is going on? Is the universe torturing me?"

"I don't know."

I sold six copies of *Beautifully Broken* and two copies of *The One That Got Away*, so maybe the universe was just trying to get me more sales. I would have preferred it in a less painful way though.

There was a lull in the people walking around, and Harper said, "I'm going to run and get something to drink. Do you want anything?"

I shook my head. "No, thanks."

"I'll be right back."

Harper took off, and I swung around to get more books out to replace the ones that had been bought.

I was counting them out when a voice said, "I brought my own book for you to sign. I hope that's okay."

I swallowed as I slowly turned back, my arms full of books, and gasped when I saw Travis standing at my table.

FIFTY-ONE

TRAVIS

I WATCHED SYDNEY FREEZE. Her mouth opened, but nothing came out, and she closed it again.

I hoped her being speechless was good. After reading the book she'd given me, I had been worried that she had completely moved on from me.

I'd been waiting for Harper to leave, so I could talk to Sydney alone. I'd seen her run out of the event room, but she'd seemed to be in a hurry, so I hadn't gone after her. I just hoped that I could say everything I needed to. Maybe I should have waited for the signing to be over, but I was here now.

I sat down in Harper's seat and took the books from Sydney's hands. I put them down on the table for readers to grab.

"What—what are you doing?" she asked.

I smiled. "Putting the books on the spot where you showed me." I raised my brow. "Am I doing it wrong?"

She shook her head. "No, I mean, what are you doing *here?*"

"I came to see you."

"Why?"

I held up *The One That Got Away.* "I read your book."

And so had my sister. I'd come home from the book signing in Iowa, and the two of us had sat down for a long conversation.

Sloan had told me she'd cried at the end and that I needed to give Sydney a second chance.

"Sydney is not Christy, Travis. She wasn't going out of her way to check up on you. She made an honest mistake. And so did you. You left your account logged in on her phone, and you know what that tells me?"

"No."

"That tells me that you trust her. You would have never done that with Christy."

Her words made me really think. "You're right. I just wish she had talked to me about it."

"Honey, everyone makes mistakes, and you two hadn't been dating that long. You need to tell her that she can trust you and come to you. After Christy, she was probably worried you'd be mad. And she was right."

I blew out a big breath. "Damn. You're right."

"Duh."

Sydney's cheeks turned pink before my eyes. "Oh."

I couldn't help but laugh. She'd sent me the book for that very purpose, but she was now embarrassed that I'd done the very thing she'd wanted.

"It was good, except…"

"Except what?"

"I didn't like the way it ended."

Sydney took a deep breath. "Why's that?"

"Because you and I are supposed to end up together."

"But that book isn't about us."

"It isn't? You gave the heroine an eye with a brown spot in it." I pointed to her eye that matched the very description in the book.

"It's a couple *like* us," she said, her head held high.

I laughed. "Good save."

"Besides, I think the book ended great. They each got their happily ever afters."

I picked up Sydney's hand. "But I don't want it with someone else. I want it with you."

She sucked in a breath. "But…but…"

"But nothing. You are perfect for me, and I love you just the way you are. And, if you ever say anything about not being pretty enough or thin enough or any shit like that, I will take you over my knee."

"Oh." She narrowed her eyes. "But I hear you have a new girlfriend."

I frowned. "From who?" *Who in the hell is spreading rumors about me?*

"From some readers." She looked around. "Over there. Those two."

He laughed. "I was talking about you. I was telling them I came to find you."

"Oh." She laughed nervously. "Does this mean you forgive me?"

"Yes. Do you forgive me?"

She eyed me suspiciously. "For what?"

"For rushing to judgment. For comparing you to my ex. For not listening to you."

"I suppose."

"You suppose?"

She sighed. "Travis, the thing is, I'm not perfect."

I opened my mouth to argue, and she put her finger over my lips.

"I'm not talking about looks. I'm talking about actions and thoughts. I'm going to doubt myself sometimes. And, if something happens between us, I want to know I can come to you, and we can talk about it. I realize that was part of the issue—me not coming to you—but I was worried about how you would react."

I pulled her hand away, so I could speak. "You're right. But you have to do me a favor."

"What's that?"

"Please don't assume the worst. You have to trust that I love you and want to be with you. And I will trust that you will come to me when you're unsure of something or feeling insecure." I pulled her toward me, so our foreheads touched. "And I said that you were perfect for me, which you are."

"Well, well, well, isn't this cozy?"

Sydney and I looked over to see Harper standing in front of the table.

"I leave for ten minutes, and Travis just sweeps in and steals my chair."

I stood. "Sorry. I had to talk to Sydney."

Harper waved her hand in a downward motion. "Sit. I'll see if I can find another chair." She put her hands on the table, leaned over, and grinned. "Does this mean you're back together?"

I looked over at Sydney for an answer.

When she didn't say anything, Harper said, "Syd, he came all the way to another state for you."

Sydney backed away and looked at me. "Why did you come all the way here? We live in the same state."

"I needed to get my shit together this past week, and I thought it would be romantic. We met at a book signing, and I came in to sweep you off your feet at another signing." I smiled. "So, did I? Did I sweep you off your feet?"

Sydney laughed. "Not even close."

I frowned, and she fell against me she was laughing so hard.

"But I'm super glad you came," she admitted.

"Oh, you are, huh?"

"Yes. Because I love you, and I think we deserve a second chance."

I grinned down at her. "I love you, too. Admit it; I totally swept you off your feet."

EPILOGUE

SYDNEY

"HONEY, HAVE YOU SEEN MY PHONE?" I called out to Travis.

"It's in here," he answered from the hotel bathroom.

Whew.

I was so worried about tonight that I couldn't keep track of basic things.

I walked toward the bathroom, grabbing my purse as I went.

As I came around the corner, my dear husband of three years whistled at me. "You look beautiful."

I curtsied. "Thank you, kind sir. You look dashing yourself."

Travis had just cut several inches off his hair and shaved his facial hair. He pulled at the collar of his bow tie. "I feel like I'm choking. This is one of the reasons I'm a personal trainer and a model. I either wear workout clothes or no clothes," he joked even though I'd seen him dressed up in several photos. He smiled at me. "But it's worth it."

"Only if I win."

Travis smiled. "Even if you don't win. It's not every day your book gets nominated for a RITA Award."

I grinned. He was right.

"I love that you know what a RITA Award is."

I knew everyone said it was just an honor to be nominated, and others scoffed at them, but at this point in my career, it really was an honor. Maybe if I was nominated several times and didn't win, then I'd think differently. But I wasn't there.

There was a knock on the adjoining door to our hotel room, and the door opened.

"Do you want to say goodbye to the kids now?" Bonnie asked. "Chad and I are going to take them down to the pool."

Two-year-old Ava came running through the door until she hit my legs. "I go swimming, Mama!"

I picked her up and hugged her close. "I heard. That sounds like fun. But you'd better listen to everything Grandma and Grandpa tell you, okay?"

She nodded. "I promise."

She wiggled in my arms, and I let her down. She immediately ran behind me.

"I go swimming, Daddy."

Travis laughed and picked her up.

While I left those two to say good night, I walked into Chad and Bonnie's room to pick up the baby.

"Hey, Noah." I picked him up. "How's Mama's big boy? You look so cute in your swimsuit."

His shorts went down past his knees, and his baby belly stuck out. He was adorable.

My nine-month-old grinned at me and grabbed at my necklace, tugging on it.

"Be careful, baby. Don't break it."

He ignored me and put the necklace in his mouth.

Travis and Ava walked in as I asked, "You'll be careful with Noah in the pool?"

Travis laughed at his mother's insulted face.

"I'm sorry. I just worry." I kissed Noah on the cheek. "I just love this little guy."

Bonnie held out her arms. "I promise to take care of him."

"Thank you," I said with a smile and handed the baby over.

"You ready?" Travis asked.

"Yep." I kissed Noah's forehead and Ava's cheek. "Be good," I told her.

"'Kay." Her answer probably meant she hadn't listened to me at all.

"We'll see you in the morning."

"'Kay, Mama." When Chad came out of the bathroom, Ava grabbed his hand. "Let's go swimming."

Chad smiled. "You two have fun."

"Thanks, Dad." Travis put his arm around me and led me back to our room. "Come on, sexy. Let's go win that award."

We made sure we had everything we needed and were off to the Romance Writers of America Awards Ceremony where I was up for a RITA award, which was thankfully in the same building.

***

Hours later, after the RITA awards after-party, Travis and I headed up to our room.

He pulled me close to him in the elevator. "You okay with not winning?"

I looked up at him. "I really am. And I lost to a great writer and a good book."

He kissed my forehead, and the doors opened.

We walked down the hall to our room, and Travis slid the card into the lock.

"But I was thinking..." I said as the latch clicked behind us.

"What's that?" he asked as he removed his tie.

I watched as he slowly unbuttoned his shirt and took it off. His T-shirt was next, and I was met with his glorious upper body. He was putting on a show for me, and he didn't even know it. He was in his early thirties now and still modeled but not as much as he used to. He ran his own gym now with a friend—plus, we had a family—so it was harder for him to find time to go to shoots.

I grinned and stepped forward. Running my hands down his chest and abdomen, I said, "I might need some of your personal cheering up."

Travis raised his brow. "Oh, yeah?"

I slipped my hand underneath the waistband of his pants and wrapped my fingers around his cock. "Oh, yeah."

He unfastened his pants and pushed them off his hips. But then he pulled my hand away and swung me around.

He slowly unzipped the back of my dress, running his finger down my spine as he went.

A shiver racked my body.

My dress fell to the floor, and he led me over to the bed.

He got down on one knee and kissed my belly, stretch marks and all. Thanks to my amazing husband, I saw them as badges of honor rather than something to be embarrassed about.

"I will always desire you, Sydney," he said, practically reading my mind.

We finished undressing each other, and I lay back onto the bed and spread my legs. "Get inside your wife, Zehler."

Travis laughed, grabbing on to my ankles, and did exactly as I'd demanded.

Once we were both spent and panting, he lay down beside me.

"I suppose we should go check on the kids," I said, eyeing the closed adjoining door.

"In a minute. I want to hold you for a bit."

I wiggled back into him. "Sounds good to me." I closed my eyes and let my husband's warmth and love surround me. Even though I hadn't won an award, I was happy because I already had everything I wanted.

MY FIVE DATES SAMPLE

CALEB

"Thank you, sir," I said to my final customer of the day and breathed a sigh of relief when he walked out the door.

I'd spent almost an hour with him, and he hadn't bought a single thing. I didn't work on commission, but it was still frustrating.

I looked around the used sporting goods store. I wanted this place to thrive, for more reasons than one, and it wasn't going to happen when people continually came in and didn't buy anything.

"It's five, guys. I'm done for the day," I told the three staff members on the floor.

"Okay," one of them said without looking my way.

Yeah, they were going to miss me.

I walked back to the break room to grab my stuff before I headed home.

My phone buzzed. It was my mother.

> Mom: Don't forget about dinner tonight, sweetie.

I groaned. I loved my family, but I had been looking forward to doing my own thing tonight.

> Me: I'll be there. Just getting off work now.

I grabbed my wallet and keys from my locker and headed for the door, but I stopped when I saw my boss—the owner of the shop—sitting at his desk in his office. I'd been wanting to speak to him all week, but he hadn't been around much.

I knocked on the open door.

Ted Goldman looked up from his paperwork and smiled at me. Unfortunately, it was strained, which didn't bode well for what I wanted to speak to him about.

"Hey, Caleb. Can I help you with something?"

I walked into the office and took the chair right across from him. "I wanted to know if you'd considered my offer."

Ted was almost in his seventies now and getting ready to retire. His wife had done so the year before, and the two of them wanted to do some traveling. While Ted had some good managers running his store, it was still a full-time job, and he was looking to sell.

And I was looking to buy.

I was one of the good managers Ted had on staff—correction, I was a great manager. I'd been working at the store since I was sixteen, minus one year back when I was twenty, making my total years of employment fourteen.

I had the most seniority *and* loyalty, and Ted was like a

second father to me. I figured I was his first choice. In fact, I figured I wouldn't even have any competition, but the look on Ted's face said I wasn't going to like what he had to say.

Ted set his pen down and sighed. "I have thought about it, but I'm going to have to say no."

"No?" *No?* I'd thought he'd at least counter my offer. A flat-out no wasn't something I'd even considered. "Did you change your mind about selling?"

A look of regret filled Ted's face. "No. I'm going to sell it to Rick."

"*What?*" I said as I flew to my feet. "*Rick?*"

"Shh," Ted said. "Close the door."

I did as he'd requested because I didn't want people listening in on our conversation any more than Ted did.

I crossed my arms over my chest. "Rick has only been here a year and a half. He's not even full-time," I argued.

Rick was Ted's nephew and had only started working here after his wife and kids left him. He was trying to make extra money to pay for his lawyer and child support.

"I know, Caleb. But, if I sell the place to Rick, he can work here full-time and spend more time with his kids because he won't be working two jobs."

"This is fucking nepotism."

Ted's chair screeched as he pushed it back and rose to his feet. "You will not swear at me, young man. And this is not nepotism."

I held out my arms. "Young man? Ted, I'm thirty-one years old. I have been here since I was sixteen. I've been a manager for nine years. You explain to me why this isn't nepotism, and I won't fight you."

Ted rubbed his hand over his eyes and sat down. "I started this store back in the late eighties. I'm the only one who's ever owned it. It's my baby. And I can't just leave it to someone …"

I sat down again. "Someone what?"

"Someone who might sell it in a few years."

I frowned. "Why the hell do you think I would do that?"

"You have nothing tying you down, Caleb. You rent your apartment, you're not married, and you don't have any kids. Plus, you don't have the best track record."

"Excuse me?"

"You quit college. You almost signed up for the military but decided at the last minute to go backpacking through Europe for a year."

"That was over ten years ago," I protested.

"I realize that, but I still don't know that you're not going to decide to do something like that again. Maybe ten years is your tipping point. And, like I said, you have nothing tying you down."

"I have my family," I pointed out.

"They didn't stop you from leaving them the last time. Meanwhile, Rick has a mortgage, child support, and children keeping him around. He's not going anywhere." Ted folded his arms on his desk. "Look, you are both excellent workers. You know you've done a lot for this store. *I* know you've done a lot. But I have to look at this objectively."

I wasn't ready to give up yet, and a plan was forming in my brain. "Have you told Rick this yet?"

"No."

Yes! I exclaimed inside my head.

"Why?" Ted asked as if he almost wanted me to have another reason.

There was still hope.

"Because what if I told you that I'd been looking for houses and that there was actually a special woman in my life?"

Ted sat back in his chair and narrowed his eyes "I'd ask why you never said anything. You always tell us about your girlfriends." He crossed his arms. "And why wouldn't you have mentioned house-hunting?"

Think fast, Caleb.

"I didn't mention the house-hunting because I didn't want it to influence your decision on selling the store. I see now that it was a mistake."

Damn. I was so impressed with that lie that I was mentally patting myself on the back.

Ted's arms fell. He believed me. "And the girl?"

"Woman, I corrected." I looked down at my feet like I was embarrassed. "I really like her." I looked up at Ted. "Don't laugh, but I think this one might be special."

"Hmm …" That was an *I'm not sure I believe you quite yet* hmm.

"You know I've never said that about anyone before." I might talk about the women I'd dated, but I'd never said any of them were special.

"This is true." He studied me, and I could tell he still didn't quite trust me. "What's her name?"

My phone started playing my special ringtone for my mother.

Saved by the fucking bell.

I held up my finger to Ted and answered my cell, "Hello?"

"Caleb, I need you to pick something up on your way here."

"Okay. Hold on one second, Mom." I pulled the receiver away from my mouth and stood. "Sorry, Ted, I have to go. Please, can we continue this conversation later?" I begged him with my eyes to reconsider.

"Fine."

I grinned. "Thank you." I turned and walked out the door. "Mom, I'm back. What did you need?"

"But, Caleb?" Ted said.

"Hold on again, Mom." I spun back around outside the door. "Yes?"

"Bring her to dinner tomorrow night."

"Who?"

Ted's eyebrows jumped to his hairline. "Your girlfriend."

Oh shit. I laughed nervously. "Yeah, okay." I pointed to my phone. "For a second there, I thought you were talking about my mom." *Awesome save, Caleb.*

Ted shook his head. "Get out of here. I'll see you tomorrow night."

"Okay." I spun again and bolted away before he could say anything else. "Mom, you still there?"

"I'm here. Did I interrupt anything important?" she asked.

Just my future. "Nothing that can't wait."

"Oh, good. Can you pick up an extra package of hamburger buns on your way here?"

I hurried out of the store before Ted. "Sure. Not a problem."

"Thank you. See you soon then?"

"Yep. I'll be there soon."

I hung up my phone and unlocked my car.

My to-do list was now buying hamburger buns, finding a realtor, and convincing someone to play my girlfriend. All by tomorrow night. I suddenly had an extremely busy weekend.

———

Get your copy of <u>My Five Dates</u> now!

ACKNOWLEDGMENTS

First, we have to give a big thank-you to all the male models who let us interview them for our book. It was one of the most fun things we'd ever done in the name of research. Golden Czermak, Christian James, Mitch Mathes, Zack Salaun, Michael Scanlon, and Taras Timofeyenko, thank you for taking time out of your busy lives to answer our questions! If you ever read our book, you might see little tidbits that came from our interviews, and hopefully, it makes you smile.

Also, thank you to Pathways Talent Services for going out of your way to respond to our questions on what your role is in the modeling industry.

Thank you to our beta readers and our ARC readers! You ladies do such a wonderful job. We are so lucky to have you as part of our team.

Thank you to all the bloggers and readers who help us promote our book. And an extra-special thank-you to those of you who read our work and post a review. We couldn't do it without you!

Thank you again to Golden Czermak—who is also the amazingly talented photographer at FuriousFotog—for the awesome photo of Chase Ketron that we were able to purchase to grace the cover of our book.

Thank you to Jovana Shirley of Unforeseen Editing. As

always, you mold our work into something presentable and beautiful.

Last but definitely not least, thank you to our families for your support and for understanding that writing is more than a hobby. We love you!

.

ABOUT THE AUTHOR

R.L. Kenderson is two best friends writing under one name.

Renae has always loved reading, and in third grade, she wrote her first poem where she learned she might have a knack for this writing thing. Lara remembers sneaking her grandmother's Harlequin novels when she was probably too young to be reading them, and since then, she knew she wanted to write her own.

When they met in college, they bonded over their love of reading and the TV show *Charmed*. What really spiced up their friendship was when Lara introduced Renae to romance novels. When they discovered their first vampire romance, they knew there would always be a special place in their hearts for paranormal romance. After being unable to find certain storylines and characteristics they wanted to read about in the hundreds of books they consumed, they decided to write their own.

One lives in the Minneapolis-St. Paul area and the other in the Kansas City area where they both work in the medical field during the day and a sexy author by night. They communicate through phone, email, and whole lot of messaging.

You can find them at http://www.rlkenderson.com, Facebook, Instagram, TikTok, and Goodreads. Join their reader group! Or you can email them at <u>rlkenderson@</u> <u>rlkenderson.com,</u> or sign up for their newsletter. They always love hearing from their readers.

Made in the USA
Monee, IL
29 November 2024

71552326R00184